Devil

THE HALLOWEEN BOYS BOOK FOUR

KAT BLACKTHORNE

Author's Note

Dear Demons,

Here we are. We made it. Welcome to this occult spin on Hades and Persephone. I know you're all eager for the devil's story and he is eager to share it. Though please keep in mind, the devil doesn't do anything in the way anyone else thinks he should. His tale is vastly different from the other Halloween Boys and the way he wanted it told is unorthodox. As a matter of fact, he's been telling us his story for three books now… have you followed the clues?

We ask that you keep an open mind as you explore hell and what that means. Because Judas and I are betting that most have a different idea of hell, the devil, and the underworld than what we're going to show. Our underworld is one heavily influenced by occult celebration and lore.

In Hades and Persephone fashion, there are some non-con themes, there's suicidal ideations, graphic violence and sex, dark demon gore and occult horror elements, among other things. For a comprehensive list please check my author site before continuing.

Now, let's do this one right. Take my gloved hand and follow me into the blackberry patch…

Xo,
    Kat

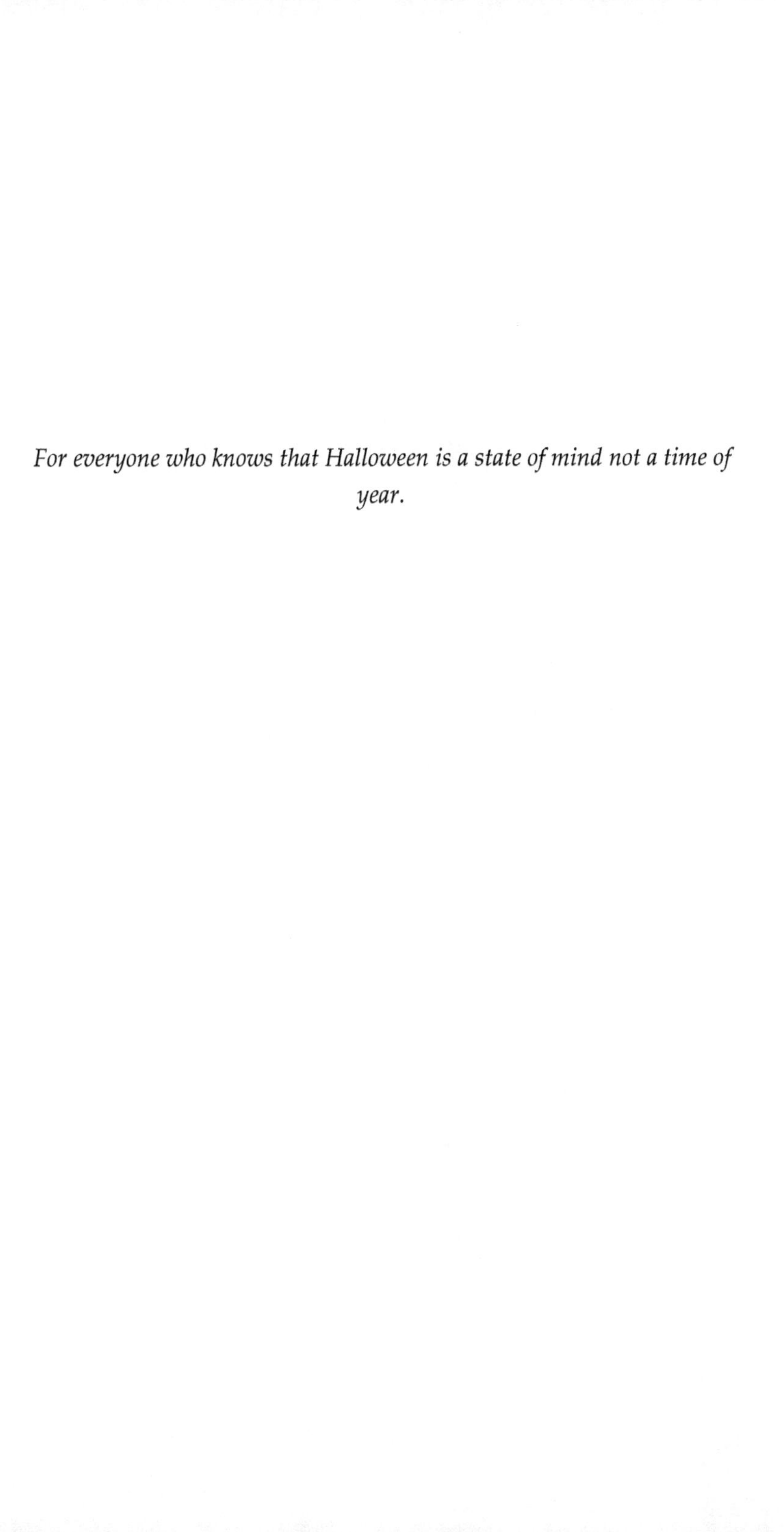

For everyone who knows that Halloween is a state of mind not a time of year.

Vibes

Devil's Playlist

IN CASE YOU MISSED IT

THE DEVIL WAITS

Footfalls echoed down the cavernous hall. Something had shifted, was shifting, in that way it only did when the course of time was on the precipice of change.

AND ALL THE songs sang
A tale so dark and true
That once day our lady of spring would return
To save hell from you

"SHE'S HERE, I brought her like I promised I would," the man dropped to his knees, gray and struggling to breathe.

"Seems she's the one that had you, don't you think, Zyre? Your soul is looking worse for the wear."

He swallowed, straining to speak. "Torture, I'm being tormented, my soul locked away and—"

With another breath his soul faded like ash into the night, carried back to his holding place, the place my bride had locked him away. Oh, she was such a good student, so eager to please me already. But there was much more for me to teach my pet.

Berries of black stained her lips
    Cursed by the devil's wicked fingertips
    Our lady of death would seek and find
    To break the curse for souls to bind

Everything was ready for her. All the leather and lace, the rooms required, the souls abuzz in wait for our Mortala's return. I had to wait for October and the thinning, radiating power of all Hallow's eve. The night I made them, the night I broke them, the night I solidified what would soon be mine. Eons I'd waited, centuries I'd searched, longing, hunting, roaming the ends of the earth and back.

Death's four horsemen rage and fight
    Against the long October night
    Oh, come Halloween!
    In Hell, above so below
    Trick her treat
    Time to learn
    Time to eat.

And here she was.
    The countdown ended here.
    Mine at last.
    And I'd never allow her to escape.

Here be the stories I've gathered on The Halloween Boys' journeys in finding their girl. Huddle in by the fire and take a sip of rum for these tales.

It all started with Ghost, the leader of the hellish crew of misfit boys. Miserable sort of fellow he was, back before he met Blythe. Blythe came riding into town, a new little fawn amongst a pack of hungry wolves, she was. It didn't take long for Ghost to set his sights on her, even Claiming her as his own, in the dark and deviously sexual way that Archdemons are known for claiming their mates.

Some say it happened at Hallows Fest, some say it happened on Ghost's grave, still others insist the claiming happened in Lamb's Blood Church. Devils help us if it's one of the last two of those. I suppose you'd have to ask Ghost himself, or Blythe, to know for sure.

That sounds like its own horror story but things with Ash Grove were never normal. The town was cursed, and as fate would have it, Blythe wasn't all that normal herself. No, Blythe was something wicked and powerful, drawn to Ash Grove for some inexplicable reason. It was found she was a reaper, death itself, and after a battle with a baphomet, she released the town and The Halloween Boys from their curses.

Now, speaking of The Halloween Boys, Dragon, the smart mouthed vampire and dragon hybrid, didn't take kindly to his friend Ghost's quick claiming of Blythe. But that's what these boys do. They fight, they fuck, they fight, they fuck. But now, a woman had entered the picture, and that shook up the crew in more ways than you could imagine.

Why, Dragon even came to me for help. That's right, The Story Keeper Pirates found themselves sailing with the Halloween Boys and their girl. We were in pursuit of Onyx's family, though I probably would have done them a favor by throwin' them overboard, because King Vladimir Drakon, Onyx's father, was a right piece of work himself.

But the devious Dragon was powerless to his crafty ways, and he stole Blythe off my ship, and took her straight to Belladonia, the city of vampires.

You know, all hell broke loose. First with a fight with his father, Blythe bringing his mother back from the dead, and the boys battling it out, mad as sin at the guy for whisking their girl away like that. But in the end, it seems they made peace with their mated bonds. Some say a blood ritual was involved. Hell, I'm not even sure that's a story I'm at liberty to share.

Which brings us to the big guy, Wolfgang Jack. An alpha werewolf and a mighty fine cook. He and Blythe ended up in Fenrir, needing to save Wolf's pack. And while his alpha werewolf raged, Blythe could breathe a bit and learn from the lunas and elders of Fenrir. With her reaper powers strengthened, she found her way to saving the lost wolves through the veil. All the while, she solidified herself as the alpha's luna, meaning she was fully mated to Ghost, Dragon, and Wolf. There was some phantom mischief in there, too, but I don't like to bother myself with the likes of circus folk, well, most circus folk.

All seemed well for our crew of Halloween Boys, until, well, I'm leaving out a pretty big player. The Devil. That's right friends, the devil had a way of hiding himself; you see. From minds, even. The stories about the devil only ever contain one grain of truth. Do you think he'd let the full story be out there? Not in folklore, legend, or ancient text, you won't find the actual devil. No, he's a quiet and mysterious sort of fellow. Not one I'd want to anger or even speak of for too long.

But he had his sights set on The Halloween Boys for ages, at least two hundred years. And for some reason, found a fascination with Blythe, too. Somehow he'd be spotted wherever she was, whispering things, hiding. The Devil was seen in Ash Grove last Halloween, then again in Belladonia at The Bleeding Heart Ball, he even was said to be baking in Fenrir. All to get close to Blythe. But why? I reckon we'll find out, because now he's stolen her away straight to Hell.

Now The Halloween Boys must make a choice. Will they stay in the comforts of a lifted curse, residing in the home they adore? Or will they make the stupidest, most irresponsible, regrettable decision imaginable and try to snatch their girl from the claws of the most powerful force of evil?

I think you already know these boys well enough to know what they'll choose.

So join me in this story, would you? I reckon it'll be a tale for the ages.

This is a story to keep.

Father Joseph

SERMON NOTES

Beloved, the holy and perfect word of God tells us His truth, and it is this. The devil walks among us, as hidden and sly as a wolf in sheep's clothing. It is important to weigh every new person you meet upon the scales of the fruits of the spirit. Do they display godly love, justice, true repentance? Or are they full of the devil's evil and worldly lusts?

Beloved, I know first-hand that demons walk among us. What if I told you that I've met the devil himself? He isn't what you'd envision. No, dear church, he is much worse. The king of lies, of deception. And he's filled with more sinister sins than your innocent minds could fathom.

Guard your hearts, for he roams the earth as hungry as a ravenous lion, searching for his next kill. His desire is to tempt, to make you wander off the holy and pure course of God. How he will lead you astray, my tender flock. The devil will entice you with things of this pagan world. Deceptions disguised as love, hope, and acceptance. But these are false gods, they are demons in hiding, and he will manipulate you into his hell.

You will think the choice was yours. You'll believe you chose the path yourself, but it was the devil all along. His plans are more twisted and deceitful than your human souls can comprehend. For the devil himself is one with death. They walk hand in hand.

So cling tight to the word of God. Use it as a light in the darkness. Never stray from the righteous and holy path. Look nary to hell and its temptations, resist the devil, and you may evade death.

Or your soul will burn for all of eternity in wicked and wretched torture.

Devil's Note

Dear Seeker,

Hello, we meet at last. You've waited for me, searched for me. Your heart has beat a little faster at my mention, hasn't it? You're skeptical, intrigued. And if you aren't wholly enamored, you're wise. If you are, however, beguiled by my presence, you're a fool like the rest of them. Here we reach my tale, and you at last uncover a pocketful of my secrets.

Congratulations on making it this far. Don't expect a good boy, for I am not a boy at all. I'm something else entirely... but you already know that, don't you?

Go ahead. Turn the page. I know you're dying for hell.

Trick-or-treat?

Judas

CHAPTER 1

The Devil

AND SO IT ENDS

> I would like, if I may, to take you on a strange journey.
>
> *The Criminologist, "The Rocky Horror Picture Show"*

A howl so dark and terrible pierced the hollow halls of hell.

A werewolf. No, *the* werewolf. The wolf of all wolves cried out, forlorn, after finding his lover dead on the ground. He had no idea just what he was or how powerful. It hadn't crossed his mind that he could be so integral in the foreboding story that was unfolding. Wolfgang was good and pure and too virtuous for the crew of sin he surrounded himself with. But he'd made a deal. He'd struck his bargain hundreds of years ago, and he'd paid the price. Sad little wolf. So sad, so terrible.

It was October again at last. The fine month of twists of fate, of orange and black, of haunted towns and ghost stories. The veil had thinned. The whispers in the chilled wind called my name. Witches chanted in fearful disdain. Demons gathered in wait for my command. Children hid under their blankets at the stories told of me. Churches again warned of my legend of torment and sin.

The werewolf mourned in the blackberry patch, clutching his

mate to his chest. Was her body dead? No, not quite. Almost, though. And it didn't matter. She was on her way to me, finally, at long last. She was known as Blythe Pearl on earth, but in hell and beyond, she was Mortala. My Mortala. My bride. My deathly dark reaper queen.

On her way home to me.

Her last love.

Did they think I'd play fair?

I am the devil, after all.

CHAPTER 2
Ghost

IDLE HANDS ARE THE DEVIL'S WORKSHOP.

> Most people will tell you growing up means you stop believing in Halloween things — I'm telling you the reverse. You start to grow up when you understand that the stuff that scares you is part of the air you breathe.
>
> *Peter Straub, "Magic Terror: 7 Tales"*

In the depths of hell, as I burned in wretched torment and transformed into the archdemon, as my bones crushed beneath the oppression of my crucifixion, the hope of her, my dark heart was set always on the hope of her for me. Why had I roamed and slaughtered and fought for hundreds of years if not for death? If not for her?

Onyx and I were reclined around the remnants of a black fire. I was admiring the way his ebony hair tinted blue in the cloudy sunlight when he sat up straight and looked to the forest, a salacious comment dying on his fangs.

"What is it?" I asked, feeling my bones rattle just as a far off and deep howl tore across Fenrir. The vampire's breath left him like he'd taken a punch to the gut as he used my shoulder to help him stand. "What is it?" I repeated, panicked now and tasting the bitter flavor of his worry.

Holding his chest, he stumbled forward, "I can't—it can't—no." The vampire hybrid took off in a flash, igniting his speed with no further explanation.

A luna with white hair raced by me, and I grabbed her arm. She shook me off with as much strength as Wolfgang and shot me an indignant growl.

Raising my palms, I apologized. "Please, tell me what's happening. What did the howl mean?"

Wolf culture confounded me, but now lunas and elders were shifting and racing into the woods. The woods where Wolfgang and Blythe were. My heart turned frozen and heavy in my chest. The woman, I recalled her name finally, Nephele, glanced at me, her voice solemn. "Someone's died." With that, she became an enormous pale wolf worthy of her apparent power and thundered off. My demon form took me by the throat, but I shook him off. *No, no. She's okay. She has to be*, I assured him, us, as I took off in a run, feeling the furs of wolves sprint past me into the forest. But I knew in the goddamn empty pit of my worthless being. I fucking knew.

My one holy charge was to keep her safe.

And I had failed.

CHAPTER 3
The Devil's In The Details

THIS IS HOW VILLAINS ARE MADE

Hollow bells were ringing at Lamb's Blood Church as worshippers lifted their voices above their hymnals. Onyx Hart adjusted his suspenders and puffed up his chest before taking his seat next to Minnie, the pretty girl with the ringlet curls. I watched the service from the flickering oil candle flames, as I usually did. I loved a good sermon.

My fascination with these boys was growing, as in thousands of years, rarely did humans pique my interest. Onyx wasn't from Ash Grove, was he? No, the truth of him was something fiery lurking beneath his wry charm. Then James Cove... so serious as he rested his chin on his fist, intent on absorbing the priest's words, as if the Bible could save him from me, from what I'd make him, given the slightest inkling of an opportunity. Not that I needed anyone's permission. But it was more interesting that way, to watch the gears turn in their simple little minds as they bargained with the horror of the homilies they fought to obey.

Minnie giggled, and Onyx looked self-assured at James's silencing glare. It was enough, and I was a step from my exit when I caught the charmer lean over his seat and subtly, lightly, brush his knuckles over James's knee. The pensive man didn't recoil. Instead, he slowly plucked a note from his friend's grip, allowing his fingers to linger a moment too *long. A moment too scandalous for the 1800s. But these boys didn't care about that, did they? Intriguing, so intriguing…*

"Did you read the note I passed you?" He shoved his hands into the pockets of his trousers and glanced away, knowing he couldn't handle the icy stare of his friend. *James, you're so lonely. Why is that? I'd like for him to ponder it for the rest of the day.*

The severe man straightened his cap before glancing past the exiting Sunday mass crowd. "Perhaps."

A horse trotted by, and the man tipped his hat.

"Mr. Moore," the boys greeted.

"Send our regards to Ellie," Onyx purred, and James elbowed him in the ribs. *Flirt.*

The old man chuckled, and the two men continued. *Always up to no good, seemingly always scheming.*

"Where's your new boy?" James murmured.

Onyx put a hand to his heart. "Why, if I didn't know better, James, I'd believe you to be jealous of Wolfgang Jack. Such a rough and tumble fellow. Not one I'd think you'd look twice at. He's your companion as well as mine. Remember the games we played as kids? He's filled out remarkably well, wouldn't you agree? Though…" Onyx's attention sharpened on an image in the distance, and James Cove followed his stare.

Two dark silhouettes stood frozen along the tree line. *Neither of the men knew they shouldn't be able to see that far. Neither of them attributed their keen intuition to being of a supernatural sort. Why would they? But the evil called to them. It sang a melody, inviting them into the haunted forest.*

"I don't like the looks of them," Onyx said lowly.

James's jaw tightened. "Nor do I."

CHAPTER 4

Wolf

DEVIL ON MY SHOULDER

> Maybe ever'body in the whole damn world is scared of each other.
> *John Steinbeck, "Of Mice and Men"*

Nothing smelled better than the scent of late summer grass intertwined with sprays from the rushing waterfalls and the salty-sweet combination of sex that still lingered on my skin. The pack was whole again—both the wolf pack and the Halloween boys pack—and it was because of her: my luna, my moon. Stepping into my gray sweatpants, I stretched and tied my hair back as I called for her. If I wasn't a gentleman, I would have fucked her five more times. That little pink sundress just begged for more of my knotting, and I wanted to give it to her. But I guessed she needed a break, and I let her have it. Momentarily. But now I was missing my mate and… I inhaled, my muscles tensing. Her scent was a translucent ribbon of black in the air just moments ago, leading down the red path into the blackberry patch that always creeped me out for some reason. The witches' stories about blackberries and the devil had rubbed off on me as a pup, I supposed. But the place was creepy even without the paranoid coven's tales. The hair on my arms stood as I followed the crimson leafy path down by the falls.

Trying not to get worked up and anxious, I reminded myself that Blythe's scent had always been faint. Some of the wolves couldn't smell her at all. Ghost couldn't see her when she first arrived, either. Then I recalled that Onyx had told me the vampires assured him her blood would kill him, though happily, it did not. There was much about our girl that we didn't understand, and even more about her mixed with us that we didn't know yet. But we had time to figure it out. We were all immortal… right?

Even with my self-encouragement, I picked up my pace and jogged into the blackberry patch. The weather had turned from sunshine and birds chirping to a chill overcast with a dense crash of thunder overhead. Raven cawed, low and melancholy overhead, circling something in the distance. I called out for her, knowing her faint scent trail ended here. She had to be here, but my luna didn't answer.

And then, as I got closer, I realized what her familiar was circling. Why he was crying. I would have rather endured the physical pain of an attack from a hundred legions of demons or slashes of ghouls than the onslaught of sorrow and rage that poured down over my awareness just as lightning crackled the sky. A shaky howl tore through my throat as I dropped to my knees and cradled her body. Blythe's body.

Shaking, I turned her over and buried my nose in her neck, searching desperately for a smell, a pulse, a rush of blood or heartbeat. Nothing I could detect. Holding her to my chest, I let out a sob of frustration. I was inadequate to help, to know what to do. Her skin was so cold. Another howl rattled me, though I already felt the ground shaking with the paws of my pack, both of my packs. Onyx appeared before me like an apparition in the fog of the rain, his arms cradling mine as we clutched Blythe's lifeless form. His green eyes glowed dark as he turned her face toward him, cupping her jaw and twisting his face in anguish. "I—I feel a little. Small, very small emotions—"

"Her smell is gone," I choked out. "What emotions? What is she feeling?"

Darkness and blue smoke wafted atop her body, covering her from the rain and encompassing us all beneath an umbrella—sanctuary of hell's gifts to the archdemon. Ghost took her carefully from my arms and answered the question I'd asked my empathic friend.

"Fear," he whispered with a quivering, worried, frightened tone that was so unlike him it made my palms tremble. "She's just barely alive, and she's afraid. Very, very afraid."

CHAPTER 5

Blythe

MASTER OF FOOLS

Humbert Wolfe

The hair on my arms stood at the caress of a frigid breeze. The dark corridor I'd entered fell into an unassuming dirt path littered with wilted red rose petals. They say the path to hell is paved with good intentions. I wasn't sure about that, or hell, since the pathway I walked was paved with death and flowers.

Every bit of barren foliage loomed over me, tinted black and creaking like something from a black and white horror movie. I rubbed my elbows, shivering as my breath came out in visible puffs. It was late September, but what was the month, the temperature, in… hell? This was hell, right? It was almost October, and instead of revisiting Hallows Fest in my beloved Ash Grove with my Halloween Boys, I'd be here, wandering this place in search of the devil.

To keep them safe, I would. To keep them alive and far from the vision of their dead bodies on the ground, surrounded by fire… I swallowed, my throat dry and my head pounding. I would endure hell and walk straight into whatever trap the devil had laid for me. Because this was a trap. I knew it was. But of what sort and to what end, I could only torturously speculate. How would I get out of this one?

The atmosphere grew darker and the wind hissed and cracked through the trees that seemed to be glaring at me overhead, whispering about my impending doom, no doubt. Looking up through the dry and splintered branches, I searched for the moon. My head hurt, clogged with unshed tears.

"Wolf," I whispered, just to hear his name on my lips. I wanted my werewolf so badly in this strange place. I still felt him slick between my thighs as I walked. My pink sundress was ripped and dirty and such a harsh reminder that I didn't belong here. Hindsight told me I should have changed, planned better, or brought supplies. But getting away from three possessive monsters wasn't so easy. I had seen an opportunity and I'd taken it, hoping they wouldn't hate me too much when they discovered I was missing.

I turned a corner in the woods to more of the same eerie woodland. Was this the trick? Some sort of maze I'd stumble around in for all of eternity? Who was this devil and why did he want to get me here?

Then the scent of sulfur invaded my nostrils, burning my throat to a dizzying degree. But I couldn't focus on the unpleasant aroma, or the freezing chill and lack of moon or stars, because branches broke in the distance. What's the scariest sound when you're alone in the woods late at night? Woods that were likely those of the very hell of legends and nightmares. How simple a sound, so small, but so meaningful. And then a soft whisper echoed around me, pricking against my awareness and heightening my fear.

"Blythe," it hissed lowly. "We've finally found you, Blythe."

A ghoul was close, and I stood, shaking in terror. It would grab me like it had when I was on the mountain—and it would hurt. Another branch broke as I stumbled forward, bracing myself against the rough bark of an oak tree. "Blythe," the ghoul whispered again. "Come to me, and I will take you to him."

I didn't know which was worse. The ghoul or the *him* it referred to.

Something whistled in the distance, and as I frantically tried to make out shapes in the dark. Something boney and sharp reached up and tugged at my hand. My natural reaction was to shake it off, like the feeling when a stick hits your leg while you're swimming in a lake. But I was without a raft in this dark pit, and I knew to take any offering of aid I could get. Whatever the small thing was that clutched my hand and pulled me to the side hadn't tried to kill me yet, and that was more than I could say for any foul ghoul. So I gripped its slender hand and followed along, down an even darker path.

My walk was hindered when my forehead bumped against something hard. "Ouch," I mumbled as the creature I couldn't see pulled my arm harder. I ducked, walking into what seemed like the trunk of a tree. "Just walking into a tree with some little helper in the dark. This is fine," I assured myself sarcastically, feeling the heaviness in my gut as my heart longed for Onyx in that moment. He would have known how to help me feel unafraid. Only moments into this journey and I was already in agony without my boys. Had it been moments or longer for them? What would they think when they discovered I was gone?

I couldn't linger on my thoughts for long, because a dull light gleamed in the distance, and the creature tugging me forward took shape. It was small and round and looked to be made of wood, much like the new form the willow spirit had taken on. Only this little wooden being was pale and striped, with long vines for hair that trailed behind it as it waddled in front of me.

"Are you a tree spirit?" I asked. When it didn't respond, I continued, dropping my elbow as I realized it was growing warmer inside the tree-tunnel. "Well, thank you for rescuing me back there."

We reached an arched door that slowly inched open as we approached. The spirit let go of my hand and stood by the door, looking down at the ground. Red glowed from the entrance, and I swallowed, knowing there was indeed no turning back now. Pausing in the doorway, I gasped, trying to make sense of what I was seeing, when something shoved the backs of my legs, pushing me inside. I fell to my knees and looked over my shoulder at the little spirit, who only gazed on with vacant eyes.

"Not a rescue," it said plainly. "A damning."

CHAPTER 6
The Devil's in the Details

A PRINCE, A WOLF, A GHOST

"It's a play party they say," Wolfgang boomed, "Samhain, or All Hallows' Eve. I don't know. A group of women in black were talking about it in town. There will be a swapping of ghost stories and celebration of the harvest. The ladies will be reading fortunes. They mentioned dressing up as something frightening."

James grumbled, "Sounds sinful to me, this All Hallows' Eve. Something of the devil."

I almost chuckled to myself as I tightened my leather gloves.

Onyx elbowed the sullen man. "Funny how sin and fun go hand in hand, isn't it, James? Live a little. We only have one life. We'll all be dead by, what, eighteen-sixty? Unless a fever claims us sooner. A night of mischief sounds delightful. We're going. Besides, the devil isn't real. I'm sure of it."

No comment from me on that one. I found it best if people believed that, anyway.

Onyx skipped up the path. "It's the first of October. The air is sweet with harvest mayhem. Be joyful, my friends."

Wolf stiffened. "Do you smell that?"

James looked over his shoulder and into the night. "Smell what? Smells like hay and firewood." The chirping of crickets was dying. The *time of blackberry evils was upon them, but they didn't know that, did they?*

Wolf shook his head. "Strange. A whiff of something foul and such anger... I—" He exhaled. "It's probably nothing."

Onyx took the werewolf's arm. "Sounds like you were in the sun for too long today. Come on. I'll walk you home."

A move Onyx Hart would regret for the rest of his long life. A walk home with Wolfgang, instead of seeking out and staying beside Minnie. Minnie, who would be taken that night. One of the many girls of Ash Grove who would die.

CHAPTER 7

Onyx

THE GREAT DECEIVER

> On some nights, I still believe that a car with the gas needle on empty can run about fifty more miles if you have the right music very loud on the radio.
> *Hunter S. Thompson*

Wolfgang was blind without his nose. Ghost was blind without his hate, and I—I was blind without her. For once, the anguish of Wolfgang and the righteous rage of Ghost were but pinpricks of sharp rain against my subconscious. Because my own feelings were loud enough to drown them out. Emotions of loss. The grief of remembrance—of how Blythe was the second love of my life I'd failed. My strength, my speed, my bite, were nothing when weighed against my innate inadequacies. There was nothing supernatural about me aside from my curse—to live with myself for all of eternity. I knew this. Wallowed in the self-loathing of it all. Blythe was limp in Ghost's arms, and Wolfgang had fallen to his knees in a howl as his pack encircled us.

The storm was so cold I worried Blythe would catch a chill, and then I remembered that she was dead. Or close to it. Because she felt the way everyone feels before they die. She felt the way I'd never tell any soul on earth because it would terrify them to know that the last earthly emotion many people had was that of terror.

No, I'd lie and say it was white light and warmth or some bullshit. But I knew the feeling. I'd looked it straight in the eye and ripped out its throat until it pooled at my feet and the feeling faded like a fog in the distance. Blythe felt like death now. She'd been touched by something *unholy*. And we'd let it happen. I'd let it happen.

"She's... gone..." Nephele whispered.

Ghost growled. "She's not. I still taste her and I taste... Wolfgang, who else was here?"

Wolfgang stood, his hair curling and dripping from the downpour. "No one. We were by the falls. She left for one moment, and then—and then I couldn't smell her."

My hand caressed her cheek. "My belladonna, so pale. So fragile and frightened." My breath caught in my chest and mixed with a sob. "Get her out of the rain. Get her comfortable."

"Don't fucking talk like that," Wolfgang hissed with a soft sadness that only fractured me further. "She's not—she's not!"

Ghost was silent, too silent, as he turned on his heel, parting the sea of wolven, and headed back to Fenrir. Wolfgang grabbed my shoulders roughly, giving me a shake until my eyes met his. His voice was graveled and pained when he spoke. "If I have to carve out my own goddamn heart and put it in her chest so that she lives, I will do it. Got it?"

I shook my head, knowing he wasn't exaggerating and knowing that he'd do the same for me, too. "I love you," I whispered.

"I love you." He pulled me close. "Let's go help our girl."

I couldn't tell him she looked and felt of death more so than ever before. Her soul was on a faraway string, and worst of all, her soul was horrified and alone. That was knowledge I had to keep and bury for the sake of my friend. Maybe Ghost tasted it, but who fucking knew what he sensed as a demon. This was my punishment for all I'd done, for those I'd killed, for failing Minnie.

This was the cruel universe taking revenge and forcing me to sit back and watch, in slow, agonizing detail, my belladonna die. And there was nothing I could do. There was nothing Wolfgang's bleeding heart could do. Ghost's tough-guy facade was powerless against death just the same. We were all fucked. We'd be tattered beyond repair in the wake of losing the woman we all loved.

But I'd have to sit on that knowledge. To know that life was no longer worth living. That my life had gone up in flames along with my farm and my courthouse. I'd have to put on one last show, one more grand lie. Because once she passed, I would find a way to end my life, too.

CHAPTER 8

Flight of the Familiars

RAVEN

Raven or Crow, whichever you want to call him, they respond to both.
Ghost by Kat Blackthorne

We held our secret meetings in the murder's treehouse. The felines, snakes, and rats complained because they preferred the ground. The ground was for worms and toads, not noble familiars. Our conversations were safer in the trees.

Cat rolled onto her back and swatted at her long, fluffy black tail. "I will start our session by asking again if any of you would like to trade with me."

The garter snake, Percy, flicked a tongue as he wrapped around a low-hanging branch. "Any of us would be proud to serve an archdemon, Cat. You betray your breed."

A female crow from my murder interrupted. "Enough of your banter. Before we begin, we should recognize the great bravery displayed by one of our own. Raven"—she held a wing out toward me—"gave his life to fly into the line of fire against a baphomet to protect his companion. He flew from a pirate ship to the land of vampires, and he went talon to paw with an alpha wolf in his spring."

Paws, wings, and tails clapped.

"Raven got Blythe, though. She's easy and nice and smells good," Cat complained.

My feathers ruffled. They didn't yet know that I'd now lost my beloved friend to the pits of hell. Worse, they didn't know my secret… the deepest secret I carried beneath my sealed beak. I'd hidden it from Blythe for so long now. If the familiars knew, that would cancel out any sort of nobility they believed I possessed. If the Halloween Boys knew… they'd kill me. Oh, the wretchedness I'd agreed to made me want to weep in sorrow. Thankfully, the subject changed.

Owl hooted, puffing his white feathery chest. "Where were you, Cat, when your companion almost died from demon chains a few Halloweens ago? And when he fought to protect this very forest from ghouls and malformed bats?"

Cat laid her ears back. "Managing two graveyards at once after he skipped town for two years. Have any of your people given you day jobs? No? Then keep your judgment to yourself."

Rat scurried across the floor and stood in the middle of the circle. "My witch has asked for intel on the Halloween Boys. I'll trade you."

I bristled my feathers as everyone looked at me. Being blessed with Blythe was an honor, but with her affections for the Halloween Boys came a host of problems. Mainly the interest and queries of other magical beings. "What do they want to know?"

"Now that the curse is broken, will they forever reside in Ash Grove or move on? Where'd they disappear to for two years, and why are they back now, and in Fenrir, of all places?"

"They will stay," I answered.

The rat clicked its teeth. "This will not please them…"

Cat jumped up on the ledge next to me, meeting every creature's skeptical stare. "The Halloween Boys and Blythe belong here as much as any of you vermin. Do they bring misfortune? Yes.

Does it make life interesting? Also yes. And you gossips know it. You weren't complaining when they saved all your precious companions' lazy asses from legions and ghouls and forest filth. So," she licked a paw and cleaned her whiskers, "respectfully, fuck off."

Hoots, squeaks, caws, and hisses sounded. Cat was brash and unorthodox, but she always had my back, and I believed her fonder of her archdemon companion than she let on. Cat was always the first to come to his defense or that of any of his friends.

With a meow, she changed the subject. "Let's play a game, shall we?"

Everyone stopped their murmurs.

Familiars loved games.

"Halloween is upon us yet again. All manner of beings will be arriving for Hallows Fest in a matter of days. We can only hide in so many jack-o'-lanterns before the smell of pumpkin gets dull again. All for what? Overhearing the vampires share stories of their sexual exploits? I'm nodding off already."

"When Halloween is over, winter is here. Life is boring again. Though the Christmas trees are fun to knock over," a tabby cat in the corner added.

Every animal nodded their agreement.

"I propose a trick-or-treat exchange. One physical tasty delight, procured however you can manage. And one gift of gab. What say you all?"

I squawked. "You're proposing thievery and gossip?"

"Yes, yes, I am."

The snake slithered. "Sounds delightful."

Owl purred in his throat. "I'm in."

The four crows from my murder shrugged. It would be a distraction that might keep the familiars from looking too closely at Blythe and her current physical state, so I supposed I'd partake. After all, it would be in her highest interest to have privacy from prying beings. "As long as we return what is stolen…"

Cat rubbed against me in that soft way felines did. "Sure, whatever you say." She winked at the others, and they chuckled. "Meet back here on the eve of Halloween with gifts and gossip. Got it? Perhaps some warm milk and tuna, too."

"A nice warm field mouse," the snake hissed.

Owl and I wouldn't refuse that. The rat feigned shock. "Cheese or peanut butter for me."

"Maybe this game isn't that bad," I agreed. "I will see you all soon."

The others left, leaving Cat and me alone.

"I can take a turn in the graveyard and give you a respite," I offered. "Just show me what my duties entail. Currently, I can't bear what a disgrace I am."

Cat tilted her head. "You are very kind for a bird. No, I actually quite enjoy tormenting the spirits. I just like to pretend that I don't."

"Why?"

"Being contrary is in my nature." She hopped off the railing. "Now, what do you say we team up and spy together?"

The thought excited me. I did very much enjoy the secretive act of gathering passive intel.

Cat looked over her furry shoulder as her black tail swished. "I know about Blythe. I know where she went and some of why, I think. Though there are other pieces to this puzzle we can uncover, secrets to be found out. We can find them and help her bozo boyfriends."

Emotion swelled in my throat. "A wondrous thing to do for her and the Halloween Boys, Cat. Thank you."

"Tell anyone, and I'll pluck out your feathers and tell everyone to call you Chicken instead of Raven."

There was the Cat I'd grown so fond of. She was helping me in her own way. And for some reason, I truly believed she could help. We could help. Like the feline said, there were still many secrets to uncover and lots more loose lips arriving for Hallows Fest. The clues were waiting, and between all of us familiars, we'd collect them each like candy in our trick-or-treat buckets.

CHAPTER 9

Blythe

SPEAK OF THE DEVIL

> Have you come to sing pumpkin carols?
> *Linus, "It's the Great Pumpkin, Charlie Brown"*

Smooth stone floors that were warm to the touch lay beneath my palms. What had I expected would happen? I'd walked into a trap. I knew that much. And if I'd accurately pieced together anything about the elusive devil, he wanted me off-kilter, scared, vulnerable, and lost. It was all a part of his game, wasn't it? But if so, why had he helped me in the first place? Visions of our ballroom dance in Vlad's castle in Belladonia sprang to the forefront of my mind. He'd whispered encouragement. He'd toyed with me in such a seductive way with every brief meeting. But why? Was it all just a trail of breadcrumbs to lead me here? And where was here? I sat up, rubbing my wrists, and took in the space. It was a large room with a high steepled ceiling.

Everything was cast in tones of gray and black. As I got to my feet to explore, I noticed the ornate red rugs, leather furnishings, shelves of books, and a large fireplace in front of the... bed. An enormous black wrought-iron canopy bed perched in the very middle of the room, draped in black lace with plush red silk bedding. It looked so inviting and not at all hell-like. I glanced around, expecting to find chains and flames of torment, but it only looked like an expertly decorated, albeit awkwardly shaped, bedroom.

A black mass moved in my periphery, and I turned, startled, to find nothing awaiting me. I could have sworn something had darted across the room. When I turned again, a nightgown I hadn't noticed before lay on the bed. And by the time I'd reached it for closer inspection, I jumped at the sound of water behind me. A clawfoot bathtub in the corner of the room under a red mosaic-paneled window steamed with rushing water. And in the same quick fashion, food appeared on the round table in the center of the room.

My heart pounded in my chest as the distinct feeling that I was not alone sank in. "Hello?" I asked, like every stupid girl who's about to die in horror movies. "Is someone here?" As I padded over to the bath and slipped off my destroyed sundress, I muttered to myself. "I'm paranoid. In hell. If this is even hell. Would have been nice if *some grumpy someone* could have stopped by and said *hi, how are you? Welcome to eternal damnation…*"

As I stepped into the hot water, I heard the squeak of something that sounded like a giggle. Sitting down quickly and covering my breasts, I asked again, "Is someone here? Please, just show yourself."

Another tree spirit, perhaps? Though I hoped this one would be less *pushy*. After a round of silence, I settled into my bath, soaking my sore muscles and washing off with the vanilla-scented bar of soap. Clearing my throat, I still felt the stare of something, so I said, "You like jokes? I have another." The room was silent again. "What's a ghost's favorite dessert?" After a pause I replied, "I-Scream."

A slender black shadow took form at the foot of the tub, ironically making me scream as it laughed with a litheness that didn't suit its menacing, translucent form. Covering myself again, I shakily asked, "Are you a ghost?"

Its whisper of a reply was worse than the laugh. Much worse.

"Demon," it answered, dragging out the word the same way the ghouls in Ash Grove did. I shuddered, looking around the room.

"Do you have a name?" When it didn't respond, only cocked a shadowy, formless head, I asked another question. "Where is the devil?"

The demon let out a low sort of hiss that reminded me of a teakettle. I huffed, "Well, you tell him to come find me."

"No one," it replied low and way too soft, "makes demands of the ruler of hell."

"I do," I argued. "Tell him."

The demon faded, as if a door of light had opened, chasing the shadow away. I hit the water in frustration, causing it to splash onto the stone floor and one of the devil's precious stupid rugs. "Maybe I'll burn the room down. What then, huh, Devil?" I muttered, sloshing out of the tub and wrapping myself in an annoyingly plush black robe. "I saw visions of the Halloween Boys dead—dying—and I'm here to stop that from happening. Don't you care at all?" My voice echoed and bounced off the steepled rafters of the ceiling. My vision caught on them. There was something familiar about the old-looking wood...

"The Lord has answered your query," the demon whisper-hissed in my ear, startling me again as the long shadow backed away. I put my hand to my beating heart.

"Stop doing that creepy stuff," I scolded... the demon. "God, what is my life?" I sighed. "What is his *highness's* answer?"

I couldn't make out eyes, but I could almost see this demon's widen. Suddenly, it held out an open and fully materialized thick, ancient book. Placing it in my palms, the demon handed me a pen. "He says to make an appointment."

"You have got to be kidding me," I spat, squinting to read the tiny scrawl. "It says his first appointment is available in... one hundred freaking years." I slammed the book shut and forced an overly polite smile. "Kindly tell your lord he can shove this up his ass."

"I'm not saying that," the demon argued as it faded away on

another stale wind. Before it did, its retreating tone nonchalantly clicked something horrific into place. "You disgrace Lamb's Blood Church with such language and disobedience."

The odd shape, the steepled ceiling, the rafters… I spun and took in the altar above the bed. *Lamb's Blood Church from Ash Grove.*

CHAPTER 10
The Devil's in the Details

A CURSED NIGHT

Their attraction was hard to ignore. The wolf and the vampire. What a peculiar pairing. One I enjoyed observing from their lantern fire. This night was different. They sensed it, though they'd be too late. Onyx's and Wolfgang's knuckles brushed as they crunched dried leaves on their walk through the forest back to Fenrir. It was a long walk, one that tired neither of them. Yet another detail they didn't look close enough into. The clues were everywhere, and they always missed them. Too focused on their earthly and carnal pursuits. Fools.

Something shifted in the air, and Onyx shoved Wolfgang against the thick bark of a mighty oak tree. Twilight fell, painting them in the orange and purple of other realms. The only time the two collided so evidently, so perfectly. The werewolf and the vampire crashed into each other in tune with the hues of changing light. Wolf moved, switching positions and pinning Onyx to the tree, gripping a hand around the hybrid's throat and squeezing.

"Harder," Onyx demanded.

With grunts of passion and heat, they shed their clothing, and teeth scraped skin. Oh, Onyx. If you'd only bite a little harder, you'd possess another bloody realization. Too bad it wouldn't matter. They palmed one another's cocks and sighed in unison while murmuring against lips.

And then, what I was looking for. Wolfgang stopped, breaking their kiss and eliciting a groan from Onyx. "What?" the hybrid asked, out of breath. "No one walks this way. Let's keep going."

"Do you hear that?" Wolfgang asked.

Onyx huffed. "I told you, friend, no one comes this way. They believe these woods haunted. They believe your community descended from wolves as well. See how right they are?" He chuckled seductively. "Now, where were we?"

Wolf accepted a small kiss before pushing his lover off and buckling his trousers. "That smell again, and this time..." He lifted his nose and sniffed the air.

So very canine, Wolf. Don't you see it?

Before his amorous friend could respond, something rustled in the distance. Twigs broke, and that eerie quiet that could only befall the forest at night permeated the once passionate expanse.

Onyx furrowed his brow and put a hand to his chest, his face falling. "I—I need to go check on Minnie."

"I'll come with you."

"You don't have to—"

"I'm coming with you."

With a nod of acceptance, the lost prince and the dormant alpha turned back the way from which they'd come, down the mountain to a town not the same as they left it. To a people part broken, soon cursed. And into the story of how their fates would change forever.

CHAPTER 11

Wolf

DEVIL'S TRIANGLE

> Villainy wears many masks, none so dangerous as the mask of virtue.
>
> *Ichabod Crane, "Sleepy Hollow"*

Pacing, pacing, pacing. I'd worn a spot on my front porch and could anticipate every creak in the wood. It needed to be torn down and rebuilt. Another thing I'd neglected. Like I'd overlooked the fragility of my luna. My luna, my moon, my mate, who lay with the faintest fucking heartbeat I'd ever heard. Nearly imperceptible. I'd heard it like this once before. That night I'd brought her to Fenrir. She'd slept for days. Her heart rate had dropped, and I shook her awake. Why didn't I catch this then? If I had…

This was all my fault. Letting her go off alone. I'd let my defenses down. I'd been a piss-poor alpha, and now Blythe would pay the ultimate price if I didn't figure out a way to fix this.

I looked at my phone, knowing the menace that would await me when I hit Call. But I did it anyway. I called the devil. And damn if I wouldn't give him anything he asked for in exchange for somehow helping spare her life. But as soon as my thumb tapped his number, the line trilled. *"I'm sorry. The number you are calling is not in service. Please redial and try again."*

"Fuck!" I roared, throwing the device against the side of my cabin and watching through heated tears as it shattered into tiny pieces.

A seasoned and motherly voice cooed from the bottom of the stairs. "A blessing in disguise, Wolfgang Jack. Best not ask for help from the reason you're in this predicament." Calliach may have been an elder, but she was the quietest, stealthiest wolf I'd ever known. I hadn't even heard her approach.

"Ames won't leave her side. He's just clutching her arm, drunk off of whatever he can taste of her with his archdemon abilities. Onyx… I know the look in his eyes. I know what he's planning, and he will completely self-destruct soon if I don't find a way to fix her."

"And you? How are you?" she asked carefully. "I'd *wager* you aren't thinking straight."

My chest gripped. She couldn't know, could she? About the bargain I'd struck with the very devil of nightmare and sin. "How I feel doesn't matter. My family needs me. My mate needs me. And I'm a useless fucking fool." I kicked an empty planter, and it flew off the side of the deck while my wise grandmother wolf watched on like a parent observing a toddler throwing a temper tantrum.

Holding on to the railing, she ascended, and I remembered my fucking manners and ran to take her elbow and help her up. I tried but failed to take the basket from her grip. After swatting my hand away, she clutched my bicep. "This is not a task you can complete alone, kind and noble alpha. You will have to do the thing you despise most if you wish to aid your loved ones."

"And what's that?"

"Ask for help, and not from the likes of the pit of darkness. You are surrounded by light, pup, if you'd only pull your head out of your ass long enough to see it." She gave a wrinkled and wry smirk as I ran my hands through my hair.

"Calliach, if she dies… I don't, I can't—"

"Hush, young one. Let us elder wolves have a look at her. We will each be laying hands on your mate, every day, and assessing her condition. We will find a way, Wolfgang, as she found a way for us. Fenrir has not forgotten her strength. It is best you remember the same."

Once I'd settled my inner alpha and his mournful fury, I joined my family and my elder in my tiny living room. Ames still held Blythe's wrist to his lips, like he was inhaling her. As if his breath could be breathed into her. With his brows furrowed, he looked so angry. I knew the rage that accompanied feeling helpless well. I contended with it myself. Onyx sat at the foot of the bed, stroking her blanket-covered legs, humming a tune and no doubt willing any good dreams left inside him to comfort her in her deep, too deep, slumber.

Calliach pulled various bundles of herbs and flowers from her basket, mumbling to herself as she worked. I was afraid to ask, to break the silence and have their eyes on me, but I did. "Any thoughts?"

"So many, Wolfgang," Ames responded lowly.

I bit my tongue and clenched my fists, acknowledging that punching my friend across the jaw for his goddamn accusatory tone wouldn't have been best in that situation. But fuck if I wasn't tempted.

"Easy," Onyx coaxed, barely pausing his gentle song. "The stress isn't good for her."

Calliach placed a hand on Blythe's throat and closed her eyes. We each watched as our helpless mate took shallow, almost unde-tectable breaths. The wisdom of the elders would not come to me until I myself became one, but I knew I trusted them and their abil-ities more than any doctor or witch. Our grandmother wolf would know. She had to know.

"This is not an affliction of the body but of the soul. I—I..."

Ames tensed his jaw and looked up through his dark lashes. "Say it. Whatever it is, don't hold back."

The elder wolf gave me a wary glance as I crossed my arms and nodded. We needed to know everything she had to tell. "I do not pretend to know what it means as I stay in the light. Though the hold on Blythe is that of a darkness worse than I've ever encountered or heard in wolven teachings. This is not from the pit. It *is* the pit. It is—" She swallowed and jerked her hand away from my mate, looking pale and frightened.

Kneeling by my elder's side, I poured her a cup of water from the pitcher on the nightstand and insisted she drink. "That's enough for today," I ordered gently. "Send someone else tomorrow."

With pursed lips, she shook her head, as if clearing it from whatever she'd just beheld within my luna. "Fear... fear so strong. Like a wild bobcat with its paw in a trap, she thrashes against it. One more wolf, one more elder... may not be enough, Wolfgang."

Onyx hummed louder and squinted as Ames pulled Blythe's wrist back to his mouth. "Go," he murmured against her skin. A soft demand and a vicious plea of helplessness. As I walked Calliach back to the fire to join the elders and lunas, she assured me that they'd continue their searching for ideas and remedies. A bitter balm to ease my worry, a stark realization of how, for once, the Halloween Boys were powerless. We'd been overcome, defeated, left entirely helpless and vulnerable. And our captor? Blythe. Always Blythe.

CHAPTER 12

Blythe

THE EVIL ONE

> I am eternally, devastatingly romantic, and I thought people would see it because 'romantic' doesn't mean 'sugary.' It's dark and tormented — the furor of passion, the despair of an idealism that you can't attain.
>
> *Catherine Breillat*

If a small part of me thought or hoped the devil was just being cheeky by asking me to make an appointment to see him, those delusions faded by the third day I had been stuck in some rendering of Lamb's Blood Church turned giant bedroom. The shadow demon hadn't reappeared. I'd slept and eaten and bathed and had imaginary arguments until I was bored out of my mind. The windows and doors wouldn't budge, and the stained glass prevented me from viewing what I assumed was hellfire and brimstone. Maybe he'd locked me in here to make me less afraid of the terrors that awaited me when a door inevitably materialized.

All the while, I reminded myself of my quest, my reason for walking into hell of my own accord. The visions of my boys drained of life stayed at the forefront of my mind. Something was coming for them, and now that I'd obtained that warning, I wasn't going to waste it and do nothing. And this stupid, annoying prick of a devil would help me if I had to force him… somehow. I hadn't gotten that far in my plan yet, but I was still making it up as I went along.

It was late afternoon on one of the days that bled into the other days, and I was sitting on a fainting couch and kicking my legs under the stained-glass window when a shadow materialized. In the shining red light from the sun, I noticed two small protrusions atop its head. "Hi again. You have horns," I said by way of greeting.

They did something of a nod, or maybe a bow, and spoke. "I'm here to escort you to dinner, per the devil's invitation."

My eyebrows rose. "Oh, now he deigns to acknowledge I exist?" I sat up and crossed my arms. "Kindly tell the devil to go fuck himself."

The demon shadow reared back as if struck. "I will not say that and nor should you." Its tone was wary as it looked over its shoulder. "Your garments are hanging over there. He requests you wear them."

With a huff of indignation, I stomped over and snatched the most beautiful, delicate black lace dress from its hanger. For dramatic emphasis, I considered tossing it into the fireplace. But then I realized that, as annoying as his timing was, this was what I wanted. Meeting with the devil was why I'd come. So I relented my display of irritation and ducked behind a changing screen. "Of course it fits me like a glove and feels as soft as butter." I cursed. "Did you know he makes delicious muffins, too? Your lord."

"I did not know that," the demon replied, unable to hide the hint of amusement in their voice.

After lacing myself into the dress, I found a vanity with crows carved into the wood and picked up a soft silver brush and ran it through my long golden-brown hair. Something stirred in my heart as I held the object and set it carefully back down. Had I seen it before? The vanity looked so beautifully familiar…

The demon cleared their throat, which I guess was a thing

shadow demons with no name did? And I turned to ask. "Is there a mirror? The one from the vanity looks like it's been removed."

"No," they replied, unsure. "Let's go. He hates being kept waiting."

"I bet he does," I grumbled, joining the demon's side. "So is there a door or—"

Air rushed around me in circles of shadow and night as we tumbled through a portal. When the smoke cleared, I was at a long table surrounded by stacks of books. I could barely make sense of what I was seeing. Shelves of books occupied the space around the black tablecloth-laden wood adorned with long red taper candlesticks. The room smelled like old parchment and ink.

And at the end of the table, he stood with one hand behind his back. The look of pure evil so brilliant it took my breath away as his ruby and copper-colored eyes stared a hole through my dark heart. Something flashed across his gaze as he took me in. Just the size of him always took me back. He was formidable... delectable... enticing...

I stepped forward, realizing what I was walking toward. I was having dinner with the most feared man in all of time and existence.

The Devil.

CHAPTER 13

Blythe

FATHER OF LIES

The prince of darkness is a gentleman!
William Shakespeare

He sauntered closer, and my breath caught in my throat. The devil had come to dinner dressed in a black suit and his leather gloves. Though his body was tall and wide and muscular, even more so than Wolfgang, it was his stare that intoxicated me.

"Your eyes," I stammered out. "They're so…"

The devil hummed low in his throat. "So what? Terrifying, horrible, evil—"

"All of those things, and like blood in an amber bottle. The shade is so dreadful and beautiful."

He took a step closer, daring me to inch back, but I held my ground even as the edge of his jacket grazed my front. It was an effort to remember how to breathe as those awful eyes looked down at me.

He ran a gloved knuckle down my bare arm. "Dreadful and beautiful, much like you, sweet death, my little terror of decay." And then he leaned in and kissed my cheek. So chaste, so warm.

My face flushed ten shades of red and my knees felt weak. "And hello. Thank you for joining me."

"Well, I was sick of dinner in my enclosure. Though the food's been great."

He chuckled darkly and pulled out my chair, ushering me to take a seat. "I don't mean for dinner. I mean here, this side of the veil."

I shakily took the glass of violet wine before me and took a sip, hoping the alcohol would burn my nerves away. "And where is here? Hell?"

He took his seat at the opposite end of the table and shook out his cloth napkin. "Blackberry wine. Like it? And this? This is a library. You've been here once before. Don't you recall?"

Something cleared its throat again before shadowed hands placed plates of food before us in unison. I looked up and thanked my horned shadow demon. "That'll be all, Amon," Devil dismissed.

"So they do have a name."

He cut into his steak. "They all do. They all answer to me. No one you see here within the town's limits will harm you."

I took a bite of zucchini so buttery I wanted to moan in pleasure. "No zombie librarians I should be afraid of?"

His rumble of a chuckle made me bold enough to dive right into why I'd come. Onyx was so skilled at warming people with his charm. Perhaps I could do the same. I'd practiced the words in my head and in my room so many times, but they came out jumbled anyway. "I saw something when I found the elder wolves through the veil."

"I'm sure you saw many things."

"I saw the Halloween Boys," I said, searching his gaze. But the mention seemed to cause him to pause. As he slowly recovered, he refilled his wineglass.

"Go on."

"They were—they were dead. Lying on the ground. Fire everywhere. It was a vision. I get those often. And this was the worst I've ever had. It's why I had to come here to find you and ask for your help."

The devil tensed his jaw and twirled the stem of his wineglass, slouching over in his seat. Chairs looked too small for him. Everything here looked too tiny, too fragile, next to him.

Including me.

"So the only reason you came here was for them. You summoned the gateway, walked through the forest of the median level, and ignorantly followed a fae, all for *them*." His grip hardened on his glass.

"Why else would I come to—"

"Hell? Yes, Blythe, this is hell. And I'm not helping you."

I stood, feeling my chest burn with anger. "All this toying with me to get me here, all those promises you made? What about those?"

He stood as well, glaring down at me with ferocity as the fire from the candlesticks shot up higher, making him a vision through flames. "Oh, is she shocked that the devil lies? Poor, pitiful, foolish girl."

"Then I'm leaving," I gritted out, throwing down my napkin and walking toward the door. A door, an ordinary door. "Thanks for nothing."

He didn't stop me. Didn't so much as budge from the head of the table as I slammed the heavy door and walked down the stone steps and onto a sidewalk lined with jack-o'-lanterns and hay bales and… with a gasp, I spun around, realizing where I was. He hadn't been lying when he said I'd been here before. But how? He said this was hell—how was I standing outside of Ash Grove High School?

In a silent wall of darkness, I jumped, feeling his larger-than-life presence. He slowly walked into view and down the stairs, with his hands in his pockets like he was going on a leisurely stroll.

He stopped in front of me, his lip quirking with a slightly amused and devious grin. His voice was pure velvet authority of an ancient horror when he said, "You're not going anywhere. You belong to me now."

CHAPTER 14
The Devil's in the Details

ARE YOU LISTENING?

A slow fog had crept into the humble town of Ash Grove. A dense atmospheric change, a chill too cold for the last day of September, and the brisk air mixed with sorrow in a way that ached bones and haunted dreams. This was it. This was where their story really took off. Oh, my friends, something wicked this way comes.

Onyx Hart rocked back and forth with his head between his knees, not on his own humble front porch, but on the stairs of Minnie's little farmhouse. Wolfgang and James approached him as twilight befell them again.

James Cove could barely contain his rage. Oh, that sweet rage that would serve me so well in the years to come. "Could have sworn we heard voices, whispers, in the woods. But no tracks, and each time we thought we'd found… something… the trail went cold."

Wolfgang shot James a worried glance as Onyx continued to grip his hair in helplessness. Wolf coaxed with a hand on his worried friend's shoulder. "She can't be far. Probably got lost picking flowers or blackberries."

"Min's terrified of the dark. Why'd she go without me?"

James's jaw tensed as he glanced back into the forest. "That new woman in town, the one spreading thoughts of harvest parties and this Halloween festivity? I don't trust her."

"You think she knows something?" Wolfgang asked, now petting Onyx's hair.

James shrugged. *"Wouldn't hurt to ask. I've no loyalty to newcomers. Like Father Joseph said a few sermons back, be wary of the wolf in sheep's clothing."*

The moment twilight switched to dark, panting was heard in the distance, and the boys all stood to greet its source. A man holding a torch breathlessly rested against the front porch post.

"Mr. Moore?" Wolfgang held the man's shoulders. *"What is it?"*

The old man struggled to breathe. "Been lookin' for you boys everywhere. They're—you need to come to town now. All men are called to assist."

And so they ran, not bothering to find a horse, not questioning how they could run so far, so fast. Human men always thought themselves more strong, more capable than they truly were, so when something indeed extraordinary happened—they tended to think it commonplace or a confirmation of their brilliance. It was a fatal flaw that I found women did not possess. Though everyone on my side of the veil knew women to be much stronger than men, regardless.

Dust kicked up as they stopped in the bustling town square of Ash Grove. Women sobbed in the arms of their husbands, and men grunted and raised their pitchforks. Who could have committed such a heinous act?

Bodies of women lay in a perfectly straight line. Some bloodied, some not. Oh, a man, too. Suppose he was caught in the crosshairs. But only one body brought Onyx Hart to his knees. His wails of sorrow were a melody, a chord that would lie beneath every song, every piece of music he'd compose again. Grief was the longest, most enduring love and form of self-torment. And this was the making of the villain. The betrayal at the hand of his kin. The match being lit that would ignite and awaken who he was.

The Dracul.

The Dragon.

I had wondered if it would emerge then, though it did not. His friends dropped next to him, the rage within them so potent it drowned out all the noise, all the thoughts and murmurs. Wolfgang and James glanced at one another, both knowing without words what they were going to do.

They'd known they were capable. James Cove prayed it away, and it didn't work. Wolfgang did every good deed available to absolve him of his violent desires. It didn't work either. But Onyx Hart? He felt no such desire for absolution. His birth mother's influence was not enough to counter the benevolence of his father, the vampire king. His head shot up from where it was buried in his lost love's matted curls, green eyes bright and burning with tears.

The voice of the dragon emerged then, as a breathless and deadly promise. "We find them. We find each and every one of them, and I will drain and drink every ounce of their blood for what they've done."

THE STORY KEEPER PIRATES begged me for this tale, along with paying a high price. The audacity Captain Vex displayed in asking was nerve well rewarded. But I didn't give them as much as I'll give you. So pay close attention to these details.

CHAPTER 15

Blythe

A ROARING LION

> A spirit of art and madness lurks incessantly beneath the balconies and behind the drapes. It cannot die, and it prevents all from being lost.
> *Albert Camus*

Glaring up at the devil, I felt like a kitten hissing at a lion. "What kind of trick is this?" I demanded, gesturing past him to Ash Grove High. "The school, putting my bedroom in Lamb's Blood Church—"

"Our bedroom."

My words died in my throat. "I'm not sharing a bed with you."

"You will. You'll do anything and everything I want you to," he rumbled plainly, crossing his arms. "I despise talking, and you do require so much of it."

Huffing in indignation, I stepped back. "For someone who hates talking, you sure do always have a lot to say to me."

"It's a part of my affinity and my affliction toward you."

"I'm going home."

"You are home."

God, he was frustrating and *handsome* and just so irritating in all his simple authority that I snapped. Marching up to him, I pointed my finger into his rock-hard chest. "This was me being nice, Devil. You're going to help me, help my boys, or I'll—I'll—"

He cocked an eyebrow. "Or. You'll. What?" He clipped each word. Then my eyes betrayed me as they dropped to his full lips, and mine parted at the sight of them. Something about this bully of a being drew me in and entranced me like none other. His eyes dropped similarly, and then his hand was on my lower back, pressing me flush to his body as his tongue wet his lower lip in temptation. I quivered at the sight of it. His gaze softened ever so slightly as he whispered, "You need to go for a walk."

My heart fluttered in my chest as my mind worked through a response. "What?"

"And then meet me in bed."

"I'm not sleeping with you."

"You are. But first, I need your help."

Pulling back and breaking the magnetism of our bodies and lips, I put my hands on my hips. "You have some freaking nerve asking me for help."

"Nerve, yes. I have a surplus of that. And you'll surrender, little death. In time, you'll give me everything." He growled, his tone laced with promise, stealing my breath again. "Don't think I can't see it written all over you… the way you suck in air in short bursts, your cheeks flushing, your knees quaking. You feel it. You have from the moment we met, and you want to give me my desires." He stepped forward and twirled a stray lock of my hair. "Say yes, and perhaps I'll reward you."

"You'll help the Halloween Boys?" I swallowed, breathless, angry at how right he was. My stupid body betrayed me each time I was with him, and he noticed. He read me like a book.

He hummed low in his throat. "Say yes first."

"Yes," I uttered without the hesitation that I should have exercised. Like a fool.

A catlike smile spread across his too-gorgeous face. "Wonderful. Look at you, so eager to obey already."

Before I could kick his shins for that comment, he nodded past me and chided. "Keep in mind, hell is not yours until you claim it. Every demon, legion, ghoul, and foul thing that haunted you in your realm? Their numbers are tenfold here. And I cannot protect you until you are queen. They'll play tricks on you, fuck with your mind. But as the queen of the underworld, you would rule over them. They would do your bidding. But until then… watch your step." He gestured behind me. "Without further ado, your tour guide to hell. I'd introduce you, but I believe you've already met."

My dress fanned as I spun, but I hit nothing, because the devil's arrogant ass disappeared in a sweet-smelling smoke. He left me less stunned by the act than what I was staring at, who I was left with. Shock and trepidation rippled across my skin as I stood face to face with his smirking, self-satisfied painted clown face.

Giving a mock bow, he offered me his white-gloved hand. "I'd say this is decidedly not a boring day for us. Wouldn't you agree, Ace?"

My jaw dropped as I stared at the chaos magician Wolf had killed and I had locked away in boredom for all eternity. "Zyre," I whispered in horror.

CHAPTER 16

Blythe

THE RIDDLER

> We are far too serious, we must learn to juggle our heavens and our hells… the game is playing us, we must play back.
> *Charles Bukowski*

"How are you here?"

Zyre clicked his heels and extended his arms with a laugh. "You agreed to the devil's terms just now, did you not? Ah, he's a crafty one, my master. You set me free just in time for Halloween. Now, shall we start the grand tour?"

"You-your master is…" It all began to fall into place. If Devil was Zyre's master, and the chaos magician was after me so he could bring me to his master, along with the ghouls… "It's been him the whole time, hasn't it?"

Zyre shrugged. "No idea what you're getting worked up about, but, yes, most likely."

"He's such a fucking liar."

"And you're surprised?" He bounced on his heels. "This is probably the dullest spot in hell. Can we at least walk and talk? Come on. The place's so fun to explore and I've been locked in that horrid little room you banished me to."

I followed several steps behind the phantom, stewing in the revelation and chastising myself for not piecing it together sooner. But I hadn't expected the answer to be lying in plain sight. If it was the devil who sent the ghouls, the magicians, the demons… why? It was too much to process, and suddenly, I felt as if I'd been asking the mysterious man all the wrong questions. Which was ironic, too, because he had all but told me as much several times.

Zyre skipped along, twirling and singing a song. "Oh, I do adore hell in October. Just wait until you see downtown."

"This isn't *hell*," I snapped. "This is Ash Grove, and you two are trying to make me believe some stupid trick. I don't know why, but I'll figure it out soon enough."

The phantom laughed. "Trick-or-treat, as the kids say." He inhaled deeply. "Smell that? Dead leaves, crisp air, the faint wafting aroma of caramel apples. Nothing beats autumn."

Despite my torment and my obnoxious tour guide, as we entered the town square—again, a mirror image of Ash Grove— my heart swelled to a level that brought tears to my eyes. Once again, just like last year, hay bales sat along the sidewalks, speared with scarecrows and skeletons. Red, orange, and yellow leafy garlands dangled above shop windows. And the pumpkins? Oh, the pumpkins were everywhere. Zyre was right. It was a spooky dream beyond compare. And whatever illusion this was, the colors were richer, deeper. The sensations of those cozy feelings of Halloween were more impactful than ever before. Like I was swimming in Halloween itself, with no end and no desire for it to ever be over.

The chaos clown put a friendly arm around my shoulder. "Told you it's perfect. Wait until when it's all lit up on Halloween."

"I won't be here on Halloween. I'll be back home in the real Ash Grove and with my boys," I corrected curtly as I shrugged off his touch.

"God, you're so dumb. Clearly the most daft being I've ever met. Though your meathead boyfriends come close."

I reared back to punch him in the arm, but he disappeared into a puff of glitter and appeared behind me to tap my shoulder and giggle maniacally. Stomping my foot, I screamed in frustration. "I need to get out of here."

The glitter materialized in front of me again, and Zyre lay back on a park bench as old men swept the sidewalks and waved hello. Just like Ash Grove. I wanted to cry. This illusion was messing with my head, and suddenly, the absence of my guys was so striking and heartbreaking that all I wanted was the arms of my demon, the bite of my vampire, and the certainty of my werewolf. God, what had I done? I slumped onto the bench next to Zyre and put my head in my hands.

"You danced with the devil and lost your head, huh?" He cackled.

"Shut up, or I'll send you back to the boring place," I threatened, not sure if I could even make good on that promise. The chaos magician sat up, and I continued. "Not that you care, but I'm now helpless, with no plan to save the lives of my guys. I'm stuck in hell with a deranged clown and an egotistical maniac of biblical proportions."

Zyre laughed again, pulling out a deck of cards and shuffling. "You know, you and I are similar creatures."

I raised my head long enough to give him an incredulous look before putting my forehead back on my knees.

"I was once made of human stuff, like you. Then I found the devil himself and traded my humanity for dark power, a deck of cards, and, of course, to be in his service. You? Same story. At least this time around."

"Very, very different story, actually," I argued against the skirts of my dress. "But I get the feeling that I'm utterly fucked right now."

Zyre patted my back. "There, there. Don't you see what this is? Mercy, the riddle. The game is so clearly laid out it's almost too difficult for me to keep quiet."

That piqued my interest. "What riddle?"

"All of this." He gestured from hell's Ash Grove to me. "You feel toyed with because he is indeed toying with you. But to what end? Why you? Oh, stupid, stupid girl. Look around. Figure it out. It's all hiding in plain sight."

"Seems to be a theme with him," I muttered, resting my chin on my fist. But if what Zyre was saying was true, and it did track with the devil's tricks, perhaps the answers were indeed closer than they appeared. I'd have to separate my desperation to get free. To save the guys, and my fear. If I was going to outsmart the king of trickery and his henchman, I'd have to be smart. Smart like a demon, like a vampire, a dragon, and a luna wolf. It was time. Time to do this without the guys' help. Hadn't that been what I wanted? This journey was on my shoulders alone, and I couldn't fail them.

Standing, I brushed off my dress and held out my hand. "Okay, Zyre. Show me around hell."

Standing, he took my palm and smirked a red painted smile. "With pleasure, my lady."

CHAPTER 17
Blythe
KING OF THE BOTTOMLESS PIT

> Cannot fix on the hour, or the look, or the words, which laid the foundation. It is too long ago. I was in the middle before I knew I had begun.
> *Pride and Prejudice, Jane Austen*

Zyre twirled and giggled as he showed me around fake Ash Grove, and I pretended to be enthralled, pretended to believe him when he said all the townspeople were real. And happy. Out of sheer curiosity, I paused outside of Magia Eclectics, seeing that it was still, in fact, the same in this illusion. Though no one was inside, and when I tugged the door, it was locked. Though, there was a sign on the door…

"Be back soon," Zyre read before slapping his knee. "You wouldn't think so, but the devil has a grand sense of humor."

"I want to go to the diner, and Fenrir, and the cemetery," I requested, still distracted by peeking into the shop that looked so vacant but exactly the same as the real one.

Zyre cupped his hands around his eyes and pressed against the shop window. "Remind me to come back for a tarot deck and that fabulous eyeshadow collection. Black shimmer is my life."

God, why was he making it hard not to laugh? I gave his face paint a once-over. "It's hard to find a good white foundation. Yours is nice."

The chaos magician clapped. "It *is*! See? Goth girls get it. Sorry about what I said at the circus that day—about your makeup. That was out of line. I'd kill to know how to do a cat eye as well as you."

I scoffed. "You should see what I can do with an actual mirror. There wasn't one on my vanity."

Zyre tapped his chin. "Wonder why, hm?" But before I could question his odd and teasing grin, he continued. "So you think you'd ever take me to Hallows Fest? I've never been but want to go so fucking bad."

It was getting late, and the ache of missing the guys was wearing on my soul. They had to have noticed me gone by now. Then the sudden shock that I could miss Hallows Fest was almost too much to endure. "Can you stop acting like we're friends? I despise you." I shoved past him and clipped down the sidewalk.

Skipping to catch up, he persisted. "But we *are* friends, Ace. Look at us—strolling hell together, working to please the devil."

"I do not care about pleasing that arrogant, lying bully of a prick."

He skipped backward, then, while juggling two miniature pumpkins he'd surely stolen off a shop's display. "Do you think I should wear this outfit for Hallows Fest or something with a little more pizzazz? I have one that sparkles."

"You know what?" I crossed my arms outside of the old church that cracked my heart open. "I think I'm turning in for the night. See you never."

He chuckled. "I can see why you're his bride. You two have similar senses of dark sass."

"Wait, what? I'm not his bride."

"Toodles!" Zyre waved before erupting into a cloud of glitter that made me cough.

"God, I hate that stupid clown," I cursed, swatting the air. But then there was Lamb's Blood... the gloomy church where I'd been with my archdemon, my boys. Ghost loved this church so much. I'd never understand it. Though it was haunting to see it, or the mirage of it, all decorated for Halloween again. Bright orange pumpkins littered the ground, piled on each other, with no order or plan. They were just scattered across the lawn and up the stone steps to the big red front door. I half expected Raven to caw at me from his favorite branch and for the guys to pop out, faces painted like skulls. They'd take my arm and pass me a bucket and say we're going trick-or-treating, just like they'd done the year before.

A sigh shook me. This was a cruel game from the devil indeed. Because Ash Grove wasn't Ash Grove without the Halloween Boys. To walk these streets and admire the Halloween decorations without them felt maddening and wrong. After stumbling over pumpkins and passing through the crimson archway, I clipped into the sanctuary, which was now a massive bedroom. I jumped as a voice greeted me from a leather armchair in the corner.

He was sipping an amber liquid from a glass by the fireplace, looking every bit as evil and devilish as he had at dinner. "Welcome home, dear."

Just his smug presence ignited a storm of anger in my chest as I marched over to the vanity and picked up an antique silver hand mirror with no glass. "Why are there no mirrors? Why does this place look like Ash Grove?"

"I see you had a lovely walk, my bride. You know, Halloween in hell is something souls aspire to for eternity." He took a leisurely sip of bourbon. "You got to waltz right in. Wonder why that would be?"

Fury roiled through me as I lifted the hand mirror over my head and chucked it at his perfect, arrogant face. I regretted my idiocy the moment the silver left my palm, because the devil only dodged my attack, letting the item clank to the ground. There was no puff of smoke, no flash of red or shouting. No, what he did was much scarier. Downing his drink in one gulp, he carefully set his glass down and reached around the chair, picking up the mirror and standing.

Twirling it in his hand, he stepped toward me. And unlike my usual steeled knees with him, this time, I took a step backward. Because I was with only him now. In his room, in his hell. And there was no one here to hear me scream, to come to my rescue. I was at his mercy, and I'd been acting like a complete idiot. Something about him dropped my defenses. What was it about him? He noticed my retreat and cocked his head.

"There's nowhere you could run to escape me. Not in this life or the next." He growled low, but his tone wasn't angry. It was something richer and enticing, making the hair on my arms stand at attention just like the candlestick flames did around him.

I held out a shaky and accusatory finger. "It was you the whole time. Sending the ghouls after me, the demons, you—you lied to the Halloween Boys."

"Ah, you've solved the easiest part of the mystery. Congratulations, Blythe. Now, will you finally start piecing the rest together so we can get on with it?"

He was a foot away from me now on his slow prowl, and my heart was racing as I gazed up at his fierce, garnet stare. "Get on with what?"

"You being mine and ruling hell with me. It is your rightful place, *Mortala*. Or are we still pretending to be *Blythe*?"

I shook my head, covering my ears. "I don't know what you're talking about."

Backing away, I bumped into my vanity, and then the grip of the devil was on my shoulders. I froze in place, breathing heavily. Why did his touch not feel foreign at all? What was it that made his eyes soften when he looked at me, that lethal man of legend evaporating, even as he commanded fear from every being in existence? His brows furrowed, as if conflicted, and with a small show of strength, he turned me around, pulling my back to his middle and hooking his hand under my chin, making me look forward.

A gasp of breath rendered me weak and dizzy at both his heavy touch and at what gazed back at me. The mirror was now in place, where it had once been missing from the vanity. And the reflection staring back at me wasn't an unfamiliar one. My eyes, my long golden-brown waves, my black dress, the dips of my elegant curves.

I was the same except it wasn't me... or it was... but I had black and twisted horns protruding from the top of my head. Her. I'd seen her on Halloween after the Baphomet's attack. She'd sat on a throne then, and she'd looked so sure, so like me but so not me at the same time...

In the mirror, I watched as Devil looked on, seemingly pleased, and bent forward, brushing his lips against my ear from behind. "Hello, Mortala. My bride. Welcome home."

CHAPTER 18
The Devil's in the Details

REVIVAL

Prayer candles flickered, and a lost and plagued James Cove sat with his head in his hands. Why'd he fight me so? This time, for the first time, I decided to ask. Sauntering into Lamb's Blood Church, I took a seat next to the praying man, and after a moment, he gifted me a cold sideways glance.

"Always loved the peace within an empty church. When they aren't empty? Not so much. But like this…" I shrugged, giving him a small smile to put him at ease. Dance with me, Ghost.

He leaned back against the hard pew and crossed his arms. "I've felt a lot of things in this church. I can't say peace has ever been one of them."

As I turned my attention to the flickering flames, he regarded me with suspicion. "New to town or just passing through?"

The smile that threatened my demeanor almost couldn't be helped as I felt his murderous desires. He was assessing me, curious about whether I'd played a hand in the murdered and missing girls. If I were the source of his beloved town's suffering. For once, James's instincts were correct, and he was listening to them.

I offered him a hand gloved in black leather, and he accepted. "Judas," I answered.

His crystal blue eyes narrowed. "Unfortunate name. Judas betrayed

Jesus and his disciples. The great deceiver, some say. An incarnation of the devil himself."

A misunderstanding, but I'll save that story for another day.

"Sometimes," I said, standing and approaching the altar, "the world needs an evil to look to just as much as it needs a light. Villains and devils are mirrors in a sense." I struck a match, and the flame twirled and danced for its master. "Everyone wants to be the hero, James. But few are brave enough to be a demon in a world that idolizes the angels." I lit a candle. "Judas to Jesus… what would humanity have done without his sacrifice?"

The boy stood then, brow furrowed, a pit of dark fury swirling in his gut. Smoke of anger, of shame, of horror at the excitement that sparked at my words. Blowing out the candle, I tapped a cross to my lips, my chest, and turned to leave, though I never really left.

"I never gave you my name," he rumbled deeply behind me. Ah, there was a hint of the monster that lurked within his bones. How easily he activated for me.

Standing in the archway to the sanctuary, I tilted my head. "No, you did not. But you will."

As I was moments from disappearing, he strode toward me with purpose. Intrigued, I waited, until his gaze met mine, burning with passion and every trait that would make him the finest king of the damned and the demons, and ruler of legions. "Can you help me and my friends, my home? I'll trade you anything."

"You are simultaneously smarter and more foolish than you appear, aren't you?" I extended my hand. "We have a bargain." His palm electrified with mine, a cog in the clock of his ticking fate, as blue smoke subtly danced around our exchange.

CHAPTER 19

Blythe

DEVIL MAY CARE

A surge of something undeniable crackled through me like a hundred bolts of lightning as I stared at his relaxed stature and the garnet tint of his furrowed stare. The devil's shoulders were wide like a mountain behind me, closing in on me, reminding me of the stories the luna wolf told me about a wolf who went insane and fell in love with a mountain, living in its caves forever. The devil was the overpass, every deep cavern of terror, and the rushing waters of horror.

And taking in the sight of me with those ebony horns... It hit me like the weight of a thousand sinful desires, colliding into me like a freight train at full speed. I met his stare in the mirror, a stare of passion that mirrored my own. Of slow restraint, ready to snap with one gentle tug.

"Judas," I whispered.

I tugged.

And he snapped.

Grabbing my horns, he spun me around and dropped his hold to my lower back, knocking every ounce of air from my lungs. And without giving me a moment to think, to reconsider, like he knew I would, his lips collided with mine. My whimper shook my bones as I wrapped my arms around his thick neck, meeting his wickedly bittersweet tongue with mine. All I wanted was him. It didn't make sense. It wasn't logical. There was no build or sorting through my imaginings.

This was wrong.

This was the only thing right.

His teeth bit my bottom lip as he scooped me up like I was his, like I'd been his forever, like I really was his bride, and carried me to the bed. Laying me back, he surveyed me with more heat in his gaze than I'd ever beheld from any man *or* monster. And I quivered beneath it, shaking my head. It was a spell—something—it had to be. This didn't add up—

"No," I breathed.

His black shirt fell to the ground, revealing his broad and muscular frame, that temping V above his low-slung pants. My mouth watered, but more than that, for some reason, my eyes teared up and my heart swelled with some sort of love. Love? *Love.*

"No," I repeated.

He shook his head. "I won't hear that word from your lips again. You won't speak it to me. Not here, not in our bed."

He took hold of my ankles and pulled me forward, reaching around and unzipping my dress while his lips found my neck and I sighed a lover's sigh into his touch. "Why do you feel so good?" I mused, tingling at every brush of his skin, the rough touch as he peeled my gown down over my hips and tossed it aside, leaving me in only black silk panties and a lace balconette bra.

"Why, indeed," he growled, pulling back and holding on to the bedposts so hard I was sure they would break as the bed shook. "You should know that this won't look like restraint, but oh, it is."

Why was a beg to *not* restrain himself on the tip of my tongue?

This was terrible. This was betrayal. This was a bewitching of the devil. It had to be. But he looked so enticing, the muscles of his arms flexing and his jaw tightening as his evil stare feasted on my half-naked form. Those hands, that jaw, his lips…

"Judas," I breathed again. *Judas?*

His chest caved in, and those amber-red eyes hooded to a slow close, as if his name on my lips was the finest liquor he swirled on his tongue. And then he was on top of me, one hand ripping off my panties as if they were made of paper. Our lips crashed together, muddling my thoughts into nothing but him. Nothing but my devil. Oh god, *my devil?*

When he pulled away to remove his pants, he sprung free, and my fingers trembled on my bra hook, barely getting it unlatched in time to admire the size, the girth, the sight of the devil himself, naked and wicked like a statue carved from the finest marble. And in that moment, awareness hit me. Of how every artist I'd ever heard of, from the beginning of time, had tried to replicate his beauty. Every poet had tried to warn. Priests had told humans to beware, and it all made sense why God himself was jealous of the Hades before me.

And I was about to let him fuck me. Or was he just taking it? As soon as my mind became hazy with thoughts wrestling to fight through, the press of his lips rendered me empty. There were no thoughts, no more questions. Nothing mattered anymore.

He dropped over me, his palms pressing into the bed and making the mattress rise. My breasts against his fiery chest and his breath like bourbon burned and stung me in a drunken intoxication of need for more, more, more.

I wrapped my arms around him, letting the feeling overtake me, as he searched my eyes, looking for something still. Had he found it? Did I want him to find it?

"You're here," I whispered, my voice taking a different cadence, my horns feeling heavy. It was the first time I'd noticed them, felt them and how my hair pooled around their sharp indents.

"Always," he purred. Then he swiped a lick at my jaw, his

hand rising to my face before he pushed two leather-gloved fingers into my mouth. I accepted them eagerly, exploring the salty-sweet, warm roughness of them. So huge. He was so huge. Larger than life, a mystery of mythological proportions. And he was looking at me, thrusting his concealed digits between my lips and letting a rumble vibrate his throat. His Adam's apple bobbed as his breathing picked up. The restraint was evident as I lay beneath him, pinned between his massive arms. I was a lamb under a lion.

A wet and wanting, confused and insatiable little lamb…

"Stop thinking," he ordered, pulling his hand out and easing it down my body. "Start feeling." Without a single stroke, without an invitation or placation of gentleness, without even removing his gloves, his fingers pierced me, stronger and thicker than any human man's cock could, and I cried out, not expecting the pain or the wetness that devoured him to his knuckles. The devil growled. "Now, tell me what you feel."

"What?" I wiggled my hips against him, suddenly feeling his hard length propped and pressing into my lower belly, his middle scratching against the warmth of hair above the pussy that was taking the thrust of his digits.

"Tell me what you feel. Do it. Now."

The answer seemed obvious, but I couldn't say no. Not because he'd just *told* me that I couldn't, but because the word would no longer form on my lips. I was incapable of no. It didn't exist. It couldn't be uttered. And suddenly, that display of his power confirmed everything. I was at his mercy. *No* didn't exist in this bed, in this exchange. But did I want it to?

"Your fingers feel so good. Painful, too." I groaned as he hooked and spread them, making sure I felt the fullness of his capturing of me.

His thumb found my clit, then, and tapped it, pushing into the pert, sensitive wetness gathered there. My moan was breathless as I moved my hands to cup his jaw. He met my stare, then, eyes full of emotion. "What are *you* feeling?" I whispered, repeating his question to me.

His jaw tensed again, and his pace inside me slowed slightly, like he was searching for the words. The devil searching for the right thing to say? "You. Only ever you, my bride."

What did that mean? It didn't matter, because I couldn't question it if I tried, couldn't sort it through, because his fingers twisted and hooked while his palm and wrist rubbed against my apex, moving my hips with them. I came hard, gripping at my captor as he only watched my face, as if he were drinking my pleasure like a vampire. Even swallowing as if I were a strong drink he swirled in his palm. I supposed that was an accurate description in that moment. When I shuddered and writhed out the aftershocks of my pleasure, he slowly removed his hold, bringing his knuckles to his nose and inhaling, letting his eyes drift closed before sucking each finger slowly, showing me his tongue, his teeth, as he did.

I opened my mouth to speak, but he simply stood. "You'll sleep now," he said coldly. "Good night."

"What? That's it?" Rising up on my elbows, I made to… something. Argue, or maybe reach for him, but a weight of fatigue barreled down onto my shoulders and neck, pushing me backward. As I sank into the bed, I faintly recalled something push into the space beside me, comforting me and scaring me and rocking me to sleep in that space between pleasure and terror that I straddled so often. And then I was asleep, in bed, with the devil.

THE SUN FILTERED in through the multicolored stained glass of Lamb's Blood Church: hell edition. A church so thoroughly defiled now by demons and devils and sex that surely it belonged in hell more than Ash Grove, even. When I sat up in a burrow of soft blankets, I rubbed my legs against black silk pajamas. I hadn't been wearing these the night before. What had happened the night before… The awareness and leftover ache between my thighs reminded me as I padded to the round breakfast table and sat among hot tea, bagels, and meats. As I took a small sip of green tea, somehow the perfect temperature, I noticed the bouquet of black roses in the middle of the table and a card with red scrawl.

Dear Blythe,
Thank you for last night.
I'll be seeing you again this evening.
Love,
Judas

I set the card down with a huff. Last night? Was I even in control of my own body? He'd touched me, kissed me, and that was more surprising than the horns displayed in the mirror. I reached up, feeling them still present.

"Horns. Cool," I muttered. "A finger bang and roses. Great." I took a bite of bagel. I didn't know how to feel. Should I feel violated? Angry? Deceived? Probably so. He beguiled me, entranced me with some spell, some devil power that made me want him so ardently, so passionately. And it wasn't just carnal want; it was the desire of lovers who'd been together for a long time. An enduring passion and strong feelings of… no, it couldn't be. It was all a trick. This was the devil, and he was playing me, confounding my mind, and luring me away from my purpose in the most sinister and distracting of ways…

Maybe I felt tricked, and maybe consent wasn't explicit, but what did I expect from the devil himself? Sweet wooing? I wanted him. I wanted even more of him, somehow. I glared at the lovely black roses he'd sent, as if he were any gentleman after a date. Stupid that they made my senseless heart flutter. Fuck, this wasn't good. Being in hell disguised as Ash Grove, the devil's devious allure, Halloween, it was all messing with my head. I had to remember my purpose here. I had to keep the image of my boys in my mind and stay on task. To save them from their fate and return home by any means necessary. That was my goal. And the devil would help me, or he wouldn't. But regardless, I was going to make it happen. If I had to lie, cheat, steal, and do some deceiving of my own, I would. And it would start with my tour with the clown and continue when I met with the devil that evening. He'd expect me to be an emotional, scared, sputtering mess. The devil he may have been, but he must not have realized that girl had died.

I had horns now. I was death. I'd find a way to start acting like it, and I would make him burn if he got in my way.

CHAPTER 20

Blythe

HELL'S A PICNIC

> The devil's voice is sweet to hear.
> *Steven King*

Zyre had made a big show of leading me to a grassy meadow, under the sinking sun of hell, and onto a quilt on the ground. There were meats, cheeses, wines, chocolates, and to my curious and exasperated dismay, a large, broody devil awaiting me.

"He's a quiet sort of guy," Zyre explained before leaving me. "But he talks more with you than anyone else."

It would be stupid to ask why, because no one would tell me anyway.

"You said once that Stevie Nicks was one of the greatest lyricists of all time, didn't you?" The devil refilled my wine, and I picked at long furls of grass, trying and failing to ignore him.

I racked my brain, wondering how he'd known that. "I said that to Ames the first time I met him."

"Yes, quite right. Do you still believe it true?"

"Yes, why?"

"Leather and Lace" by Stevie Nicks and Don Henley played around us as if there were stereos in the trees. Another display of my picnic date's power. I narrowed my gaze and bit into a purple grape. "Is this really hell?"

"Indeed, it is."

"Doesn't look like it."

"Hell is different things for different souls. For you and me, and the residents here, this is our dark paradise."

"And for others?"

"For others, hell is more of an internal state than a gruesome destination. Hell is the shadow of self all beings must eventually contend with, in one life or the next."

I took in the patchwork fall foliage and the faint smell of smoke and ash that tainted the otherwise perfect breeze. "And you rule over it all?"

"*Rule* is a very human word, my dear. I am more like a guardian."

After moments passed and we sat in the silence he valued so much, I murmured as the wind blew through my hair and the sun glinted, so lovely, in his deep red stare. "You're going to have to let me go back."

"No. You aren't leaving," he said with stern finality.

And everything from his tone, his demeanor, the way he observed me as if I were the most interesting puzzle to solve… the way he spoke more with me than anyone else yet gave up next to nothing of himself. His words and declaration haunted me, terrifying me with their wayward truth.

Maybe I was truly stuck here with him.

"Have you always been—" I gestured to the large storm cloud of a man in front of me. "Actually Hades?"

He snorted, then popped a grape into his mouth and stood, offering me his hand. "To interrogate me, you must be my dancing partner. That is the law of this land, a law I happened to only just now implement."

Rolling my eyes and biting back a smile, I took his leather-covered palm in mine and let him pull me close. "I'm not interrogating. I'm getting to know you. Isn't that what you wanted?"

He spun me out and back in as music softly played across the meadow. A dance floor just for us. "Yes, I have always been a devil. I can recall no time before. I am a force, as are you."

"I was born human, though." My gaze caught his, and my breath hitched, and in a moment of candor, I confessed. "I'm annoyed by how attracted I am to you."

The corner of his mouth quirked. "Likewise."

It was a struggle to focus on conversation and not the way he affectionately gripped my hand and held my waist. Or the way the line of his strong jaw complemented his broad shoulders and nearly seven-foot-tall height. It wasn't just his physical splendor that drew me in. It was his mystery, the gentleness hidden behind such power and authority.

Judas was arguably the most formidable being in all the world, yet his strength was not a booming, loud thing, I was learning. His power was as quiet as he preferred to be. A hidden and reserved nature that contradicted any perception of who you'd think he was upon hearing his mythological title.

I pushed down the flutter that erupted in my lower belly. "Is this how you spend your days? Walking around this little copycat of a town. Isn't the devil supposed to, like, be doing grand and terrifying things?"

"Is that what I'm supposed to be doing? Huh," he teased. "How do you know I'm not already?" Air hooked in my lungs and flushed my cheeks as he clutched me by the small of my back and danced with me, slow and close now. The atmosphere evolved into a milky shade of blue while fireflies flickered around us. "My job is to look after this place and all its levels. I ensure balance. You'll find that, on this side of the veil, balance is more paramount than most things. The notions of good and evil merely come from mortals making sense of the balance we on this side of the veil inherently comprehend."

"That's not an answer. That's another immortal nonanswer. What do you do in your free time, for fun?"

He rested his forehead against mine, and I felt his fervor and smelled his vanilla and birchwood scent. It was intoxicating. *He* was intoxicating. After long moments of swaying, holding me close, as if he were afraid I'd fly away, he answered. "I enjoy baking. And photography."

My eyes were caught on his lips and the way they parted when he noticed my regard. "That wasn't so hard to share, now, was it?"

"It's half a lie," he whispered lowly. "I lie a lot."

"Oh?"

"My free and untethered thoughts are constantly and unabashedly of you."

Heat warmed my lower belly at his unexpected declaration. It could have been a lie, as he said he liked doing, but it didn't feel like one.

A gloved finger tilted my chin. "Why are you always wearing gloves?" My voice sounded breathless and betrayed my wanton desire.

He leaned down, the air from his answer like cherries against my aching lips. "Why, indeed."

I shouldn't have—I don't know why I did; maybe I was truly entranced by him and this place—but I rose on my tiptoes and closed the distance between us. And in a moment of pure insanity, I kissed him. A kiss that brought forth a longing sigh from the devil's lips as he wrapped me in his embrace. It wasn't a kiss of lust, but of something else. Something far more frightening.

Something far more damning. And I'd spend the rest of the night pretending it didn't happen. Telling myself I did it only to manipulate him into letting his guard down and allowing me to escape. That it wasn't my enthusiastic doing, but my mind being seduced by his allure. But obviously, I wasn't as strong as him. He could admit his lies, and clearly, I could not.

CHAPTER 21

Onyx

BURNING

Do you believe in destiny? That even the powers of time can be altered for a single purpose?
Bram Stoker, "Dracula"

"I'm going to fuck you right here against this tree." Wolfgang growled, shoving me against the bark, splintering pain down my spine.

I glared at him through my eyelashes, his pants of breath rough and primal. "I don't want to."

The werewolf, who was a good bit wider than me, pressed his thick and hairy forearm into my neck, forcing the air from my throat. His other hand jerked at my belt as he growled. "I didn't ask if you want to. But I know, Onyx, that you need to."

A strangled scoff of a sob rendered my reply hollow. "You forced me away from her, marched me down the godforsaken path to Hallows Fest—the last place I want to be right now—and now you're going to fuck me against my will, too? Seems a little dark for you, Wolf."

While he pushed his arm harder against my throat, the pain and dizziness mixed with heat and lust from his emotions poured into me. His calloused hand pulled my cock above the waistband of my boxers and gave me a hard jerk. My eyes rolled back. The sensation of something other than sorrow, of Blythe's fear, of the impending death of my wife and my subsequent demise, was indeed… distracting.

"Remember this tree? I do," he growled in my ear, his breath warm and full of promise. "We walked this path to Hallows before it even existed. You and I loved each other before we ever knew it."

The hole where my heart should have been constricted. "Under similar circumstances. A romp in the woods, a scream in the night, and a scene of horrors awaiting us."

"Sounds like your dream date."

Something resembling a rough chuckle strained from my chest as he continued his caring assault. Wolfgang knew me, and I knew him. He knew I could push him off, and he would have let me. The werewolf would have let me hit him, make him bleed. He'd allowed it all before. But I didn't have any fight in me. Perhaps he was right. Maybe I needed a sensation other than misery.

"You don't think, after all these years, that I don't know where that thick, emotional little mind of yours is going, huh?" He palmed me harder, and I gritted my teeth, resisting the orgasm he expertly knew how to coax from me. "Blythe's not going anywhere, and you're not going anywhere either. Except Hallows Fest, with me, tonight."

"Fucking why? What does it matter?"

He pushed into my throat harder, blurring my thoughts, compressing the little air he allowed me. "You fucking matter, Onyx. You dense piece of shit. And not only would Blythe want us going to Hallows, but a tree spirit told me to go."

My eyes opened, then, finding his hooded gaze and untamed beard. "Told you to go? Why?" I gritted out, suppressing a moan. His hold on my cock was unrelenting and smooth, and he knew exactly what the fuck he was doing with every pump of my shaft.

"The little wooden thing cornered me as I was chopping wood. They always have a reason, and they love Blythe. The spirits want to help. I didn't tell Ghost, but you and I—" His lips crashed into mine, hitting my fangs, drowning me in his earthy, sweet taste. "We can help figure this shit out."

"Okay," I breathed, the first little spark, the tiniest of embers, glowing to life inside me. Even my sleeping, mourning dragon curled at the idea. If the spirits were talking, then we'd be right to listen.

His fingers lightly rippled along my balls, and I sucked in a strangled breath, holding on to his arm as he gritted out "good boy."

"Fuck," I moaned, my body tightening in protest, in surrender, in a crackle of wood on a new fire. My release shot out, coating his palm, as his kiss found me again, gentler this time, as his hard grip and push softened into me. "Thank you," I whimpered, letting the hot tears fall. "I don't know—I—"

He pulled me into that big wolf hug of his, and I collapsed into his touch as he petted the back of my head, emotion clouding his tone, too. "She needs you. I need you. You're a motherfucking dragon *and* a vampire, and you're the smartest, most caring person I know. We *will* find a way."

I didn't know what I'd done to deserve someone like Wolfgang Jack, or what any of us did to warrant his love, but it was awe-inspiring in each manifestation he blessed us with. After drying my eyes on his shirt, I allowed his words to stoke the flame inside me. He was right, as usual. This wasn't a time for me to cave in on myself and my fucking self-centered internal landscape of turmoil. Blythe didn't need that. She needed a dragon. My queen *needed* her dragon. Her vampire king. And that I would be for her. Though it may be the hardest test of my lifetime. My love, my wife, my boys, needed every ounce of my cunning, my perception, and my empathic gifts. They required my charm and ability to see things in a different light. Because something about this wasn't fucking right. This was a riddle in plain sight, and the answer was some-where close by. I could feel it.

I swallowed down my own pain and dark thoughts and held my werewolf's hand as we stepped into night one of Hallows Fest.

For her.

EVEN UNDER PRESENT CIRCUMSTANCES, Hallows Fest always felt like fucking home. So many freaks like us, so many monsters and vampires I hadn't seen since last year. I wished Blythe was on my arm, dressed in something slutty. But I pushed those thoughts away. It wouldn't help me to dwell on them.

I was in awe, as if it were the first time I realized it. "There are so many people here. The wealth of magic and knowledge in this place…"

Wolf nodded. "A concentration of a lot of fucking power, indeed. But where do we even start?"

"Let's roam. Things at Hallows have a way of finding you out when you need them."

Wolfgang raised his eyebrows. "Optimist now, are we? I need to forcefully fuck you more often."

The side of my mouth rose, and I licked my fang. "That's a thrilling prospect, and I wholeheartedly agree." I scanned the area, wondering where Blythe would go, remembering the spots I'd seen her gravitate toward last October, when I was watching her from afar. "Let's start at the willow tree," I suggested as a herd of shifters spun and brushed past us, their fur shedding against our black jeans.

"Do you think Ez and Vince will be here?" Wolf asked, his sheer size parting the crowd of freaks. "And what will you do if they are?"

I snorted. "I'd say they'd be fools to march their coven here after what happened in Belladonia, but Vincent is the fool of all fools, so it wouldn't surprise me. And to answer your question, I'll make my dearest uncle squeal like the little pig he is."

"That's my boy." Wolfgang hit my back as we parted the willow branches. "No witches yet, it seems."

"Two covens now. Wonder what that means. Is it like a battle of the bands? Should we get wristbands? Do they have merch for sale?"

Wolfgang chuckled as I paced around the tree roots, not knowing what I was looking for. This place vibrated something in my dragon's chest. My mother had told me to listen to him more. Sure, Mom. Why not?

Wolfgang lifted his nose and furrowed his brows before slapping me on the shoulder. "I smell someone I've been looking for. Find me when you're done hugging trees and communing with nature."

"Fuck off." I grinned, still circling the tree as he disappeared through the willow's vines. This was where Blythe's beloved willow spirit had previously resided. It was where the witches took up camp at Hallows each year. Maybe it was just a basic tree, or maybe it was more. Or maybe I truly was losing my mind and *communing with nature.*

I slumped against the bark and pulled out my harmonica. One of the only instruments not destroyed by the blaze inflicted on my farmhouse. I missed that goddamn house. Maybe the guys and I would finish rebuilding if—when—my belladonna woke up. Puffing into the dented metal, I hummed our tune, the one I'd written for her and completed in blood in Belladonia.

That seemed like so long ago now. What a shit show that bloody ordeal was, and for what? So I could disappoint an entire city of my half-blood immortal fang family? Perfectly on brand for me. I huffed the melody with irony into my harmonica until something caught the corner of my eye.

A slight shimmer. Something not quite natural. When I looked, it was gone. But if being undead for hundreds of years had taught me anything, it was that if you thought you saw something out of the corner of your eye, you fucking did. My muscles tensed, knowing it could be anything. A spirit, a curse, or some Hallows Fest asshole fucking with me. So I continued to play and look at my boots. And on cue, it glimmered again, a shape taking form. *You don't like when I look, so I won't look.* My eyes strained within my periphery to make out the form of a... woman?

Continuing my playing, I was mulling over a smart-ass remark when a chord struck my soul. A sound I'd memorized within the core of my being. And then the voice said my name again.

"Onyx," she said.

Blythe said. I trembled, my heart lodging in my throat and sweat staining the harmonica against my lips. Pausing, I turned my head just slightly, knowing I couldn't not look at her. What was this? Some sick joke? I'd kill the phantom or fool playing this game with me. I'd tear out his spine with my bare hands and lick it clean of blood for fucking with my emotions, for using my wife against me. But then her shaking voice sounded again, and I felt her this time. Her emotions hit me like an earthquake of feeling, of *her* feelings. Those couldn't be manufactured with a spell or prank. This was her. Somehow.

"Blythe? Belladonna?" I stood, dropping my stupid instrument. "Love, where are you?"

"Onyx, are you here? Please—" My wife was a shadow of black pearlescence, mixing with smoke from campfires and the laughter of creatures in Hallows swaying on the willow vines.

Taking a desperate step forward, pushing my overwhelming desire to cry and scream down my ribs and clearing my mind, I repeated as she continued to fade. "Where are you, belladonna? Tell me, and I will tear through the universe to find you."

"I'm—"

Fear, overwhelming panic, surged from her.

"I'm in—"

She screamed.

"No!" I lunged for the shadow of her as she disappeared, and she dissipated like smoke in my palm. "Fuck!" I screamed. "Blythe!" I yelled, over and over again, but it was no use. After a moment, the vines parted with force as Wolfgang rejoined me, puffing as if he'd run at the first sound of me.

"What happened? Breathe, friend."

Pacing, I pulled at my hair in frustration. "She was here. Blythe. I felt her. You're going to say I'm crazy, but I swear on everything I am—I saw some fucking ghost of her—oh, fuck—does this mean she's—"

"She's not dead." A rough voice swished through the willow vines and stumbled onto the tree roots, bracing himself on the tree as if walking on land was foreign to him. "Well, not in the way yer thinkin'. And I sure could tell you where she is. For a price, that is. For a story." The pirate captain smirked, stroking the bells in his beard.

Captain Vex Beard, The Story Keeper, was here.

CHAPTER 22

Blythe

WICKED TEACHER

> The enemy that sowed them is the devil; the harvest is the end of the world; and the reapers are the angels.
>
> *The Bible*

Hell had always been a mythological place of suffering. Fire, brimstone, and eternal damnation. Payment for sins, and all that. At least that's what I'd overheard in the Easter services my mother would drag me to when I was a kid. Each year, the church itself disturbed me more than the tales of demons. Maybe that should have been my first clue that something was off about me. Though those memories were fuzzier and harder to access than ever before. I'd never fathomed that I'd be walking through hell, captured and touched by the devil, and on a nature walk with one very annoying clown.

"Keep up, Ace. We're almost there. You'll like it, I swear," he cooed.

"I know what this is," I called after him as he skipped ahead. Zyre had the energy of a toddler, and though he was showing me around, I felt a lot like a mother hen chasing around an overgrown child in a Halloween costume. He stopped to talk and perform for everyone, card tricks all day long, stupid knock-knock jokes when there was a silence. This was it. This was my hell and punishment, wasn't it?

"No shit. You're just now figuring it out? But notice the path is lovely cobblestone, and though it's not the Hallows Fest of your Ash Grove, it is quite nice." He twirled. "I do hope the candy corn stand is back this year."

Candy corn stand in hell. Sure, nothing surprised me now. Despite my reluctance, I followed him, noting the stone path flanked with flickering jack-o'-lanterns. My mind was never far from my boys. What were they doing? Did they miss me? Did they even realize I was gone?

I spoke up, thinking I may as well take advantage of my idiot tour guide. "Do you think the guys know I'm gone? Or is this like… me being gone five minutes to them?"

"Or five years." Zyre snorted, and my heart dropped into my shoes. Instantly, I regretted my questioning. "Doesn't matter, Ace. You're not getting out of here."

"Yes, I am," I murmured, and this little outing was just another way for me to plan my escape, to scope out the exit routes. Maybe if I found the forest I'd arrived in, a spirit would help me get out, or I'd recognize the path I'd taken and I could follow it home. There was a way in; there had to be a way out. And whether it had been five minutes, days, or—god—years, to my boys, I knew they'd be waiting for me.

We rounded the perfectly manicured bend, expertly decorated in autumn fare. The smell of pumpkin was bittersweet in my nose, making me fall in love reluctantly. *It's all a trick,* I told myself. It had to be.

As we turned the corner, Zyre extended his arms. "Like I said, not as rock and roll as Hallows Fest, or so I've heard, but it's adorable, all the little stands."

I swallowed. It *was* adorable. Where Hallows Fest was chaos and immortal mayhem, this plot in the fake Ash Grove was bustling with vendors dressed in autumnal leaf crowns. Women wearing billowing orange dresses, men in suspenders, and people laughing around fires, drinking what smelled like hot cider. We passed a booth where a woman dipped and swirled caramel on bright red apples, smiling and bowing her head slightly as I passed. Zyre clapped with glee and jumped in place in front of his candy corn, returning with a paper cone of sweets for me as well.

"So this is a fall festival of sorts?" I asked, marveling at the celebration of colors and smells around me.

"It is as old as time, Ace. You could say Halloween was inspired by this place. A worshipping of the season change, the thinning of the veil, harvest, Samhain, whatever you want to call it —it all started here." He put an arm around my shoulder, tilting his cone into his mouth and chewing his treats. "Feel it? I know you do. Feel how ancient and old it is, how charged this place is. Why, magic fucking abounds!"

I huffed a breath, passing a puppet show of green dragons, ebony demons, and gray wolves. There was no argument I could make, as what he said rang true. This place indeed felt like the start of it all. I walked through the very birth of Halloween, and the realization and dark magic thrummed through me, causing my horns to tingle somehow and my heart to lighten. "It's not... terrible," I conceded. Something familiar caught my eye near the side of a stretch of booths filled with cups of pumpkin spice brews and steaming cinnamon hand pies. Could it be? "I'm going over there for a moment," I informed my companion, hoping he wouldn't join me.

Thankfully, he was distracted by the puppet show, watching with rapt attention and stroking his white-painted chin. "Don't wander where your feet can't lead you," he mumbled, absently waving me off like a fly.

I rolled my eyes, weaving through hell's patrons, who eyed me slightly. Some even bowing as I passed. Weird. Until finally I was parting the strings of velvety willow vines. A gasp shuddered through my lungs. This tree... it wasn't a hologram. Or maybe a copy like the town. It was the willow tree from Ash Grove. My fingers inched into the grooves of the bark, remembering my time there a year ago. The witches, the willow spirit... Somehow, despite the commotion and clapping and laughter right outside its vines, the inside of the tree was silent and still. Hope sprang within me. Was the answer in the trees? Could it be a portal home? Was it home, somehow? Rubbing the bark with my palm, I eased over the tree roots, circling it. I had no idea why, but it felt right. I was close to giving up when a sound echoed, and I froze.

A buzzy instrument. But it wasn't the sound of it that weakened my knees. It was the melody. It was... mine. The song Onyx had written for me was one I'd recognize anywhere. It played in my soul, in my mind when I couldn't sleep. It was the lullaby of my heart, and it made every part of me ache with want for my vampire.

"Onyx?" I asked in the direction of the sound.

I rounded the tree and stopped. A shadow, or something like a reflection in an antique silver platter, shone back at me. Him, it was him. Onyx's black hair was messily combed back, emphasizing his widow's peak. His skin was pale and his face a little duller than usual. He stood, green eyes glowing, and turned the left side of his perfect jaw to me.

"Blythe? Belladonna? Love, where are you?"

He was here. Onyx was here. Tears welled in my eyes as I reached for him. But I stopped short, not wanting to burst whatever spirit bubble this was.

I looked around, making sure Zyre wasn't nearby. "Onyx, can you hear me? I'm in hell, Onyx—the devil, he has me. I'm—"

He said something else, inching closer to me as tears streaked my face. Louder, I said, "Onyx, I'm in hell—"

Suddenly, Onyx slashed in half, parting like two plumes of black smoke. I screamed, falling backward as a huge looming figure with the presence of more evil than I'd ever encountered stood in his place.

"Stop! Bring him back!" I screamed as the devil stood before me, wearing a black cloak and staring down at me with red fury in his gaze.

His voice echoed and rattled my bones as he spoke, chilling me with fear and hate and anguish. "There is no more Onyx, or Wolf, or Ghost. There is only me for you now, Mortala."

Tears welled and fell as I stood, looking up at him and gritting my teeth, hating that he was seeing me cry. "I will beat you," I threatened. "There is only them for me."

Something flashed across his downturned gaze then. "You're never leaving this place. You will never see them again."

Heat struck my cheek in a flash of bright orange, and when I turned, it was too late. The willow tree erupted in an inferno. Its branches crackled black, the vines alighting in flame. "No!" I screamed, dropping to my knees. If it had been a portal, it was now going up in a blaze of ash. My willow tree, my Onyx—

The devil stood, watching me like a psychopath as I cried. I heard Zyre in the distance, but all I could focus on was the heat on my face as I turned my back to them, feeling utterly lost and trapped. This had been a mistake. A huge fucking mistake.

And I wanted to convince myself that it was all a dream. But then something cold and metal pressed into my palm by a burning tree root. I gripped it tight and slid it into my pocket, holding it within the fabric once it was hidden.

Onyx's harmonica.

If it was here, there had to be a way.

I had come to find a way to save my boys, and now I shuddered, on my knees beneath the fires of evil incarnate, hoping my boys would find a way to save me. Please, let there be a way home.

CHAPTER 23

The Findings of the Familiars

CAT

My tail swished in the window of Magia Eclectics. Witches should know better than to trust a black cat in the window, but these witches didn't know better. Marcelene, in all her foolish pride, was worse an entity than even my bone-headed archdemon. At least my guy had sense. Sometimes. The elder witch's skin was wrinkle free now, and her curls bounced with all the vibrancy of her granddaughter's. She paced the shop, anxious, glaring out the store window over and over.

The front door opened, and she jumped, startled. What has you so afraid, Crone? Perhaps the splitting of her coven was affecting her more than she let on. *Wah, ha, ha.* The reaper decoration chimed in mechanical eeriness that matched the rest of the Halloween decor. Ash Grove was nothing if not a stickler for their stupid traditions.

An old witch with long gray braids approached the crone. "You must speak with the demon."

That perked my whiskers right up. Finally, something interesting. Something I wasn't supposed to hear. *Go on…*

"Bite your tongue, Opal," Marcelene snapped. "This is all because of him. You don't think he'll kill me again? You don't think the archdemon hasn't been waiting for the excuse?"

"This resistance is self-preservation? What of Ash Grove? There is one much worse than the graveyard keeper, and you know that, don't you?" Opal pursed her lips. "Yesenia will find out. Either from you or from them..."

Marcelene sighed and rested her forehead against the shop counter. "I've bested them all before, and I'll do it again."

"This is greater than you, sister—"

"No more of this." She waved a hand. "Light the sage incense on your way out."

"Come with me. Come do what is right as Halloween approaches," Opal urged with concern. "The Medicine Thicket Coven will not stand idly by."

"I'm safe here. The wards here are strong. They hold," Marcelene muttered to herself, head still pressed to the countertop. "No, this is fine. This is all fine."

Wow, the crone had officially gone bonkers. Ghost would be delighted. Though I hated delighting him. But these were interesting tidbits of information, nonetheless. Who was Marcelene afraid of more so than Ghost? What part did she play in this incident with Blythe? Stretching my back, I hopped down onto a pumpkin as the worried witch spun out of Magia, and I followed her anxious little ass all the way to Yesenia, who was coincidentally already in the next spot I planned to visit. Blythe's friend— well, my friend now too, I guess, even though I hated that word— wrung her mint-filled hands outside my cemetery. Yes, *my* cemetery. Ghost had been a piss-poor guardian, in well, *ghosting* us, for two years. He'd only come back to visit the damned and the lost souls maybe three times. Lazy bastard demon. So self-absorbed. Killing all these souls and forgoing his promise of pain and torment. Disappointing.

The witches murmured as I pranced over. "Always mint and herbs. And never, say, a fresh salmon filet." I jumped up onto the gate, preferring the high ground. Hey, some cats were mouse cats. I was a bird cat. Trees for me, please.

"Cat, the gate. It won't open for me," Yesenia whispered, horror lacing her tone.

I suppressed a yawn. "Like I said. Salmon filet. It's me you need to please. Not this hunk of iron."

"I've heard of Blythe, and I fear…" She held her chest. "I just wanted to come here first to see something, but… this is unfounded that I wouldn't be let in."

"The Medicine Thicket Coven have long been keepers of hollow grounds." Opal furrowed her brows. Witches, always getting their undies in a bundle if the wind blew wrong. Give me a break.

Still, usually the gate talked back to me a little, and it had been silent since my approach. So I ran a single claw along its bars. "Open up, drama queen," I told it. It didn't budge. Again, I demanded, "I am the familiar of Archdemon Ghost. Stop playing games. Open."

The ground inside the cemetery rattled. Souls were restless, and the damned hung on my every word. Yesenia lifted a palm to her mouth. "We must go to her, Opal."

"My stars, child. I will not be going anywhere near the reaper. This is… you know what this is, Yesenia." Opal backed away slowly, pulling out a blue crystal from her robe. "I will inform the covens."

Scratching the iron again, my ears laid back. "Hell's gate has never closed to Ghost. Would never close to Ghost."

"Cat, you know the one who controls that. Why wouldn't *he* want to be accessed?" the young witch asked needlessly. Of course I knew the devil ruled over hell, and Ghost, and well, everything. But god damn, why would he lock us out? Unless…

Raven cawed above us, circling like a vulture. Creepy beings, birds. I loved them. The witch took off in the direction of the wolves, and the crow and I followed. My suspicions were correct that Blythe had gone to find the devil. What I hadn't expected was that he'd keep her *there* and keep the Halloween Boys *here*. I wanted fun gossip, a little mischief to break up the monotony.

Maybe a fun murder to solve, and yes, a way in the mix to aid Blythe. This? Well, this was bad.

WOLF WAS PACING outside the tiny cabin when we approached. He was with two men. One I smelled immediately. Plum and jasmine and drama. Onyx Hart. The other smelled like saltwater and fish, which wasn't entirely unpleasant. They stood outside as if afraid to go in, afraid of Ghost, no doubt. Probably wise.

When the werewolf noticed us, he gave Yesenia a short nod, then he whipped me a small regard before looking up and pointing to the sky. "Where the fuck were you?"

The witch and I stopped, and Onyx even stopped his glaring at the fish man, to watch the commotion. Raven cawed, an eerie and sad sound. If I had a heart, it might have saddened it. Wolf yelled out, "You're her familiar. A sacred fucking calling. The most important task of any animal. And you left her in a field to die?"

Raven circled us, crying.

And that itchy little spot in my middle where my heart probably was filled with anger. Or maybe it was just fleas. "Where the hell were you other than getting your dick wet and passing out? Shut the fuck up, maybe?" I hissed. "We're here to talk to Ghost, and you losers, too, I guess."

Wolfgang growled low in his throat, and Onyx, surprisingly calm, patted the overgrown dog-man's shoulder. "Hi, Yesenia and Cat. Welcome to the shit show," he said to me and the witch, who, to her credit, held her ground.

"We have much to discuss. Should we all try to go inside? Or perhaps out here is better?" She cast a wary glance at the cabin, no doubt fearful of what lay inside. Though the trepidation in her gaze wasn't wholly for the archdemon. My friend feared something else. Or two somethings.

"Who's going in?" Onyx asked, crossing his arms and glaring at the wobbly man as he pulled out a long pipe and filled it with tobacco. This guy didn't give a shit. I liked him already.

Wolf was still standing with his arms crossed and shooting death stares at Raven, who still cried above us, circling the dark and starry October sky. "He's more cross with me than he is with you. You go."

"Fuck that. I call *not it*." Onyx shoved his friend.

"You can't. I call not it first," Wolfgang replied. "I am four seconds from letting my alpha wolf out. The full moon is soon, and I will rip Ghost's head off if he back talks me over the body of *our* mate again."

Yesenia rubbed her temples as the smoking man in the hat sauntered over. "Sounds like you all need a hero, and here I am. Ah, I'll go speak with the boy."

I huffed in my throat, trotting past them and waiting for the stupid but brave man to open the door. This would certainly make for interesting gossip at the tree house later. No one was beating me at this Halloween game.

The humans reluctantly agreed, and the man made his way inside, and I after him. Ghost, in his weak human form, clutched Blythe's hand to his mouth. His face was sullen, with gray under his eyes. He hadn't eaten or drunk or showered. Damn, he was bad off. My fur prickled atop my skin. I didn't like seeing him like this and hoped this could help. Maybe the witches could aid. Maybe the smelly man could assist, too, somehow. Though I doubted it.

The archdemon's pale gaze flicked up briefly above Blythe's wrist. "Vex," he said lowly after a moment. "I'm not in the mood for pirate nonsense. If you didn't notice, my claimed is hanging by a fucking thread."

"Son, yer fallin' into madness and obsession. I see it in your eyes."

Jumping onto the bed, I padded at Blythe's feet. She was too cold, way too cold, despite the fire burning in the hearth. Curling up on her feet, I purred, and Ames tensed his jaw while giving me a sideways glance. He was glad I'd come, glad I'd brought help. You know,

I didn't particularly like the guy, but what did that have to do with love and loving someone? All we familiars did, at the end of the day, was love. *Ew, okay, enough of the sappy shit.* I quieted my purr to listen.

"Yer the captain of yer boat, and it's sinkin', son. You're not going to fix anything by wasting away in here, your mouth to your girl. There's no helping her if yer dead. Well, deader than you are. Not sure of the demon rules of life and such."

"I'm dead if she dies," Ghost replied hoarsely. "I am nothing if she dies."

"You're a coward, then," Vex said absently, rifling through Wolfgang's kitchen cabinets and pulling down a bottle.

Ghost growled. "Excuse me?"

"Coward to not fight for her, to not fight for your crew when they're under attack. Sitting here on yer sinking vessel gettin' drunk on your sorrows."

The archdemon ran a hand through his hair and sat up slightly. I studied the bearded man who jingled when he walked. Was he full of coins? Bells? But devils, was he actually getting through to my thick-headed companion?

"Under attack?" Ghost questioned weakly, moving his lips from Blythe's wrist. She was breathing shallow little breaths.

The pirate removed the cork with his teeth and spat it out before taking a double gulp of alcohol. "You heard me. Blaming everyone here and not the one who's not."

"Who's not—" He sat up. "Tell me what you know right fucking now." Standing, he strode forward, and the pirate opened the door and walked backward onto the porch.

"See, fellas? I got him to come outside." Vex congratulated himself as Wolf, Onyx, and Yesenia regarded us from around a fire. The witch pushed past the men and up the stairs into the cabin, leaving the door open as I pounced down the stairs, momentarily distracted by a very springy cricket. The fire was warm, though, and Ghost reluctantly sat by it. Though his gaze flickered from us to the open door in worry. He really was obsessed with Blythe. It was cute in an unhinged way. Also, the guy needed a shower worse than the drunk jingle man.

"I take it Hallows Fest was productive," Ames said.

"Yeah, I saw Blythe's ghost," Onyx replied.

Ghost stood. "You fucking what?"

"Not a ghost. Not a dead one. Mostly—" Wolfgang stood, getting between them. "Vex, fucking talk, would you?"

"She isn't dead. Not fully. Not yet anyhow. And what you saw was really her." Vex took another drink.

"Our mate is in bed right now," Ghost argued.

The pirate opened his mouth, but the witch bounded down the stairs, joining us in a flurry of curls and the smell of mint. "She—there is darkness all around her. But she's holding on. Her love for you all keeps her like a tether to her body. Though it is slipping… she is being… persuaded."

Onyx groaned. "I swear to god if you all don't start talking like normal fucking people…"

Vex boomed over their collective bickering. "Your girl's in hell."

Yesenia added, panicked, "Did any of you make any bargains with the devil?"

Wolfgang stilled his pacing. Onyx opened his big mouth first. "Hell? *The* hell? And of course not. I'm an attorney. You think I'd make a deal with the devil? How stupid would someone have to be…" He looked to Ghost, who was staring at Wolf, who was staring at the ground.

Oh, this was juicy. When I'd started this game, I thought maybe I'd find someone's porno stash, not uncover deals made with the devil himself. My tail swished with excitement. But also, poor Blythe, that sucked… I looked at the fire. *Hell.*

The witch and the pirate seemed to disappear as the two Halloween Boys glared at the werewolf, who finally looked up and met their stares head-on but didn't address them when he spoke in the low, growly tone of the wolven. "How do we get to her?"

Ghost was gripping the sides of the log he sat on, holding

himself back. I jumped onto it next to him. I wasn't about to miss a fight between them. They had destroyed a field in some squabble a decade ago. We familiars had taken bets. It spanned a week. It was *epic*.

"Gettin' there is one foolish way to perish." Vex stared into the blaze, taking another sip and stroking his beard. "Contending with the one who took her? Well, that'll be worse than a hundred deaths."

Yesenia wrung her hands, nodding. "Yes, yes, it would be."

Ghost pulled his gaze from Wolf. "Took her? You think…"

Vex chuckled roughly. "Oh, the devil took your girl, son. Be sure of that."

Ghost stood and fisted his hands. Blue smoke inched over the grass around us as the werewolf huffed slowly. The vampire pulled at his hair, shaking his head. They were losing their shit. I looked up and made eyes at Raven, who was perched in a tree, almost invisible in the darkness of night. Yeah, he was watching as intently as me.

Yesenia took a few steps back. "I-I have spells. The Medicine Thicket Coven and I have herbs and teas that could aid in calling her back—"

"No," the voice of Ghost rumbled. "We will retrieve her."

Vex looked at Ames as his body slowly grew and shrouded in blue smoke, his eyes wide and his brows raised. To his scrappy credit, Vex didn't take a step back from the transformation. He only watched patiently. Dude was either the bravest man I'd seen or the dumbest. I was still deciding.

"Yes, we will," Onyx echoed, eyes glowing green and slitted like a serpent in the night.

I startled when the werewolf let out a howl, communicating something angry and charged with his pack.

The pirate shook his head in astonishment with a small smile. "Fellas, one does not simply walk into hell and challenge the devil himself. I can assure you—you wouldn't make it past the first level without succumbing to the dark torment he inflicts.

Goddamn, I barely made it out with all my wits when I went very long ago."

"Not sure you kept all your wits, buddy," I murmured. The crow squawked a nervous chirp of a laugh.

And then after a moment of fire pops and crickets chirping, the voice of Ghost the archdemon rumbled from high above me. "I promised that I would chase after her soul—we all did—and if that leads us to our end, then so be it. Boys, we're going to hell… to kill the devil."

CHAPTER 24

Blythe

HONEY-TONGUED DEVIL

> I don't ask you to love me always like this, but I ask you to remember. Somewhere inside of me there will always be the person I am tonight.
> *Tender Is the Night, F. Scott Fitzgerald*

Arms I didn't want brought me back to Lamb's Blood Church and deposited me in bed. Alone in the dark, I thought of him through a pounding headache as I stared at the rafters my demon had once fucked me on. I lay at the base of the altar where my boys had made me theirs. But none of this was mine. When I first arrived, I'd thought this mirage of Ash Grove was meant to lure me into a false since of security. But now I knew it was more sinister than that. The devil had crafted an image of the town I loved, my home, steeped in memories of my men and the first place I ever felt true belonging—and he'd done it to break me.

To tear apart these walls board by board. To burn the willow tree after finding a glimpse of my vampire, to make me sleep under the same kaleidoscope of colors as Ghost's attic. To shiver me in the same draft from the hollow walls of this stone church and lead me through a pumpkin-covered town, a Samhain celebration like Hallows Fest. This was all a cruel facade. An act of torment built just for me. Putting me in this place alone and without the men who infused it with life, mayhem, and passion… well, this really was hell, wasn't it?

And my horns that pressed into my pillow were as useless to save me as I was here. What place did a reaper have in hell? I was as powerful as a goldfish in a bowl and the devil knew it, exploited it. I was wasting time. In some future reality, my boys lay dead on the ground while I lay on a bed in hell at the mercy of a psychopath in leather gloves. But I could barely best a ghoul. How would I go up against the father of evil himself? The stuff of nightmares and folktales gone bad had carried me to bed like a child after a fit.

Hot, useless tears streaked into my hair and ears, and I glared at the ceiling. No, if I were in hell, then I would become hell. I would become hell for him. He would want to release me just to get rid of me. No more doormat, scared bunny, running teenager. This ended now. Sitting up, I noticed I was in a black silk nightgown I didn't recall changing into. That freak. He'd touched me against my will. He'd entrapped me to think I liked it, too. It was a violation of epic proportions. Images flashed through my mind of what my guys would try to inflict on him if they knew. No, they couldn't know. I'd take care of the devil myself. I had to. There was no other way out of this.

The devil wanted me? Well, he was about to get every bit of me. Every dark, twisted, fucked-up, intolerable part. I'd be his bride. And he'd regret ever bringing me here. No doors in this room, I noted again as I touched the stone walls. That couldn't be true. After my experiences in Ash Grove, Belladonia, and Fenrir, and now hell… I knew a thing or two about doors. I was a door.

That thought resonated in my body like a wash of cold water. I touched where the sanctuary door should be and felt it in my bones.

I am a door.

Smoke cleared, and the doors swung open. Hope surged within

my chest as a rumble of thunder crashed outside. Going outside to wander the streets and forest was a bleak possibility. The devil liked this church. Maybe there was more to be discovered right here. I'd learned this past year that monsters like him liked hiding their secrets in plain sight. Vladimir's potions of vessence, his spider familiar, Zyre and his wolfish disguise… Devil couldn't be so different, could he?

I fought the urge to go upstairs, if only to be in my archdemon's attic in some other reality. Instead, I slipped down the narrow stairs to the basement. It was so creepy I'd never explored it on my own before, and I was always too preoccupied by Ghost anyway. But dark basements seemed like somewhere the devil would hide something.

Sure enough, a musty hallway led to a stream of red light pouring from the sliver under a door while music scratched from a record player. The door was familiar. I noted its splintered wood and old knob… Opening it, I realized it was the same room, the same door from Belladonia—when I'd stumbled upon the devil as I wandered the streets. The same record player buzzed something instrumental and eerie, and the room was washed in red. Stepping in, I spied the same ropes of developing photographs. This time I'd check to see what they were. This time I wouldn't be distracted by the devil's stupid, artificial, enigmatic charms. This time—

The door slammed shut behind me, making me jump and spin around.

"You should have stayed in bed," the devil growled, looking down at me in that assessing, predatory way as he took a step forward. I took a step back, frightened within my bravery but still brave all the same. The two feelings, I'd learned, could coexist.

"You should have stayed in hell," I gritted out, bumping against his photo table. "Or you should have helped me save my Halloween Boys."

The devil scoffed as he slowly rolled up one sleeve of his red button-up shirt. "You speak to me as if I could not obliterate them with a thought. You speak to me as if I couldn't make them forget you ever existed." He sauntered forward and placed a palm on either side of the table next to me, pinning me in, his hot breath hatefully caressing my face as he towered over me with simmering garnet eyes. "You speak to me as if I don't have eons of methods I could implement to torment you, break you, coerce you into doing, or being, anything I desired."

He didn't speak in threats. Not in the ways of phantoms or demons or kings, at least. But with the assured promise of ability and unwavering magic the likes of which I'd never encountered and tried to tell myself he didn't possess. But he did. He was. And I knew I was in over my head with him. But I had power, too. I was a force all my own, and his threats only charged my desire to outdo him.

I met his stare, and his gaze fell to my lips as I spoke. "You're not the only one with power. I will find a way to undo any damage you cause. I will find my boys, and I don't care what you do to try to stop me. You've already tried to trick me with the Ash Grove setup. You've already fucked with my head and made me think I wanted you sexually when I didn't. Do your worst, Devil," I spat, knowing I was mouthing off to the lord of the underworld, knowing it could cost me my life.

His deep gaze lifted to meet mine, and he simply corrected me roughly. "Judas."

Heat swirled in my lower belly, and I felt my body betray me as my own stare dropped to his full lips. His strong and chiseled jaw that begged for the scrape of my teeth. The bulge in his neck where that deep baritone resided. The place his words ushered forth every infuriating feeling known to man. Every interaction I'd ever had with him was so charged, so full of meaning and feelings of intense passion. Why? Was it just what he was, or was it something more?

Remembering myself, I shoved those thoughts and denied my aching, melting body, and replied. "No, you're not Judas to me. You're only the devil."

Darkness flashed across his eyes as he glared at me in challenge. "Then I suppose I better keep acting like it, then."

Then his lips were on me with a force that pushed the air from my lungs and into his mouth. Our teeth hit together. It was a roughness of longing, not of pain. A deep ache of need. A loneliness seeped into me so deeply that I wanted to cry and hit him at the same time. "Stop fucking with my emotions," I gritted out against him as he set me on the table and pressed into me.

"I cannot," he gruffed, cupping a hand around my head and hooking his other hand under my knee. "I will not," he added.

I groaned in agony of want and frustration, knowing he had just admitted to messing with my head, my desires, my body. But I couldn't stop him. And even in my right mind… did I really want to? It would be a lie to say I'd never fantasized about him, wondered and ached to know more. Like I hadn't imagined this very moment on the table when I'd stumbled through his door in Belladonia. Like I hadn't sought out paths to figure him out, to make him smile. There was no resistance as I wrapped my arms around his broad shoulders and neck, dipping my head back and allowing him access to my throat, my chest, my everything.

He growled as he dipped to nibble my neck, the soft touch of him drawing a moan from my lips as the lines of photos dangled above me. In the red light, the devil looked at home in all his sinister glory as I reached between us and unbuttoned his shirt, easing it off his sizable frame. He stood between my knees, shirtless and broad, before dropping to his knees slowly. "You are the only one I have ever or will ever kneel before."

His words pierced my heart in a way that shouldn't have been possible. But I supposed anything with his magic was possible, I was feeling what he wanted me to… I think. I swallowed my nameless emotions (that would stay nameless) and ran my toes lightly against his biceps. "Kiss my feet," I said, not even recognizing my voice or the command.

His eyes lit up, and there was a slight curl to his lips that left me breathless as I watched him take my bare foot in his hands. He planted a slow kiss on the arch before bringing my foot to his face and rubbing it against his stubbled cheek. "When I'm on my knees for you, my sweet death, I will do anything for you."

Through a haze of heat and the sudden heaviness of my horns, I watched as he sucked my big toe into his mouth, lapping at the pad of it with his tongue. The movements sent jolts of want to my pussy. My pussy that was weeping onto the thin silk of my short nightgown and begging for him.

"You'll do anything for me whether you're kneeling or not," I replied roughly, my voice betraying my arousal. "You'll help the guys. You'll let me escape. I'll make you."

"I am very curious to see what you'd make me do, Mortala." He rose up on his knees, draping my legs over his shoulders. With one push, he parted my thighs, and I leaned back on my palms. Heat flooded my cheeks as he eyed me: no panties, soaking wet, spread bare for him. This was delirious, and magically induced, no doubt. I'd absolutely regret it tomorrow, but hell if I didn't spread my knees wider and pull up my nightgown farther.

"And I'm very curious to see what that wicked mouth of yours can do." I wanted him, needed him, and it wasn't the first time, was it? Brushing the confounding thoughts away, I focused instead on the fire in his gaze and the firm grip of his hands as they eased underneath my ass and squeezed. "But," I amended, as he dropped closer to my center, "I want you to know that I'll be thinking of them. I'll be thinking of my men and not you."

He raised an eyebrow and narrowed his gaze. "Is that a fact?" His voice held all the same power as the thunder echoing outside. "So you'll be thinking of, what, Ghost's tongue?" Before I could answer, I gasped. The devil opened his mouth, unfurling a long, red forked tongue. "Like this, is it?"

"Oh my god." I breathed in both terror and delight as he swiped it up my center, sending shivers of thrill and heat pulsating through me.

Growling, he pulled back for a moment. "No, and I still don't think you fully realize that you're with the devil himself now, little death. And you are mine. You belong to me. But go ahead and try to think of them if you can, because I can be whatever it is you want from them."

A groan fled my throat as he pushed his tongue inside. Thick and throbbing, it writhed inside me, curling and rippling. The fork of it pierced my cervix into that hard push of pleasure and pain that Ghost so often coaxed from me. Within moments, I was coming undone, my ass thrashing in the devil's firm grip. Knowing he'd brought about my orgasm, he retracted his tongue and pressed his face into my wet and sensitive pussy, breathing in and pushing against me before growling.

"And what of Dragon?" Suddenly his hands warmed against my ass as if they were heating pads, and then a flurry of need and happiness and every good and amorous emotion imaginable poured into me. I let out a giggle and ran a hand through my hair, struggling to sit up. Joy, oh the joy and passion I felt… My vampire's gift was in the devil's palms, and he smirked as I met his gaze. "But that's not all you like, is it? You like this—"

With speed and ferocity, he attacked my cunt, sinking his teeth into the lips of me. I screamed out before a lightning bolt of orgasmic pleasure struck me like an electric shock of ecstasy. The sounds that came from my throat were carnal and wild as the devil drank from me, eliciting release after release until I was sure I'd die from coming. When finally he had his fill, he pulled back and wiped my blood from his lips and stood. "And then, what of Wolfgang? The werewolf has his own specialties, does he not?"

My sore, blood-soaked, and overworked pussy trembled with heat and excitement. This was so wrong, so terribly cruel and awful… and every moment of it thrilled me. The devil towered over me then, like a lighthouse in a storm. Only he was the storm, too. He was the ocean, the sky, and everything grim and wonderful in existence. And he looked at me with hunger and want and… something else. Something I couldn't, *wouldn't*, name. Because naming it… the way he tucked my hair behind my ear so tenderly didn't make sense.

Neither did the way he ran his knuckles down my arm, making me sigh into his touch. And when he dropped his pants and pressed the head of his cock against my center, I didn't scoot back or push at his chest. Instead, I inched forward and wrapped my legs around his waist. My lips found his, and our kiss was all passion and every bit the color red of the room. Power, pain, magic, and need. The devil slid inside me. My body stretching and straining at his girth, at the way he filled me as if we'd done this a thousand times before. My body melded into his like water against a stone, and we began to move. Slick and with both intensity and grace as lovers who'd been dancing this way forever. He moved in and out of me, holding me tight, his breathing heavy. Then he took my face in his hands and searched my eyes. Searched…

"Stop," I whispered out, trying to break our trance.

"Never," he replied earnestly, picking up his pace and making me moan. "I'll never stop."

Waves of emotion slammed into me with every beating of his cock. Feelings of sadness, of hope, of joy, and remorse. Then a deep sense of waiting, so much waiting. Tears streaked my face. "Quit making me feel this way. I don't want these emotions. Why do this?" I begged, holding on to his shoulders and bucking against his thrusts. The graze of my clit against his girth and our slick desire propelled me to another climax.

"Everything you're feeling is true, my bride. Feel it, feel me." He took my palm and pressed it to his chest. "Feel me," he said again, desperate this time, resting his forehead against mine. "That's it. Don't run from it. Surrender."

And so I did. As our breaths intensified and our bodies mixed together, time and space stood still. My tears fell and crashed into the thunderous orgasm that shuddered through us both. The devil breathed a groan as I whimpered in his hold, not expecting to feel so vulnerable, so held and seen. I didn't know what to think of it or how to make sense of it. Was it a gift or just another cruelty?

But before I could even dry my eyes or dare question him again, the burn, a now familiar burn, swelled inside me. "This is from your wolf, right?" he said, breath ragged in my ear. "I do enjoy the idea of keeping us joined together like this. Though the wolves are a bit rough around the edges."

A whimper escaped me as I accepted the stretch and remembered my wolf and Fenrir. "I love him. I love them," I sighed, gasping and digging my fingers into his back.

"I know you do." He wrapped his arms around me tight, bringing my head to rest on his chest. So intimate, too intimate. But for some reason, I liked it. Maybe that was what he wanted, what the embodying of each of my guys was meant to do to me. To make me into this weak and crumbling mess of a person. But I couldn't pull away, couldn't fight it or yell at him. All I could do was rest too comfortably in the devil's arms as the record scratched in the corner of the red room.

MOMENTS PASSED in that slow but quick way that time stops post earth-shattering sex. I sat up, and the devil's grip fell to my low back as I leaned to see the contents of the glossy pages that dangled above me. Those ember eyes burned like coals as they watched me reach up and pinch a photo off its clip. Terror and confusion died in my throat, though I still dripped with him between my thighs. "This—how is this a photo of me at the diner...?" I took in my stained Fleetwood Mac shirt, my messy pulled back hair, and my anxious expression over my coffee mug. "This was the day I met—"

"James—or Ames—Cove," Devil answered for me. "Yes, it is."

I wiggled out of his grasp and onto the table. He allowed it and stood back, crossing his thick arms and surveying my panic as I yanked down photo after photo. "Me at Hallows Fest in my fox outfit. Trick-or-treating with..." I rubbed the pads of my fingers over the glossy image of Ames, Wolf, and Onyx in their skull mask face paint, arms thrown around me as I laughed, clutching my orange bucket of candy. My chest tightened and my eyes burned. "You've been watching me."

"That's a bit of an understatement. Go deeper."

"Stalker," I accused on a confused breath.

"Hunter," he corrected. "Seeker."

"You've used them, lied to them, played them." My quiet anger rattled my tone, making me sound weak. Maybe that was what his amazing sex was meant to do—make me fragile again. The photo trembled in my hand as I pulled it closer to my chest.

"Yes." He stepped forward and growled down at me. It was more like a lovers purr than the malicious declaration it was. I hated his magnetism, hated that I was drawn to him, that I found myself leaning forward and wishing for his touch again. Magic, dark, twisted magic, all of it had to be.

"Why?" I demanded as another photo caught my eye, and another, and another. Pulling them down, I added them to my sacred stack. Ghost transforming and having me in his graveyard, on his grave… Onyx holding me in the rain as fire surrounded us on the steps of Belladonia… Wolf as his alpha, pinning me to the ground in my red hooded cloak.

Such intimate moments, our moments, and somehow, here they were on black and white and colored glossy paper. "Why me?" I trembled again, amending my question, making it better, or whatever he and the spirits had always asked for. Feeling him near, I wanted and *didn't want* to push him away as he rested his palms on the table and leaned forward, grazing the photographs with a soft glance before lifting his sincere stare to mine.

"Because you are haunted just as I am."

Yes. Something inside me resounded. I shook it away. *No, no, no.*

Why are you fighting it so hard?

His deep baritone rumbled in my thoughts, and I sucked in a breath, meeting his intense gaze. I gritted my teeth together and snapped back in my mind. *Because this isn't real.*

The devil raised an eyebrow in challenge and flicked through a couple of the overhead pages before plucking one. He admired it a moment before flipping it around. Reluctantly, I took in the image of me on my knees in Onyx's cottage. The devil stood above me, holding a glass of whiskey.

As I stared, his voice echoed in my mind again. *What if all this is real and not a lie? What if I'm not tricking you? Could you try to believe that? If only for a moment.*

My attention snapped back to him. "Sounds like something someone who's tricking me would say. And get out of my brain."

"Get in my bed, and I'll consider it," he replied plainly, a slight tilt to his lips. "Come, it is time for sleep."

My fight was gone, fucked out of me, and on the photos I clutched to my chest as if they were gold. His eyes widened slightly as I laced my fingers with his, and I hid my annoying smile that didn't make any sense in this situation. "Don't you dare burn these or I will burn you," I threatened when we made it back to our room. I mean, his room… whatever room it was.

His dark chuckle warmed my lower belly like cider on a cold day. "That I would love to behold, but first, I would like to watch you sleep."

"Stalker," I grumbled, climbing into the huge four-poster bed and sinking into the fluffy black comforter. My thoughts and mind quieted amid the cracks and pops of the nearby fire, and despite the images of my burning willow tree and the pained sound of Onyx's voice, the devil's presence as he eased into bed and by my side warmed me with comfort and safety. A sense of belonging and familiarity that couldn't be magic ushering forth a somber sleep of which every moment I regretted. What was happening to me?

CHAPTER 25

Blythe

GARNET WORDS

> Nothing is absolute. Everything changes, everything moves, everything revolves, everything flies and goes away.
> *Frida Kahlo*

The shade of his deep ruby red wings matches the shades of his glimmering eyes as he clutches me close and soars through the night air. I laugh as I look below, my hair whipping around us, at the jack-o'-lanterns and fake spiderwebs strewn about Ash Grove. "I love Halloween through the veil." I sigh, resting my head on his shoulder as we glide.

"And I love you," he whispers in the voice of a mountain. My mountain. "It's yours. It will always be yours."

When I awoke from my dream, all the doors were open to me. I bathed in a hot bath, then brushed my hair with a heavy brush that fit every groove of my palm and slipped on a pair of flats that curved to the arch of my feet. My black jeans hugged my curves just like any pair I'd broken in before, and the corset top slipped over my breasts and hugged my form as if I'd chosen it myself.

There was even makeup in my vanity filled with my shade of cool-toned foundations, gray eyeshadows, and deep reds, plums, and ebony lipsticks. Trickery. Just like the dream. The very real-feeling dream. I cursed to myself as I dabbed on red gloss. I wanted to look pretty for me, not for any other reason. Certainly not for Devil. Definitely not for the tall, handsome, mysterious, lying devil. Okay, maybe I was dressing up for him just a little bit, but only in hopes of lowering his defenses and getting him to either let me go or help the guys. That was the only reason.

Down the steps of Lamb's Blood Church and over the array of pumpkins that littered the yard, I found the air crisp with the smell that only exists on mornings in October. The leaves crunched beneath every step, and the pavement was damp from last night's storm. Everything was so Ash Grove—every shop window was decorated with hale bales, scarecrows, and plastic bats.

What if all this is real and not a lie? What if I'm not tricking you? Could you try to believe that? If only for a moment.

The devil's voice echoed through my mind as clearly as it had in the red room. Could it be real? Could it somehow be that I was indeed in Ash Grove right now? But how could that be possible? It was the only possibility I hadn't considered. If somehow this wasn't a trick, this wasn't a lie, then how was this possible? A man waved to me as he swept the stoop of his hardware shop, and two women stopped chatting to smile at me as I passed their park bench.

The looks of awe and curiosity that flashed across their faces didn't seem like illusions. Not even the kind someone as powerful as the devil could craft. And the way he moved about this place was so not underworld ruler-like. Though his demons did treat him as such. So did Zyre. There had to be a missing puzzle piece I wasn't seeing. Some clue I'd overlooked in my insistence that this couldn't be genuine.

And what about Onyx at the willow tree, his harmonica cold and solid where I'd left it on my vanity table? He was here, they were here, somewhere, somehow. Was it possible to find them again? Onyx hadn't been a trick. He'd been real, and something the devil didn't want me to see. Something he didn't want repeated. So for that reason alone, I had an arrow pointing me in the direction of realness and emotion. The devil had shown his hand by burning my tree, by banishing my gateway to my guys. But I would find another, and another, and another. Until finally we were reunited and they were safe.

The diner was bustling, and my chest tightened. I wished that I'd walk inside to my guys all huddled in our booth, elbowing each other and teasing our favorite waitress. I experienced a moment of sorrow and hope outside the swinging door as someone passed, giving me an awkward bow as they did. I froze as I overheard voices I recognized.

"My lord, cutting off your connection with Ash Grove in favor of… alone time… with her in this level of hell was not the wisest of decisions."

"What makes you say so, father?"

"The Halloween Boys. When they realize something is amiss, they will be desperate, untamed. They would do anything for—"

"Silence. Do not bother me with such things now."

"My lord, I know you have awaited this return for some time, but there are other factors to consider—"

"Blythe, my dear, your place is not lurking in doorways but on my knee," the devil's heavy voice boomed. Blushing at being caught eavesdropping, I swung open the diner door and slinked inside. The devil sat at a booth, at the booth Onyx and I preferred, and tapped his knee where it took space in the aisle. He was too big for a diner, for a booth. It was ridiculous seeing him somewhere so quaint, so trivial. I did as I was told, passing the back of a bald head of a robed man seated across from him.

When I perched on the devil's leg, his thick arm snaked around me, locking me to his side. I gasped as I made eye contact with the older gentleman across the table. "Father Joseph?"

His steely eyes betrayed nothing as he simply cut a slow bow. "Miss Pearl, it is a pleasure to see you again."

"W-what are you doing here?"

"Having coffee, dear child."

"No, I don't mean this fake diner. This fake Ash Grove. hell, with the devil. Why are you—"

"Fake?" He raised an eyebrow at Judas. "Is this what she believes?"

Then the priest stood, his metal cross necklace clanking against the table, and smoothed his robes. "May god have mercy on us all. May he forgive us for what is to come." He prayed, touching his rosary to his lips.

"See you at mass, Father," Judas said by way of goodbye, sipping his steaming coffee from a greasy diner mug.

I wiggled, trying to get out of his grip, and when he only tightened his hold, I turned to look at his beautiful, perfect, arrogant, and chiseled face. "Why is Lamb's Blood Church's priest in hell?"

"It is a lovely time of year to visit. Did you notice the jack-o'-lanterns appeared? I do love when they're all lit up at night."

"You're changing the subject," I protested.

"I know the jack-o'-lanterns are your favorite."

"They are... how do you know that?"

The devil poured a refill and swirled his finger through the rising stream. "How indeed?"

"Why are you here? A copycat hell diner doesn't feel like your scene. This is where Onyx and I go each morning."

"Who?"

"Onyx Hart, Dragon—"

But he was chuckling darkly, and I shoved his rock hard shoulder. "You're vile."

When I looked back to the table, it was filled with stacks of waffles, fruits, bacon, and all my favorite items. My stomach begged for every morsel, and I couldn't even pretend to be too mad to open my paper-napkin-wrapped silverware and fork a whole waffle right up to my face. Devil looked on, amused, as I took a bite. Then he took a bite of the opposite corner. I laughed. "We are some kind of twisted Lady and the Tramp, right now."

The devil ate my scraps with one hand. He kept the other lodged around me as I nibbled from our shared plates. Residents came in and out, giving the devil a wave as if he were just another guy in Ash Grove, as if it were just an average Tuesday in October. And as if he and I were just… together. Like this was our morning routine before going off to our jobs, then meeting at home later and lying on the couch to catch up on the show we watched together. Why did this moment, this glimpse of a false life, feel so real? Was it all an elaborate illusion meant to lure me into… into what?

On the tip of my tongue was the question and the hope that he'd give me a real answer. But then the bells jingled and a dramatic *aww* shocked through the bustling diner.

"Look at you two." Zyre spun on his heels, looking fresh in a new velvet green suit with a black- and white-striped shirt. His clown makeup was bright white to accentuate the black diamonds over his eyes. I wondered what he looked like without his getup, or what he'd looked like back when he was fully human. He grabbed a napkin to dab his fake tears. "Mom and Dad eating breakfast. So wholesome. I told you," he said, waggling his finger between the devil and me as he plopped into the seat across from us. "His broody mystique and devil flames of hell thing grows on you after a while. Though I just passed Father Joseph. Odd fellow, isn't he?"

And for the first time since entering this hellish mashup of Halloween in Ash Grove, I burst out laughing, tears rolling down my cheeks. The hilarity of being in a diner with the devil and a deranged clown calling a priest—probably the most normal of us all—odd—

And then I felt the devil—no, Judas—bury his face in my neck as he squeezed me close. My back vibrated against him because he was laughing , too. A true laugh, of happiness, of contentment. My entire heart almost dissolved onto the sticky linoleum flooring under the florescent lights. How many people throughout eternity had heard the devil laugh? To be the source of that had my mind

and heart spinning and beating like bat wings in the night. Was I…
crushing on the devil?

When we stood outside the diner, Zyre juggling miniature pumpkins for onlookers on the street, Devil put a hand on the small of my back. "I love the smell in October. When it's cloudy and the air smells like smoke from burning leaves and wax from sugared candies. There's something about it that nothing in any realm can compare to."

His words spoke to my heart, my soul, my obsession with all things dark and haunted.

"Would you like me to show you around hell a little more?" he rumbled in my ear, like it was a lover's secret, not a demented request. But the truth of it was, I'd always been enticed by both. How could he know that?

"Yes," I replied. No sooner had the words left my lips than he'd cradled me in his arms in that bridal pose that harkened back to the times he'd me called his. My protest died at the same moment deep red leathery wings sprung from his back. My mouth fell open at the sight. They were a ruby red and shaped like bat wings with hook-like claws protruding from the ends. They suited him somehow. Like they'd always been there and I was just now noticing them. Sort of like my twisted horns. It was exactly like my dream. My mouth went dry at the distinct feeling that this was all real.

What an evil sight we were to behold. People had sure stopped to watch us. Old ladies held on to their husbands' arms and diners strained to look out the windows at us. Men stood around their shops, clutching their hay bales and plastic bat decorations in their hands. But they weren't frightened. They all… smiled. One woman covered her expression as her eyes filled with tears. I couldn't comprehend why, but my heart swelled with the answer. Somehow, they were all mine, and I was theirs. And I was his. I was so much *his*.

"Wave to our people. Wave to hell, Mortala," Devil purred in my ear.

I did as I was told, offering a weak wave, just before he shot into the sky. I clung to him like a kitten to a high tree branch. He chuckled darkly in my hair as I burrowed into the crook of his neck. His neck that smelled like vanilla and fire and leather, warming my core along with the fear and cool air of the sky.

"You won't see much hiding in there. Though I can't say I mind having you hold me so tight. Perhaps I'll go even higher if this is my reward."

"Don't you dare!" I squeaked, peeling my face away from his skin. Reluctantly, I looked over the vast view of hell, of Ash Grove in hell. It was as breathtaking as the being that held me close, his mighty wings gliding on a strong wind. The trees were a patchwork quilt of yellow, orange, and reds of the most lush of autumns.

Smoke snaked from chimneys and leftover pumpkins flickered with old flame. I recognized many things like the Brew Pump and other abandoned gasoline stations and unassuming portals to other worlds. Maybe one of them would take me home if I could get away long enough. The path to Fenrir was just as wide and proud, as if still tramped by the paws of mighty lunas and my beloved Alpha. And downtown was as vibrant and decked out in Halloween as ever, with all the fare and tacky plastic my heart could dream of.

It was a mirage or something. It had to have been. But it felt so true, and it looked so real and so much like home. "Is this all real?" I said, awed. "Please, just tell me if this is a trick."

"Can't it be both?" he asked in that sly way the devil always and never answered. But in an effort to ease my turmoil, he did finally add, "It is real. It is my home, our home, and my personal level of hell. The best and truest level."

Yes, that's true. I felt it in my soul. In the purest form of my being, I knew what he told me was the truth. But how? The devil circled to a gliding stop above a jagged black mountain peak, easing us into a flat enclave bordered by sharp protruding stones. When he set me gently on my feet, I braced myself against an enormous rock and looked out over Ash Grove. As I did, a concerning bright red caught my eye.

When I realized what I was, I covered my gasp. "Fire?" I asked, feeling his looming presence tower close behind me.

"Bordering our home here is a wildfire. One that is inching closer by the day."

Shocked at his straightforward candor, I spun around. "Why don't you stop it?"

"It is a product of events passed. A consequence of the way of things. A grove of ash. Even I am not above reaping what I sow."

"What does that mean?" I urged. "We can't just... let it burn everything down. Even if this is, you know, hell."

The corners of his mouth quirked. "Then what shall we do, my bride?"

I sucked in a breath, feeling the bats scatter within my ribs again as he pinned me in and rested his arms on the rock above me. *Don't look at his arms. Don't look at his arms,* I pleaded with myself. "Why do you keep calling me that?"

"Because it is true... and you will stop the fires."

My heart beat furiously as my gaze dropped to his perfect cupid's bow of a top lip. "How?"

"Come a little closer and I'll tell you. The answers you seek are in my kiss." He rocked his hips into my stomach. "They exist between my thrusts and your moans."

"Judas," I whispered, already breathless at the idea of having him like that again. As if I hadn't secretly fantasized about it a thousand times since I met him. As if the events of last night could even put a dent in my desire for him.

He rumbled low in his throat and closed his eyes. "The answers to every question you have are in the beginning and ending of my name on your tongue."

My thoughts and soul clouded together, and suddenly, my horns felt heavy on my head as he leaned into me with the restraint of a caring lover. And I didn't know why, but two stories came to mind and tumbled out of my mouth.

"In Belladonia, they said the lady of death, the belladonna, found a lonely vampire, and he fell for her. He died, or lived in agony. The details are fuzzy…"

"Vampires are not good storytellers." The devil towered over me, sheltering me between his biceps, and dipped his nose to inhale my hair.

I swallowed, remembering the second story. "Then the lunas of Fenrir told me of a wolf that fell in love with a mountain. Then she went to live within his caves…" I trailed off, tingling at the feel of his thumb as it stroked down my arm. "All the stories feel the same now. With you."

"Because they're all about you, Mortala," he thundered before his lips were on mine with a fury and and intensity so powerful I moaned into his cherry liquor taste. "Did you just have cherry alcohol?" I asked, still bewildered to be accepting and embracing a kiss from the devil himself.

"No, and that's not what you're tasting," he growled. "And my restraint is slipping and will surely break if you keep looking up at me with those tragic eyes."

"Then I'll keep doing it," I dared, watching his stare ignite like a spark of ember within a desolate cave. "Get on your knees for me," I ordered.

The devil cocked a brow at my audacity.

"You said you'd only get on your knees for me, right? And you'd do anything for me while you're down there. "I'm going to tell you what I want, and you're going to listen."

Narrowing his gaze, he tilted his head before raising his palms. I thought maybe he'd fight me or ignore my order, but instead, he slowly lowered to his knees before me. "As you wish, Mortala."

My heart thrilled with excitement at the words and the sight of him, evil and powerful, kneeling before me on the cold slab of rock. "I want to make a bargain with you."

His eyes lit up, and my mind whirled with every piece of intel I'd gathered in the past year. Everything I'd learned of hell, every riddle from a spirit or a witch, everything thundered into this moment of claiming my own power and authority as death, as my own dark lord.

"I'm listening."

"You will spare the Halloween Boys from what I saw in my vision—"

"I cannot do that," he interrupted.

Anger threatened to roil through me, but I gritted my teeth and altered my words. "You will keep the Halloween Boys from their end."

The devil rubbed his jaw, seemingly tasting my words. I'd crafted it well. There were no loopholes. The devil would spare them that fate by promising they wouldn't die, like I'd seen them do, and in this, I could ensure their safety. I could save them.

"And what do I get in return if I agree?"

"I tolerate you occasionally."

"Not nearly a good enough bargain."

"What do you want?"

"You, all of you, with me forever and all of time," he replied without hesitation. The devil was better at bargains than I was, of course he was, and the sky rumbled in agreement. This was wrong and right and heartbreaking all at once. But what other choice did I have? With every moment I spent here in this level of hell, as he called it, my guys were closer and closer to their doom.

If I was the thing Judas wanted, then I was the biggest bargaining chip, the strongest card. I had to play. Death, the ace of spades, reaper. This was my destiny. Judas was right; all roads led to him. To save them was to surrender, to keep them alive was to say goodbye.

I swallowed my pain and extended a trembling palm. With a sideways smirk, he took my hand and lifted my knuckled to his lips. "Sealed with a kiss," he murmured into my skin. "No harm will come to them, and you will stay here with me for eternity."

Sucking in a deep breath, I wanted to cry and rage and punish this god of deception who looked as haughty as a king on his throne, even as he knelt. "While you're down there looking pleased with yourself, the least you could do is please me," I said on a shaky breath. My heart needed distraction, feeling, heat. Anything but the sorrow of the realization of what I'd just done.

Without hesitation, his hands were on me. "There is no one in all the realms that can make you feel as good as I can, Mortala. None more evil. None more skilled." As he looked up at me and eased down my jeans and panties, he said, "I could even wipe the memory of them from your mind if you like."

"No," I pleaded. "No, never." His touch was electric against my bare thighs, and I loathed the way it made my inner thighs wet with want. "I hate this. I hate you," I whimpered as his lips pushed against my sex.

"I covet your hate," he growled while pushing his tongue against my clit. Moaning softly, I leaned against the cold rock behind me, trapped and devoured by a bear in his cave. "Let your hate drip down my chin, Mortala. I will swallow every drop, and you in turn will take mine, too."

"No," I protested weakly on another whimper. The swipes of his tongue against my slit had me shaking and writhing as his rough hands squeezed my ass. My hips betrayed me, thrusting forward for more, allowing him more access, begging for more of his mouth.

"That's right, Mortala. Give me your delicious hate. I am your devil, your fool's bargain."

He knew just what to say, how to lick and suck at my clit, and my stupid body shuddered into his sandpaper chin, giving him the orgasm he chased. As he rose to his feet, my weakened knees made me wilt before him, and my traitorous hands reached for him of their own accord. No, he wasn't forcing me. This wasn't magic, I realized. This was me. This confusing torrent of feeling, the rush I got when I touched him that mixed with heavier emotions than should exist within me. I didn't know how or why, but the contradictory truth was that I was shattered at the thought of saying goodbye to my boys, and my mouth was watering at the sight of the devil's cock as it sprang free in front of my face.

Could I belong in hell with him? *Yes.* That echoey woman's voice purred inside me as I took the devil between my lips. My jaw ached at how wide I had to open just to accommodate his tip as his grip tangled in my hair, easing me harshly forward. "They were just practice for me," he hissed. "You are mine."

The head of his dick filled my mouth and pushed past my lapping tongue as I sucked harder and harder, reveling in his hiss as he leaned an arm on the jagged rock. He might have been making me choke on his cock, but I was making him come undone. Good, I hoped it hurt. I hoped his orgasm ruined him like mine had destroyed me.

I licked against his girth and ridges as he pummeled in and out, slicking between my lips and groaning with every slam against my throat. He pulled my hair and directed me. I hated the way my heart beat faster, my pussy still wet from him and aching for more.

"I'm not going to come in your mouth," he gritted out. "So you can stop trying so hard for that."

With a yank on my hair, he helped me to my feet where I stood and glared up at him with hot tears of anger and want in my gaze. He was so tall, so domineering, and now I belonged to him. I hated that. *I loved that.* Fuck. The corner of his mouth lifted in a wry and dark smirk as he removed his shirt and tugged off mine. My breasts were heavy, and my nipples pricked in the cool air. He surveyed me up and down, no hint of malice in his assessment, only a parted-lip sigh of awe. "Look at you. How I've wanted you, my death. And now I'll never let you go again."

"Again?" I questioned as my eyes fluttered closed at the feel of his heated palms encompassing my tits. His body pushed against me, and his cock slid against my middle as I suppressed my moan. "I don't like this," I lied.

"Don't you?" He flicked his thumbs against my pert nipples and prodded his enormous cock harder against me. One hand slid between us and dipped against my sex. "Lies. How I adore lies. And now I have a few of yours."

I swallowed, leaning into his horrid and beautiful touch. "I'm not lying." I doubled down, knowing I was caught and screwed regardless.

He hummed in appreciation. "Yes, another." He slipped three fingers inside me. I gasped at the intrusion and the feel of the frigid rock against my bare back. He hooked his grip under my knee and removed his fingers as I reached down to guide his cock. Chuckling like the evil legend he was, he goaded me. "Done lying so soon?"

"I hate you," I gritted out, lining him up with me.

He pushed in slowly, both of us letting out a groan of ecstasy at how perfectly our bodies fit together. "Say it again."

"I hate you," I repeated on a whisper that sounded like anything but hate as my body responded to him. My hips bucked back and forth, grinding my clit against his sizable girth.

"Mortala, Blythe." He whispered softly into my hair as a hand cupped my jaw. He tilted my gaze to him, and something inside me broke at the sight of those big jeweled eyes.

"Judas," I whimpered, my hands finding his jaw as I kissed him passionately. "It's all real?" I asked desperately, knowing the answer, feeling a torrent of emotions that were at odds with each other.

"It's all real," he confirmed, pounding in and out, pushing me closer and closer to the cliff's edge of my release. "Give in. Let me have you."

It was a plea, a demand, a trick disguised as a lover's request. And maybe if his cock wasn't buried inside me, I would have questioned it, would have fought it. But what could I say? Anyone would be weak with the literal devil between their thighs.

"Yes," I moaned just as my bliss waved through me like a

hurricane of passion and feeling. The devil's own release roared through his cry, echoing through the mountain.

And I was no expert at making deals with the devil, but it felt like the deal had been struck, the ink dried and spilled down my thighs, the bargain sealed with his kiss on my lips.

The Halloween Boys were safe.

And I never would be again.

CHAPTER 26

Onyx

PRINCE OF DARKNESS

"The strength of the vampire is that people will not believe in him.
Garrett Fort

We sat in a sickeningly sweet rose garden, each of us exchanging glares. I was probably supposed to speak first, but I liked watching Vladimir and Vincent squirm. Elysium seemed to be amused by the setup as well. My mother twiddled her thumbs anxiously, pretending to prune roses to busy herself. While my companion stuck out like a bulky wolf in a sleek viper pit.

"Get on with it." Wolfgang elbowed me, huffing at the vampire men's haughty glances in his direction.

"Feeling uncomfortable?" Vincent drawled, swirling his wine as he lounged on an iron patio seat. "Why, I might as well if I were you two. Waltzing into Belladonia after abandoning us in our time of need, then demanding an immediate meeting with us." He shot me an antagonizing smirk. "My dearest nephew, you didn't need to bring along your guard dog. You're relatively safe here."

Wolf puffed up his chest and leaned across the ornate outdoor table. "You won't feel so safe with my maw clamped around your delicate little neck."

"Gentlemen, please. We are in the presence of the queen," Vlad drawled, rubbing his temple. My father looked gaunter than usual, paler, and I wondered why that could be. He'd gotten everything he'd wanted. He'd used me and killed countless others in his quest to bring my mother, Queen Cassiopeia, back from the dead. Though the longing stares passed between her and the vampire slayer didn't go unnoticed by me or my father, it would seem. Interesting, I mused to myself, observing the emotions in the party like a spread at a banquet. Intrigue, sadness, relief, anger... so very interesting.

I stood, plucking a rose from a bush and twirling it between my fingers, then gave my mother a soft peck on her worried temple. "Forgive me, mother, for I am about to sin," I whispered slyly. She only shook her head as if she already knew.

Pointing the rose at Vincent and then to Vlad, I declared, "You both are heinous, wretched creatures with no good use to rub between you. In fact, all the realms and spaces between every door in Belladonia would be better off without you having ever existed."

Vincent leaned back and crossed his arms. Wolf looked on approvingly. My father only steeled his red gaze as I circled them. "There is no hope for you, no penance for your ghastly actions. Vince has lied to me my entire life, pretending to be a nobody coven leader, which suits him quite well, and the phantom circus thing? Adorable." I patted the rose atop his platinum blond head, and he swatted me away like a fly before I addressed my father. "And you, devils help us. Striking deals with devils, sending demons to prey on girls in Ash Grove, forsaking your one and only perfect child." I held my hands to my chest. "Tragically, you are evil incarnate."

"Did you come to air your precious little feelings, son, or is there a point to this display?" Vladimir's vampiric drawl dulled on like an untuned symbol crash in my ear.

I put the rose between my teeth and leaned against the table in front of Wolf, who crossed his burly arms and huffed in amusement. "Flirting right now is so like you," he muttered.

"It is, isn't it?" I confirmed, admiring how he was the most appealing looking thing this garden had ever seen, aside from Blythe. The alpha wolf was too good for this horrid bunch of roses and blood suckers outside Vladimir's floating castle, but he'd insisted on joining me anyway, and for that, I was thankful. With a rose between my teeth, I spoke, strained and ridiculous. "You two and the whole of Belladonia will be apologizing to me."

"Excuse me?" Vincent sneered.

"And to the girls you killed in Ash Grove. And for the countless other atrocities you've committed in your too many thousands of years of pointless, painful existence." I spit the rose onto the table.

Vincent stood, haughty vampire that he was, and protested. "And what makes you think you have the authority—"

"I am the king," I said plainly, looking to Vlad and quickly to my mother. "That's what you all wanted, right? Well, here I am, King Onyx Hart Drakon, ready to take up my kingdom. And my first order of business is this."

Elysium chuckled and clapped his hands. "Bravo, friend, bravo." His chair whirled and clicked in agreement, and I smiled, giving him a nod.

Then everyone began talking over each other. The vampires bickering, my mother attempting to smooth it over, and the slayer cackling like a kid on Christmas. "Oh, this is madness," Vincent spat. "Apologize to him. Why, I'd never—"

"No, no, not with words, dear uncle, but with actions." The bustle fell silent as I plucked the petals from the crimson rose, watching them fall slowly in my father's direction. "You and your covens, along with this town and this darling, creepy little castle of magic, will accompany me and my friends on a little trip."

Again, silence. It felt like a courtroom, but I was the judge now. I was the judge, and this was their justice. The gavel in my hand bloomed as I dropped another petal. "I'm calling you in, calling you out, and hoping you each die a terribly painful and agonizing death in the process."

"And to where is this trip?" Vladimir asked lowly, eyes full of emotions I fought against tapping into.

"Oh, you've been before, Dad. You're going to love it."

"I'm waiting with bated breath."

All eyes on me, I took it in, my first act as reluctant King of the Vampires. A title I never expected, never wanted, and never intended to take on. But I would now, and for no noble reason. Not to help them but to damn them. Not to save the town but to punish it. To call in its debts, to harness its resources. I was a king of ruin and torment, and I would gladly watch it burn if it meant salvaging the one and only thing I cared about in this world. Wolf's hand lay heavy and supportive on my shoulder as he stood next to me as I commanded.

"We're fetching my wife, our mate, from the devil himself. You will accompany us to hell, and you will be my army."

WOLF

My alpha wolf was fine tuned to every scent, every new print in the soil, and each tug between summer and winter that October brought. Hallows Fest ushered in new smells, old aromas, and friends along with foes. This was my first Halloween as an alpha, and already, my obligations seemed to outweigh my abilities. With Blythe fading in my cabin, I returned with Onyx to her short breaths and Ghost's intensifying rage. My pack looked to me for orders, their claws out and teeth bared. They were ready and awaiting my word.

The lunas would do whatever I asked, and it would be a request, not an order. Even still, the responsibility, the burden, was on me. Because what I'd be asking was more than any of them deserved, a greater battle than even the wolven of old undertook. Onyx had wielded his power and diplomacy with all the charm and elegance befitting a vampire king. He was a king, he'd always been one, and something swelled in my chest at witnessing it first-hand. Finally, after so many trails of torment and doubt, King Hart was commanding his people. Though not without his demented style that made him all the more charming. The looks on Vladimir's and Vincent's faces still made me chuckle.

Now it was my turn to take my title as alpha into my hands and honor it in the way it should be. I just hoped I was making the right decision. Oh, and with an audience of pirates taking notes as to my every move. Letting them make camp in Fenrir may have been a mistake. Though the wolves and the Story Keepers were getting along well, almost too well, with all the drinking and partying. With the way Nephele was following around Lena, a pirate with wild black curls and curves almost as lovely as Blythe's, had me both happy for the luna, but also wary of letting our defenses down in her lovesick haze.

But I was one to talk, because what I was about to risk would cost all of Fenrir for the sake of my mate. I was no leader on how to behave when in love, because I was willing to risk them all to save her, and my time to organize was now. With Blythe somehow in the devil's clutches, I couldn't comprehend the type of torment her soul was likely enduring at his hands.

This was going to be hard. I paced outside my cabin, leaving Blythe and Ghost inside and Onyx picking a banjo on my porch. He was acting so level-headed, so secure, so very un-Onyx-like, that it was concerning. I found the pack around a large bonfire, interspersed with pirates. Vex gave me a wave and offered me a pint of rum. Usually I'd refuse the stuff—it was basically lighter fluid—but I accepted his offering.

"Here you go, boy. You look like you need it," he said.

"You here for story time?" Nephele asked me, wrapping her arm around Lena, who giggled and leaned into her luna.

"We are the story keepers, after all," Lena smiled, her gold tooth glittering in the firelight.

Taking three deep gulps from the pint, I tried not to cough at the burn. Damn, no wonder the pirates were happy and out of their minds all the time. I cleared my throat, and the pack looked to me. My pack, my people, and the crackle of the fire and stares of dirty faced story-keeper crew.

"Lunas, stellas, sols of Fenrir," I began. "I've decided that we're going to hell. We're going to find and free Blythe, even if that means taking on the devil. Though not all of us. You may volunteer and Nephele and the elders and I will have final say over who—"

Giggling paused my speech. And then roaring laughter from every wolf in the pack.

"Wolf, dear." Nephele stood, slapping me on the shoulder and taking my pint. "We've already decided. The lunas and I have already chosen the wolves who are coming with us and the ones staying to provide for the pack."

"What?" I asked in disbelief.

"You thought we were waiting for you or something?" a luna piped up from the crowd, eliciting more laughter. My own smile threatened to tug at my lips as Nephele finished my rum. "Now, either stay for the stories or get back to your mates. We're ready for hell when you are."

It was as if the breath was knocked from my gut, though I should have expected nothing less from my pack. They were sharp and decisive, and I certainly wasn't the only one in charge. They'd declared that they intended to follow me to hell and then went back to their eating and drinking, as if it were just another ordinary day for them. The pride I felt threatened to strangle a sob from my chest, and I knew that if I started crying, they'd punch me for interrupting their story time with our wily pirate guests. So instead, I walked back home. Back to my mates. And then onward we would all go to hell. Together.

CHAPTER 27

Ghost

DAMNED IF YOU DO

> If I cannot sway the heavens, I will raise hell.
> *Virgil*

Onyx was a dragon and a vampire. He let emotion, fire, and lust control him. Wolfgang was an alpha werewolf. The moon, his hidden and carnal urges, and his sense of loyalty drove his every action. I was unlike either of them. I pondered as I gave my claimed's wrist one last kiss before prying myself away. My lips hadn't left her skin but for the briefest of moments over these past weeks, and when I stepped outside, the chill of October and the fog of withered leaves twisted with my blue hell smoke as it wafted along the frosted grass.

They'd all be looking to me to lead them on this journey to hell. A place I scarcely dared think of and a foe only the foolish sought after. The devil. But the devil had gone and angered the wrong one this time. He'd underestimated us—me, and my boys—and the lengths we'd travel for our mate. What was his game and why the blurry lies and prolonged stalking? Then again, what was prolonged to evil itself? We'd fallen into his web, believing he was a friend, and yet he'd been waiting for her, or waiting to punish us with this specific sort of misery.

Rage churned behind my ribs. Fuck. That old familiar hurt and devastation that was my ever-present companion for every goddamn year of my pitiful existence before meeting her. I was an ancient thing, and I'd been set in my ways for a long time. The only thing big enough, meaningful and true enough, to shock me out of that state was her. It was only and always Blythe Pearl, my claimed. I'd brought her into this world and I'd kept her here, sharing her with my friends like a well-loved book passed back and forth, shared and talked over. All the while, the biggest threat to her walked in and out of our lives. Either blinding us with his abilities or manipulating some extension of our curse, the devil waited, didn't he?

I hadn't realized I was growling, didn't know I'd even shifted into my demon form and traversed the distance from Fenrir to my cemetery until I stood outside the gate. "Open," I vibrated in my throat.

It didn't move.

"It's not listening anymore," Cat said lowly from somewhere above me. "Hell's gates are… closed."

My bones rattled as I squinted my eyes shut and gritted my teeth. Of course he did. Of course he locked it. But it wouldn't stay that way, not for me, not for a fucking archdemon. Opening my eyes, more fiercely determined than ever, I peered through the iron bars and called. "Wake up, sleepers."

The ground rumbled and quaked in response. The same as it used to do for her, my claimed. Fuck, everything reminded me of her. She was everything. She'd seeped into every fiber of my being, my town, my cursed life. And I'd sooner forfeit the entire world than let him have her. I'd burn hell to the fucking ground to get her back.

Dark shoots of shadow sprang and erupted from the hollow ground. Swaying and twitching in the autumn breeze. The veil thinning in October. The devil couldn't have picked a better month for his defeat. I recalled a murderer I'd put in this graveyard fifty years ago. He'd lure teenagers into his house, sedate them, and kill them. Burning their bodies in a furnace in his basement. Fifty years of torment, a night of agony at the hands and fists and teeth of the Halloween Boys, wasn't a fraction of the justice he deserved. But I opened his mouth to allow the wretched thing to speak in radio tones of static.

What… archdemon?

There were hundreds of them. They'd been rotting, writhing, suffering. Each of their deaths only a vague memory to me, but the slow torment of me and my boys—they shuddered through every moment of every day.

Still not enough.

"You have been given a gift this day, a gift you do not deserve, as you don't deserve the holes in the ground you inhabit now. I'm calling upon the damned to army with me to hell. You will fight, you will kill, you will do as I command."

They were silent, swaying like shadowed and dark forces often depicted by humans in horror films. Any one of them was enough for decades of literature and lore. The evil in a single entity of theirs enough to maim and traumatize a mortal for life. And I had a cemetery full of them, all fixated on me right now.

Cat hissed from the tree branch above me as the murderer floated closer, cocking its head at an unnatural angle to look at me through the iron bars. Its radio frequencies chimed, then, through static, searching for the mismatched voices and words to piece together. They weren't even allowed their own voices here, but I'd allow them to manipulate human-generated sound waves occa-sionally. *And… we… get… what.*

It strained, darkened, pulsing through the tones of a woman, a child, and ending with a word from a rock song. I bared my teeth, my demon on edge and ready to rip heads from bodies. Oh, hell would be a relief, and unleashing of Ghost.

For some reason, I glanced up at Cat, who perched on a naked tree, staring down at me with slitted eyes. Maybe I'd grown some-what fond of my unwanted and reluctant familiar. Maybe.

The Damned waited. I considered making them wait all night

but didn't want to waste time, couldn't afford to waste time. We needed this now, all our forces. Halloween grew near, the veil thinned, and Blythe was in his clutches. This had to happen now.

"You get death," I responded lowly, though the bargain pained me. They didn't deserve it, and I was a coward for offering it, but the more help, the more forces to invade the levels of hell, the better. And there was no humiliation or cowardice I wouldn't stoop to for her. I'd become a slug if only for one more moment with Blythe.

Radio static sounded like a flurry throughout the graveyard before silence befell again. The creature straightened. *Deal.*

I wasn't a vampire thirsty for blood, nor a dragon greedy for flight. My soul was long gone and had never been as pure as a wolf as it chased the light of its luna. No, there was nothing good in me and nothing I craved. Nothing I desired but death. And I'd give the damned their death in exchange for mine. My death, my reaper, my life. Because that's all I was: demon, an archdemon, and hers.

THE GROUND THUNDERED beneath the immortal footfalls outside the gates of hell. Silence befell the forest in a way that only occurred when danger was present, and this was indeed a great convergence of terror. Wolf eyes met mine throughout scattered trees, haughty vampires from dozens of covens crossed their arms and bickered quietly among themselves. And at the head of the gate, Raven cawed at my boys as I approached the iron.

"I thought hell's gate was metaphorical, not actually the gate to hell," Onyx purred, flashing his canines beneath his glowing green eyes. He was as bloodthirsty as I was, and yet even still, he could manage levity. Yes, I loved the fool.

Wolfgang stretched his triceps, looking up at the gate, or the bird, I couldn't tell. "Have you ever known Ghost to be a demon of nuance? Our friend here's a pretty black and white guy." He gave me a weak smile, and after a moment, regarded me. "We're doing this. We're breaking into hell."

"To fight the devil," Onyx added as we huddled together at the base of the iron-guarded cemetery. Taking a deep breath, I looked out among those that we'd forced, coerced, and threatened to our aid. Only the wolves were friends. The others and the damned that lurked invisibly as dark spirits were as evil as what we'd face beyond the hollow ground. Good. The more wretched the better for what we were to face. Feeling tugged at my ribs as I assessed my two friends, friends who had surpassed friendship, lovers who'd over-encompassed love. Was there even a word in any language for what they truly were to me? No, I didn't believe so. At least in hundreds of years of existence, I had not found one.

"There's a strong possibility we don't all come back from this." They looked at me with serious expressions, and I etched their strong and unique features into my mind's eye. "This could be... our last adventure, boys."

Wolfgang's jaw steeled, but Onyx only wrapped his arms around us. "This could be the devil's last adventure. Not ours, never ours."

The werewolf cleared his throat, and I tasted his determination mixed with sorrow. Wolf's emotions tasted like steeped teas and warm spices. "Everyone accounted for?" he asked.

"Every haughty coven in Belladonia and Hallows Fest and beyond is here," Onyx replied, looking out over the vampires he commanded. The balls it took for him to go and claim the town like that, and in front of Vlad... I'd marvel at that for a while. Onyx Hart was a determined son of a bitch.

And Wolfgang. I felt his deep concern and his conflicted feelings as he told us of the lunas, stellas, and sols who were joining us. He knew the risk and cared deeply for his pack. But the fact that he'd enlist them to walk through hell with us meant he'd give even his beloved Fenrir to save Blythe.

When my boys had first shown interest in my claimed, I couldn't deny that I'd felt possessive and wholly against the idea.

But seeing them here now, standing with me outside of hell's gates, willing to kill or be killed at the hands of the devil for her… There were none more worthy of her than they. Perhaps not even me.

"And mine are ready as well," I replied lowly, turning to assess the gates.

"Yours?" Onyx questioned. "Not sure how many demons cat could take."

My familiar hissed from an above branch, and Raven chirped a laugh.

"You'll see," I murmured, touching the gate. "The devil has closed the door to him. But if we all three try, I believe we can open it."

I could call on hell smoke. Onyx's vampire half was made in the fires. And Wolfgang could rip through veils. The three of us together had potential we'd rarely explored to its full extent. Now was the time to try and coax out whatever the best or worst of us had to offer.

"On three, we pull this piece of shit with everything we got." The guys nodded and grabbed on. I counted us down, and we pulled, our hands burning soon after with hell's flame. "Something's mad," I encouraged.

"Not as mad as me," Wolf gritted, the strength in his hold budging the very metal of the gate.

Our palms burned as we pulled. Agony and hate rattled into our bones. Hell was waiting, and hell didn't want to be entered by anyone's accord other than its own. "Hell doesn't want to let us in," I gritted out.

"Well, too fucking bad. Hell stole our girl." Onyx puffed, heating his hands with dragon fire. The iron bars of the gate hissed in response.

Something panted behind us, and I noticed Cat drop from her branch to speak with a woman.

"Are you sure?" Cat asked lowly. I wasn't going to stop pulling, but this fucking gate was barely budging.

"What? Who is it?" I snapped.

Wolfgang answered, likely smelling her before she arrived. "Yesenia."

"How nice of the witches to show up," Onyx quipped sarcastically. "Go back to selling lipstick and tarot cards, Yesenia."

I didn't disagree.

Wolfgang huffed in anger as he put more strength into his pull. I was sure none of us had ever seen anything he couldn't lift or budge. Wolfgang could carry whole oak trees on his back. The dark magic infused in keeping us out was intense. The thought that went into locking us away from her only sent shocks of rage through my body as Cat pressed her black paws on my feet.

"What?" I growled as she looked up at me with big slitted eyes.

"Blythe—"

We stopped pulling and stood, breathing heavily and looking down at my black cat familiar. My chest tightened. We'd left her guarded by the lunas. They wouldn't let anyone take or harm her, that I knew.

Cat straightened, her chest proud but her whiskers sunken. "She's gone, Ghost. Blythe's stopped breathing. Her pulse is gone. She's dead."

I couldn't hear what came next over the pounding in my head, the swirling tornado threatening to burst forth within me, and the influx of emotions from Onyx and Wolfgang scraping against my tongue. Wolf howled, guttural and long, before huffing along with his body changing. I followed, strengthening within my archdemon form. The sorrow, the failure, the fury buried us in blue hell smoke. Something roared, and fire ignited around us as a long reptilian tail swished.

Yesenia's voice called from somewhere in the distance. "The devil has her, her soul, her essence. You can reach her yet, but you're running out of time. She's given up—"

This time when I punched the gate, the bars wavered. And when Wolfgang in his alpha form, looking like a beast of nightmares, pulled on it with all his strength, they moved and bent for him. With a roar of fire, hell's gate shuddered and squeaked, knowing that dragon fire wasn't from it but from someplace greater, someplace good. And with a thrash of his dragon tail, the bars splintered. My archdemon pulled them off, prong by prong, then, tossing them to the ground. And when I stepped over the broken, gone gate of hell. The ground thundered and lowered like a road, going down, down, down, all the way to level number one.

Hell awaited us. The alpha and the dragon followed behind me as I led the charge into the darkness beyond the hollow ground. With rage fuming within us, we traversed. For her, for her soul, to retrieve her.

Yes, hell awaited us.

But hell awaited *him* , too.

And we'd surely bring hell to the devil now.

The Halloween Boys

HIGHWAY TO HELL

T he boys and I had long since shifted back to men as we walked forward, about a half a mile ahead of the armies of immortal misfits behind us. We could only imagine the bickering happening between beings as opposed as vampires and wolven, and our heavy hearts and churning anger thought it best to create distance for a while. It would take time to reach the first level. Unless, of course, the first level reached us first.

"My father found my mother's soul, and Blythe brought it back," Onyx said, looking at his Doc Marten boots as he walked.

"Blythe is a reaper. She is death, so she can't be dead. Her human body might be, but her soul is here. I saw it at the willow tree. We'll find her."

"Yes, but we have to make it to her first. When are you giving everyone a rundown?" Wolfgang asked me.

My jaw tensed.

"Everyone's looking to you to lead this, Ghost. You know the most of hell. Where are we going? What are we up against? You mention levels… these are things we need to know."

"Wait." Onyx stopped and kicked the ground. "Hold on. This is pavement."

Wolf and I raised an eyebrow at one another. "Yes, and?" the wolven asked.

Onyx let out a huff and ran his hands through his hair. "It's a highway. Guys, this is the literal highway to hell!"

I knew that despite our dire circumstances, both Wolfgang and I were containing our smiles just to fuck with him. Getting Onyx riled up was one of our small pleasures over the many years we'd spent together. Fuck knew they'd teamed up and gotten me worked up hundreds of times in our friendship.

"Obviously," Wolf said absently.

"Have you not heard the song?" I asked, knowing that would set him off.

He punched my arm hard and chuckled. "Fuck you guys. I know what you're doing. And you know this is fucking rad. We're on the highway to hell right now." The vampire hybrid looked around. "It's like, eight lanes, too. Hell get a lot of traffic?"

"Sometimes," I answered, still staring ahead of us, waiting for what was to come. But I stopped and watched as the crowd that accompanied us neared. Wolfgang was right. It was time to give them a rundown, though I wasn't sure how inspiring I could be. This was a fool's mission for us. For them? Guaranteed suicide. Something like guilt trilled beneath my skin at the thought that I was no better than Vladimir sending demons to fetch his bride. Here I was, sacrificing communities for mine. But would I change, send them away, or go back? No. They would die, and I would let them. As long as it got me closer to her, so be it. I never claimed to be the hero in this story. We were the villains.

Vampires and Wolves stopped and snorted, already irritated with each other, and looked around, waiting for my word. The atmosphere on the highway to hell was a permanent half night. Just enough light coming from a gray and faraway place to see but not enough to see fully. Like everything else in hell, it was a game, a trick. We looked like a black and white comic strip in this lighting.

"Thank you all for coming, for joining this fight for one of our own who's been dragged to hell by the devil himself," Wolf began, ever the patient and true leader.

The members of his pack were in their wolf forms, and they sat on their hind legs, listening intently, while the covens of vampires crossed their arms and looked on with disdain. I didn't blame them. Though Onyx smirked, seeming to enjoy their displeasure. He addressed them, then, with a bored tone, waving his hand. "Listen to Ghost or don't. But if you do, you're more likely to return to your arrogant and selfish lifestyles."

A cold voice called from the crowd piped up. "And if we don't return? What happens then?"

Onyx's eyes flashed green, and he took a step forward, cocking his head. "Vincent?" There was surprise in his tone, like he hadn't known the coven leader was here. "Well, I reckon you stay to be tormented." He smiled then, a wicked look, as if he hoped that would be the case for his horrible uncle. I hoped the same.

"That's correct," I answered. "Since we're all some form of immortal here, you can hope for death, and you may get it, depending on what kills you. More likely, you'll be trapped on the level at which you fall. And that fate…"

A brusque voice chimed in from the middle of the group. "Means yer tormented for all eternity. Don't it, Ghost?" Captain Vex stroked his bejeweled beard with twinkling eyes. Looking around in shock, I noticed dozens of pirates had joined him.

"Why the hell are you here?" Wolfgang chuckled in amusement.

Vex approached and rubbed my shoulder in that fatherly way of his. A way I was never accustomed to being treated but allowed from him for some odd reason. "You boys stayed for our fight. We'll be stayin' for yours."

Then my throat really did constrict with feelings of care. Feelings I didn't want to or plan to bother with. But I gave him a short nod of thanks before swallowing my emotion and looking back to the crowd with the pirate captain and my boys by my side.

"There are seven levels of hell that I know of. Though there may be more. Some say as many as nine, but only the devil knows for sure. Where we are now is limbo, the highway to whichever level spits out at us. We will fight through each or find our demise, likely both."

Wolfgang elbowed my rib. "Little bit of hope wouldn't hurt, old friend."

I rubbed the back of my neck. *Hope.* What did I know of hope? This journey into the depths of chaos in search of the soul of my claimed was the craziest thing I'd ever done. Though at the same time, I supposed it was the most hopeful as well. Perhaps the most hope I'd felt in my existence was from her. That Blythe could see me, love me, and be mine. I had hope that I would not fail her. Or that at the very least, between Wolfgang and Onyx and me, one of us would reach her. One of us would rescue her and keep her safe from then on out. That was my hope, I supposed.

"It's uh…" I searched for the words as hundreds of skeptical eyes stared back at me. "It's been done before, though. I've made it through hell."

"Aye, as have I," Vex concurred.

Onyx whispered, "How many pints of rum do you think we need to get that story out of him?"

Wolfgang let out a labored sigh. "Standing in the thruways of the underworld, and we can't be serious."

Rubbing my temples, I shook my head and looked back to the

faces of the haphazard army before me. Silence fell. The kind of quiet that spooked humans in forests. It was quiet here, like death, like someone watching. We felt we had time, but I knew our moments were sand in a hateful hourglass.

As persnickety as the vampires were, and as optimistic as the wolves were, they knew it, too. We all felt the keen awareness of exactly where we were. The place we'd either long avoided or, for some, long sought out. And we stood on its highway now, awaiting the slam and crash of the Mack truck of dark reality that charged inevitably forward.

"We will encounter various demons in hell," I began, only having to project my voice slightly over the crowd. "There will be the typical kind—the breeds you expect, the ones from bible stories and campfire tales. The shadow beings that thrive on chaos and blood. The monsters, hounds, creatures of nightmares." Vincent crossed his arms and leveled me with a hard stare, a stare I met right back. The coven leader should watch himself, because the demon he met might just be me. Onyx snorted, sensing my emotions and agreeing.

"And the others?" Nephele asked, sitting cross-legged on the ground in her human form, her long white braids almost glowing in the dim and hazy gray light.

"The others were once human," I replied lowly. "The rapists, the pedophiles, the abusers, the kinds of mortals we Halloween Boys hunt and kill on the other side of hell. Only now we're on their turf. They're angry. Here, they remember us, know us, and they've been stewing in their fate for ages. Waiting for us to come home…" I looked over my shoulder at Wolfgang and Onyx, wishing for anything but the solemn gazes they passed me. Then I spoke to them in a warning plea. "They'll be rabid and risk nothing to get a hold of one or all of us. And… *one* of us needs to make it to her."

My meaning registered across their faces as Wolf crossed his arms and Onyx shoved his hands into his pockets. But I held their focus until, one at a time, they offered me a slight nod. They understood. There was no other way.

"This place will also battle for your mind." A dark, ancient voice spoke in the crowd, parting the sea of vampires and wolves as he strode forward, black and red cape billowing behind him. Onyx's intake of breath was audible as his father, Vladimir Drakon, continued. "You will be tested, tempted, and tried as fiercely as your body is burned. Should you succumb, either physically or mentally, you and your soul will stay trapped on the level where you fall. To burn in a wonderland of regret for the rest of time." The vampire's cool red glare met Onyx's, perhaps expecting a response or show of emotion.

My friend offered neither, instead turning on his heel. "Let's see what all the rock songs are about, boys," he quipped, leaving a stone-faced ancient leader and absent father behind him. Wolfgang and I followed him. Deeper into hell, foes and friends at our back, in pursuit of the hope that had been stolen from us. To fight the thief of that hope was our destiny, our curse, our holy calling.

The Hell Trails

He only came to watch me die or fail. Those were the only options in his mind, and if I were honest, maybe in mine, too. This was court, and I was on trial. Could I lead a people? Could I take control of the sickly rose that was Belladonia and its doors to realms unknown? My father clearly didn't think so, with his cliché cape and long, gaunt face full of impassive disapproval. Speaking to the vampires, informing them of hell. They listened to him. They mocked me. I hoped they'd all perish here and allow me to start over. Some king I was. A half king of pity and inadequacy. Vladimir knew it, Vincent knew it, and the people of Belladonia knew it, too.

"Get out of your head," Ghost grumbled, brushing his shoulder against mine as we walked along the highway. "I have a surprise for you."

My attention perked up, and I looked to him and Wolfgang. "What kind of surprise?"

"It's just up here," Ghost replied, motioning toward a dense blue fog of hell smoke. "Thought I'd share."

When we reached them, my mouth dropped. "You're fucking serious?"

Wolfgang covered his mouth in a chuckle. "How many years have Onyx and I begged for this, and you vehemently said no? That you're the only one allowed to have one?"

Ghost mounted his bike with a sideways smile. "We're in hell now, boys. They're endowed with my ghost rider abilities, too. Hell smoke, pass through shit, demon speed." He shrugged, as if these brilliant masterpieces of motorcycle demon engineering weren't the most incredible things I'd ever seen.

Wolfgang revved his engine, and it roared to life. Knocking his head back, he howled, informing his pack that we would be moving ahead. "This is cool, man." Wolf sat up and tied his hair into a knot.

Sitting on my own black bike with neon green fucking flames on the side, I rubbed the handlebars and found a switch. I could have kissed the archdemon. "Stereo speakers? You shouldn't have, sweetie."

"I really shouldn't have. You're right," Ghost grumbled, his pale blue eyes narrowing as he kicked off his kickstand.

My bike vibrated to life, sounding like a storm cloud of bats as I fiddled with the sound system. After a moment, "Highway to Hell" by AC/DC thundered over the three roars of machinery. I'd speed into hell to get farther away from my father and my wretched people. To get closer to my likely doom at the hands of the devil and for the favor of my stolen bride. Damn, if that wasn't the most rock and roll thing I'd ever done.

Wolfgang laughed. "You would." Then he took off in a blaze of blue smoke that matched the blue moons on his bike. Ghost eyed me for a moment. "Whatever happens, I got your back. All right?"

Some hollow hole in my heart ached, and all I could do was nod. I wished I had the fucking nerve to say "I know, and I love you, too." But it was all I could manage, and he understood. He revved his engine and peeled off in a blaze of smoke.

The speed and power paired with the thumping bass were everything I needed. And I must say, the vibes were immaculate as I caught up with the boys. All until Ghost raised a fist to halt us. Before I could speak, Wolf lifted a finger to his lips. He heard something in the distance. And then, clearing through the fog, a line of them snarled and charged forward.

"What the fuck are those?" I asked.

Wolfgang responded. "Three-headed hellhounds. They're nasty motherfuckers."

These weren't just dogs with multiple heads. They were the size of grizzly bears, and they were charging us with massive teeth as they panted and shook the pavement with their footfalls. Dozens and dozens of them unleashed.

I looked to the guys. "Here we go."

"Here the fuck we go," Ghost rumbled in his demon voice.

"For Blythe." Wolfgang dismounted and shifted into his shadow wolf form, amber eyes glowing.

The engine purred beneath me as I shot forward, igniting fire around us like a barrier of flame.

And the first battle began.

Fire proved helpful against the hellhounds, singeing their leathery gray skin. Ghost was a beast, tearing off the jaw of one and decapitating another. Wolfgang tore through the hounds as if they were dolls made of paper. Likewise, the ones foolish enough to lunge for me died by fire. If these were the best hell had to offer, this was going to be easier than I anticipated. But somehow, I knew that wouldn't be true. By the time the lunas caught up with us, we'd left them scraps of maimed hounds to finish off. The vampires didn't get their hands dirty, and I rolled my eyes in their direction. They would be sullied. They'd fight when they had to, but surely they'd allow a wolf to die before lifting a finger. How embarrassing to be half a part of such arrogance.

Speaking of arrogance, my father approached me as the guys spoke with the lunas and pirates, the vampires listening on, feigning disinterest.

"You will be a better ruler than I, son," Vladimir said, stepping over a puddle of hound blood as I retrieved my bike and pushed it forward.

I snorted. "Even with so many *weaknesses*? Oh the horrors of caring for those in need. Perhaps I should keep their blood in little vials for my spiders instead." I was referring to his past comments, of course. How he'd dangled women and children in front of me, even weaponizing my love for Blythe. The events of Belladonia would long haunt me, but somehow, his words even more so than the terrors we faced there. My father had a gift for knowing everyone's weak spots, like he needed supernatural abilities to know mine. Mine were obvious.

His cape floated behind him as he walked beside me, and we pulled away from the rest of the group. "You believe your weakness to be care? Your need to protect the innocent?"

He was far more conversational than I'd ever heard him before, and for the briefest moment, I wondered if he was a phantom disguised as the vampire king, but that didn't make any sense.

"Tell me, then, what's my weakness?" I jumped when my motorcycle tires hit rough dirt and left pavement. The terrain was changing.

Vladimir looked around with glowing eyes. Just like mine, only red. I hated that they were just like mine. "I vow to tell you sometime."

I rolled my eyes, "Sure—" Something screamed behind me, and in a flash, my father attacked it. A lanky, shapeless form shuddered back into the forest, screaming as it went. Something tapped my shoulder, and I turned, but when I did, piercing pain struck the back of my head, and I fell forward.

Screams ignited around me as I lay frozen in the dirt. Was this my father's plan? To separate me from the group and watch me suffer. To trap me in hell for stealing his kingdom?

If it was, he'd surely succeeded. I'd let my guard down. My last coherent thought was that my weakness was being a gullible idiot. And how much I'd miss the sweet taste of Blythe's blood. And then the world was fading to her favorite shade of black.

Nephele was in the middle of her debrief when I interrupted her. "I don't smell Onyx anymore." In my panic, I turned and ran toward his scent trail. The green ribbon of his smoky plum scent cut in a sharp stop at his bike. In the distance, I saw Ghost, and when I made to shout to him, the pavement cracked and rippled beneath us.

Everyone was shouting, then, as the ground split in two. Though I was frantic to find Onyx. Ghost bellowed over what now became a cliff. A cliff that was growing into the sky, separating him from us.

"He must know!" was the last I heard from him. Then the ground beneath us halted its tremble and my feet sloshed into ankle deep mud and liquid.

The atmosphere changed to a dingy olive shade. The waters resembled a sewer, while blackened vines with barbs hung all around me and the lunas. Nephele held on to my arm for support.

"We were sorted," she breathed.

"Sorted how?" I asked, kicking through the mud, incensed that I'd let us be separated, wondering where Onyx and Ghost had gone, and really fucking mad that I couldn't smell anything.

"Sorted into our level of hell." She looked around. "I only know what the elders told me before we left. They surmised that something like this might happen. Hell is like a well- oiled machine; it's placed us where it believes we belong. But if we don't accept it and continue our pursuit of good, it will sort us through other levels until we eventually reach our destination." The luna grabbed a long stick and plunged it in front of her, using it as a makeshift walking staff, and stomped through the eerie netherworld swamp. "Come, let's keep moving," she ordered, and all of us wolves fell in line. We marched to the sounds of goopy brown water beneath us, though somehow it was becoming deeper and deeper until it was to our thighs.

I was disoriented. There were no scents. Nothing made sense here, nothing was right. "I'm glad you're here to lead us, Nephele," I said to the back of her white braids.

Something shrieked from a vine above us and dropped. It was like an enormous sharp-toothed rat. It writhed and hissed and had a long black tail. I made to grab it, but the luna pushed it under the water with her walking stick, impaling the creature as it rippled and bubbled the liquid. "Someone has to," she said coldly. "It could never be you."

Hurt stuck me as if I were the skewered rodent. "What?"

The other lunas sloshed past me, casting me cold stares. "You heard me," she repeated. "Stay or come, but we don't need you, Wolfgang. We never have. In fact, no one does. Why do you think your own micro-pack has abandoned you in hell?"

Her eyes were glazed white as she shook her head. "You're a disgrace, and you've failed us all. Your grandfather would be so disappointed in you, Wolfgang Jack."

The wolves marched ahead, spearing the overgrown rats as they dropped with murky splashes and leaving my heart twisting within me. They were right to be angry. I'd made a grave miscalculation in asking them to come. I hadn't anticipated us being split from the larger group, but as wolves, our instincts were all we needed to survive in any environment. But the thought of my grandpa… Each step had my feet sinking deeper in slime until I was half wading after them.

"Wait up!" I called out, though the only thing I heard were

snickers in response. They'd finally had enough of me. I'd finally gone too far, asked too much, led them astray for the final time.

My layer of hell was one where my pack no longer needed me. Cast out, isolated, a lone wolf. This was indeed my hell, and it hurt like hell. It hurt worse than any real or imagined flames of torment could. Killing swamp rats only made me feel better momentarily, until finally, I could barely hear the wading of the lunas in the distance. They couldn't get away from me fast enough.

My heart broke with every paddle through the water, and I remembered my last swim at the waterfall with Blythe. God, she'd looked so beautiful. Naked, hair wet, her supple body wrapped around me as I took her under the falls. Did that even happen?

For some reason, I felt confused. Like maybe it had been a dream, maybe nothing but the swamp had ever existed. A scream pulled my mind back to reality, and then another scream. I swam faster, fighting to catch up with the lunas. More gurgles and screams, and something thrashed in the water ahead. Something much bigger than the rats.

"Help!" Nephele cried out, more pained than I'd ever heard the warrior.

My biceps and abs burned with effort as I propelled forward as fast as I could. "I'm here!" I shouted. And no sooner did I arrive than a spiked-back, scaled monster with a long and massive jaw erupted in front of me, wrapping its rough tail around my body and digging its claws into my shoulder as it yanked me under the murky tide.

I fought on land. I didn't know shit about water, except that my lungs burned and I was disoriented. My size, for once, was a liability, not an asset. It made me stiff and caused me to sink faster. The long reptilian monster was a giant crocodile, I realized as I narrowly dodged the snap of its jaws. And for a moment, as dirt and bubbles flitted past and the crocodile spun toward me again, my lungs burned and my mind spun in dizzying directions of doubt. My pack didn't need me, neither pack needed me. I was an extra. I was unnecessary. My time spent trying to be useful was me begging to be needed, to be accepted.

But I was neither. If anything, I was only in the way.

The creature's tail hit me again, burning my temple and positioning me for its death strike. Blythe had Onyx and Ghost. Both were more suave, more charming than me. I was a fourth wheel and no one's first pick. The lunas had each other. They had no need for an alpha sol. Maybe the most selfless thing I could do would be to let the creature drown and kill me. Locking my soul here where I could no longer be a burden to those around me.

Yes, maybe that was the right thing to do.

In the murky brown before me, all I could make out was the open mouth full of jagged yellow teeth coming for my head, and I didn't swim away. Why would I?

Staying there and drowning in my weaknesses could have been the best course of action, right? And then, for some reason, as oxygen struggled to reach my brain, I remembered a flash of Blythe laughing around a campfire. When I'd brought her to Fenrir last October and made her a plate of meat. She sat among the elders and felt like mine.

She looked at me like I could protect her, and fuck if I didn't try to. Then I remembered that I was in water and recalled jumping off my grandpa's boat when the fish were scarce. Sometimes he'd jump in and try to grab me a scare me, too, much to my delight.

Maybe they didn't need me.

My pack, Blythe, the Halloween Boys.

Maybe *I* needed them.

And maybe that was okay.

That was okay.

Jaws wrapped around my throat, and my fight returned. My fight may have been selfish, but if it was, then so be it. A bubbled groan pulled from my mouth as its teeth cut into my palms. Blood bloomed in the water around us, darkening it further, and I found my strength, pushing on the creature's thick trunk for leverage and pulling its maw open, open, farther. The crocodile spun, trying to fling me off, but its teeth, protruding and burning into my hands, caught on bone. And through the lack of air and agonizing pain, I held firm.

In its frenzy, it breached the surface, allowing me a stinging gasp of thick and peppery air and the final opportunity to crack its skull. The creature went heavy and limp, splashing into the bloodied waters and ripping the flesh of my hands along with it. But they were mostly intact, and I was alive. Nephele clung to a vine, screaming, as another one of the beasts circled her. She was bloodied, as if she'd just endured a battle similar to mine.

"I'm coming!" I yelled, swimming after her.

The water gurgled, like jets had just been turned on, and I stopped, feeling something brush against my leg. Spikes dipped and fell beneath the surface, attached to the back of fifty or more of the crocodiles. We were surrounded. Still, I swam toward her, scales brushing against me and sets of jaws opening to greet me, thrashing against each other and fighting for the chance to devour me. If I was going to die, if my soul would be trapped in this swamp for eternity, it would be in pursuit of saving someone else. I moved my arm, and incisors brushed against my skin as another croc wrapped its tail around me.

It jerked me under the surface just as music blared. Was this dying? My brain was short-circuiting and hearing Journey's "Don't Stop Believin'." Onyx would never let me live it down if he knew this was the song I died to.

But then as swiftly as it came, the crocodile released me, and I kicked to the surface. When I did, arms grabbed me, hauling me up and over the side, onto a hard wooden surface. I coughed, pointing behind me. "The lunas—Nephele—"

A man knelt in front of me, his long beard jingling as his magic jukebox played behind him. I knew this place. No, this ship. It was the Story Keepers, and Captain Vex had pulled me from my demise. He moved the wet hair from my face as I sat up, breathless and still bleeding. His mouth formed a straight line, and his red parrot ruffled on his shoulder. "There's no more lunas, son. They're gone."

My voice scratched in my throat as I screamed for Wolf, who only got smaller and smaller as the ground beneath me rose and shifted higher into the sky. I considered jumping, but my archdemon form deflated, leaving me as a man, and suddenly I was dropped onto a shaking container.

I hadn't prepared them for this, didn't consider that hell would split us up, but the possibility that we were now being shuffled into our respective circles of woe... I should have known this would happen. The devil wouldn't want us relying on each other, and the underworld would want order.

It would want us where we belonged in order to pay for our centuries of sin. Mine would be the worst of them, the most debauched and baleful. And as the smoke cleared, my thoughts were of my claimed. The boys would be okay. They'd get through wherever they were sent. At least I hoped so. But Blythe, she was in the hold of the devil, and why he took her or wanted her... rage had my fists balling up as I turned and punched a lamp off its stand.

My breaths were heavy as I oriented, and the carpeted floor shook beneath me. Wait, *a lamp*? Chatter pulled my attention in the narrow car, and I took in the sight of men in bowler hats, smoking cigars and turning newspaper pages. Stepping over the lamp, I pressed my face to a frosty window, seeing the front of the old train and dark smoke billowing and trailing over us. We snaked around a snowy mountain pass, and the cart shook as the smell of bourbon and cologne tickled my nostrils.

"What the actual fuck?" I asked, walking down the aisle. No one spared me a glance. I screamed, a roar of frustration and a plea to erupt into my demon form, but no one turned to look, and Ghost sure as hell didn't appear. No, looking down and assessing my suspenders and brown slacks, I knew I was stuck in my human form. A train ticket trembled in my hand, the name one I hadn't seen in hundreds of years. Not only that, but worse. I was trapped not as Dr. Ames Cove, the hell-riding, leather-jacket and skull-face wearing therapist and serial killer. No, this body, these clothes, this time period was one I recalled vividly, but only in my nightmares.

I wasn't Ghost or Ames or the leader of the Halloween Boys in this train car. The ticket in my hand screeched the name of someone who died a long time ago. An aspiring priest, a hopeful young man. I was James.

James Cove.

I paced the train car as it shook and rumbled down the track. Snow was falling softly outside in light drenched in frigid blue. How was this my hell? I gritted my teeth. My boys were likely fighting to the death somewhere. Blythe was locked away in fiery pain at the devil's hand. And I was wearing glossy penny loafers as men played cards next to me, oblivious. I looked for something else to punch and decided to scream again instead. My frustration was doing nothing to calm my mind or silence the men's low and distracting chatter.

"Can't punch your way out of this one, can ya, big guy?" A woman's surly voice pulled my gaze as she sat under low light in a corner booth. She puffed from a long cigarette holder and bobbed her heel beneath her billowing dress over her crossed legs. I didn't recognize the jade of her eyes, but the scarlet of her hair was unmistakable as I slumped into the velvet booth across from her.

"What the fuck are you doing here, Ezmerelda?"

She took another drag of her cigarette, seeming at home in her pastel, spoiled princess getup. "Sent to torment you, I suppose."

I hit the table in anger, clinking the wineglasses, and the vampiress *tsk*ed. "Obviously I was banished to the same circle of hell as you, dimwit. Keep your demon rage in your pants for five minutes, would you? Yes, we all know you're such a big, strong, evil guy," she said patronizingly, as if she were cooing to an infant. It only made me want to scream again as I darted my gaze, searching for an unlocked exit.

"We have to find a way out. If we scale down the mountain, we could reach another level, and get out of—"

"How are you so old and yet so stupid?" Ezmerelda interrupted, refilling her glass of red wine. "Truly, I do have a heart for archdemons. One of my closest friends is one. But oh, your breed is horribly short-sighted at times." She took a sip and raised her eyebrows as I crossed my arms and glared on. "Nice hat." She eyed my newsboy cap, and I resisted the urge to rip it off and throw it.

"Okay, Ezmerelda," I growled lowly. "Why don't you tell me what we're supposed to do since you know everything?"

"Where do you think this train is going?" she asked, flicking the ash from her smoke. "I'll tell you where. Nowhere."

"Nowhere?"

"The Train to Nowhere. And look around. You brought your friends."

I raised an eyebrow but looked over my shoulder at the men. They weren't my friends. I didn't recognize them… but then I saw the long gray beard of a man playing poker. Horror prickled my skin seeing the stout man across from him. "They shouldn't be here," I murmured, my voice strained with concern.

"Oh? And why not?"

"Because they're murderers and psychopaths, and because I killed them," I answered, disturbed to see the contents of my graveyard, the damned, clean and looking alive and drinking so merrily.

The Red Vampiress giggled, lifting a lace-gloved hand to her berry lips. "Looks as if hell sees you all as the same. Well, except for the fact that you're aware of our state and they are not."

"There must be a way to break down the door. If we can get to the conductor, maybe we can take control of the train and—"

The vampiress let out a belabored sigh, as if I was the stupidest person she'd ever spoken to. "No, ghostie boy, no. Nowhere." She giggled again. "Oh, you'd rather be out fighting, wouldn't you? Don't you think he knows that? That hell and the devil, in their eons of shadowy wisdom, know precisely where our punishment is best served. You're stuck, darling. There is no escape."

"How can you be so calm about this?" My rage had my palms rattling the table. "Maybe since you care for no one, you have no one to love or look after, Ezmerelda. And I may be a piece of shit demon, but I at least have that. I have her, and I have the guys, and I will find a way to break out of this and get back to them." In a fit of anger, I stood, knowing I wasn't getting anywhere with trying to converse with a churlish, egotistical vampire.

So, for the next hour, or two, or maybe it was a day, I proceeded to tear the train car apart. None of the reimagined damned so much as glanced at me. And every bit of carpet, furniture, and wine bottles I smashed against flimsy doors only momentarily broke or shifted before materializing in their original form. Madness. This was fucking madness, and the pompous vampiress looked on with dull amusement, still flicking her ash and dispensing wine until I conceded some form of defeat and rejoined her, resting my head in my hands.

"Great, so my hell is a train to nowhere with all the men I've killed and the fucking red vampiress to witness my mental break-down." I looked up. "Thanks, Judas. Very creative."

"Oh, he doesn't know you're here. Not yet at least. I mean, you'll know when he knows. Trust me. In fact, that's likely the only thing you boys have on your side right now. The element of surprise."

I perked up at that and met her gaze. My first thought when we were separated was that it was Judas's doing. But if it wasn't, then we still had the element of surprise in our favor. "How do you know that?"

"I know lots of things."

"Tell me more, then."

She poured a glass of wine for me, and I only stared at the burgundy liquid, still fighting the urge to heave it against the wall if only to watch it reappear in front of me again. "The devil is in his Hades and Persephone era. You four horsemen shall watch what she does and make peace with the aftermath."

"What the fuck are you talking about?"

"You know the stories, same as the stories about you and me and our kind. The devil has stories of his own, does he not? And what's the one about him whisking away his goddess to the underworld, hm?"

"You're saying he's taken her as what, as like a—a…"

Ezmerelda hummed a wedding march, and my eyes widened.

"No," I growled. "He can't."

"Can, has, did." She giggled. "What's one to do when the devil steals their girl?"

"Rip him apart," I responded, looking over the exits for the millionth time.

She sighed, tapping her manicured nails along her glass. "James, be reasonable. It's the only way you'll get out of here."

"What about you? Don't you want off this train?"

Ezmerelda looked around, and a small moment of honesty softened her expression. "I don't know."

"She needs me, they need me, and I'm just sitting here." I slammed my fists against the table again. Feeling emotions I didn't want to feel rising to the surface.

"Would we sit here?" she mused quietly, sitting back. "Sit here and think after them for the rest of time? Like a train passing through snow, never to touch, always to remember."

I put my head in my hands again, and to my humiliation, tears welled in my eyes. "For her, for them, I'd do anything."

"I know, James," she whispered, placing a hand on my arm. "And that's why your hell is nothing."

Her words bounced in my mind like a pinball. It made sense. This was my perfectly crafted hell. Where I wanted or desired the flames, the fight, the battle and pain, my place of great torment was a soft and quiet thing of no purpose, no outcome, no escape. My strength, my powers, were nothing here. I was nothing here.

"I'm nothing," I confessed through half sobs, knowing she'd meet me with ridicule. But surprisingly, her grip tightened on my arm before she tilted my chin up to look at her.

"Then be nothing," she answered with a small smile. And I noticed her teeth weren't sharp. They were normal mortal teeth; she was a normal human here, too. Still fine looking, but not with the same exaggeration of features her vampire form afforded her. Was this a form of Ezmerelda she'd lost long ago? Perhaps the version of her before she turned into the infamous red vampiress of nightmares? She looked like an ordinary woman on a train.

So we sat in silence.

Doing nothing, being nothing.

My breathing evened out and my tears dried to my face. I watched the snow fall, fighting my thoughts, silencing my roiling rage into a mound of soft fallen snow. It was the opposite of Ghost and his hell's fury. It was the opposite of Ames Cove and his control. To just… sit.

Ghost and Ames couldn't help me here. I was stripped bare and raw and until I was the form of myself I thought had died, the form I wanted to die. But on this train, maybe *he* was who I needed to be. An idea sprang to life, one that certainly didn't come from my demon or psycho killer sides. But I'd already wept in front of Ezmerelda. My pride was long gone.

I turned around and tapped a man on the shoulder. "Game of cards, old chap?" I asked.

He acknowledged me and tipped his hat. "I believe we have room for another player."

Ezmerelda raised curious eyebrows as I exited to join them at their booth. I had no idea what my end goal was, but I had my ass handed to me in four rounds of cards with the men I'd slaughtered. The damned were good at poker, I surmised.

Then I shook their hands and found the next booth, drinking bourbon and smoking with the occupants, before joining the next and discussing the current events in their newspapers. By the end of the day, or week, however long it was, I'd met and befriended each man aboard. For once, I knew their names and faces aside from blurry recollections of their bloody ends at my hands. I stood at the front of the train, unsure of what to do, but the slight curve of Ezmerelda's mouth encouraged me to continue. Something was happening, even if I had no idea what. I was following a different lead altogether here.

I cleared my throat. "Gentlemen."

The men stopped, looking up at me from their cigars and drinks.

"It's Sunday," one of them shouted.

"It's the preacher!" another answered.

I swallowed. Emotion, guilt, every emotion I never wanted to feel bubbled up, but I would let them out. I had to. It had to be the way to her, to them, so I'd do it.

"Yes," I said unsurely. "I am Father James Cove, and my sermon today is a short one."

The men straightened as I led them through a prayer. A prayer for their souls, a prayer for strength. Somehow, all the words from my early human days were still there. All the bible stories and studies were lurking inside me and waiting for use, eager for a break from their dormancy.

"Forgive, and you will be forgiven," James Cove said. I said. "Luke 6:37. It's a passage, a theme in the Bible, that I have never played well with." I sucked in a breath. "What is forgiveness when there is so much pain? When others go about with their wrongs with seemingly no consequences. No, forgiveness isn't easy for me." I walked the aisle, the damned following me with their gazes. "'Father, forgive them, for they do not know what they do.' Jesus said that from his cross. From his death, he begged forgiveness for his transgressors. It is… what we must say to those who willfully harm us."

The train shook and rumbled beneath my feet, and Ezmerelda met my stare with wide eyes before nodding, encouraging me to continue.

"*I forgive you* is what we must say to the forces of darkness that threaten to nail us to crosses. *I forgive you* is what we must say to the evil that seeks to entomb us. Forgiveness should be handed out freely," I said loudly over the screech of train cables as I held a booth as we jerked forward. "To our friends, the ones who anger us, to the devil himself, we must forgive."

The lights flickered and the sounds of the men's resounding *amen*s flustered around the train. The clanking came to a stop, and the train hooted like a giant tea kettle. Wind rushed at my back as doors opened behind me and a skeleton conductor saluted me, motioning for me to get off the train.

When I looked back, the men were no longer men, but black shadows of the damned once more, and they were lodged firmly in their seats. I found Ezmerelda and extended my hand. "Come on."

She sat for a moment, so at odds with the horrifying entities around her, a doll amongst demons, and I thought for a second that she may want to stay. Maybe a part of her wanted to stay, and somehow, a part of me felt the same. The James Cove part. Blythe had always reminded me that he was there, and she was right. Maybe I needed to stop ignoring him so much. Maybe James Cove could command the train every now and then and show me that my humanity wasn't my curse after all.

But then Ezmerelda stood and took my hand. "Let's go get your girl." She smiled with a fixed sadness in her eyes. Had it always been there, or was it plainer now without her vampire magnetism to hide behind? I wouldn't question it. We stepped into the snow together, knowing and meeting for once as humans again.

We followed a shoveled stone path down a snow-covered mountain hill as the train sounded its horn and chugged away behind us. Going nowhere, with two fewer nothings.

When I opened my eyes, the sky was… pink. And then, like a storm cloud moving into my vision, my father appeared and offered a hand.

I took it and rose to my feet, rubbing my head. "What happened?"

"We were attacked, and suddenly we were here. Our station of penance, I presume, though I see no other vampires."

"Convenient," I cursed suspiciously, eyeing the ancient vampire. "My fucking hell-curse would be to be stuck with the father who didn't want me in a…" I looked around, more confused by each thing I beheld. A pink-lit cotton candy stand, teacup rides swirling, game stands, a merry-go-round, and dirt path. The rides looked old, like this was some fair from long ago. "A carnival?"

Vladimir shrugged his broad shoulders. "The devil is crafty. If we are here, you can trust that it is the place of the utmost misery."

Glaring at him, I replied. "Oh, I believe you."

Turning on my heel, I left him behind, inspecting the stands instead. I picked up a baseball and jumped when the attendant appeared. "Three tries, and you win a bear or a bat."

I stared at him in dread. Stared at his emerald eyes, slicked-back black hair, the fangs, the silver jewelry… "You're—you're me," I stammered out.

"You gonna knock over the pins or what? I don't have all day," he said.

I threw the ball like it was made of snakes, knocking over the top pin and backing away. The mirror image of me smiled sinisterly. "What, don't want your other turns?"

"What is this? Do you see them, too?" I asked when my back hit my father's looming shoulder.

"I've counted maybe forty *yous* here… so yes, son, I see them, too."

"I am not your son," I mocked as the cotton candy me stepped from around his booth, swinging a baseball bat with nails protruding from its shaft.

"You two causing trouble?" he asked, and I noticed my name on the tag sewn into his striped shirt. "Because I don't like trouble in my carnival. How about you, boys?"

A dozen more surrounded us, taunting us with things I would most likely say. "Well, Vlad, looks like you get your wish. You get to kill me after all." Flicking my wrists, I snaked fire toward the four near me. They jerked and wailed in surprise. "Dragon fire works in hell." I smirked, squeezing their middles. "Because Dragon fire comes from some place better. Some place the devil can't touch." With a quick movement, I burned them in half. Then I turned to focus on the three more that were left. My father's face and hands bloodied with his own kills.

For some idiotic reason, that irritated me. Did he take pleasure in slaughtering my look-alikes? I took to a fistfight with the three mes who charged with swinging chains. I grabbed the shackle, wrapping it around my doppelgänger's neck and squeezing until he dropped. The other two descended, getting in punches to my jaw. One assailant laughed in my same chuckle and taunt. "Scared, are ya?"

Rubbing my busted lip, I chuckled darkly, looking at myself reflected in this hell projection. My hair perfectly combed, holes in my carnival uniform that I surely would have put there myself, and scuffed converse sneakers. "No, man. You may look like me, but you don't know me at all. Because I'm not afraid." I was upon him in a moment, shoving my hand through his chest and finding a long, wet spine. His eyes widened with death. "I'm fucking giddy," I growled. "Don't you know? I've fucking always wanted to kill myself." With a yank, I pulled out his spine.

Casting a look over my shoulder, I saw Vladimir, blood dripping down his chin as he fed on one of my fallen doppelgängers. I wondered if he'd dreamt of killing me like that and feeding from me if only to taste and search for a hint of my mother. His red eyes caught mine, and he stood, not bothering to wipe his chin, his eyes that same shade of deranged that mine became so often.

"There's more." He gestured to the rides ahead. It lit up with flashing colors and upbeat tunes. "Shall we?"

Something that I didn't want to swell in my heart did. How often had I had similar fantasies as a younger man, wishing to find my father? And then after discovering what I was—wishing to kill with my father. But this man wanted nothing to do with me. He'd gotten what he'd hunted for, killed for, what he'd killed my own fiancée for.

"Do whatever you want," I responded. But I sure as hell was killing more of me. If the devil thought this was my torturous hell, battling and murdering myself, he'd be gravely mistaken. This was a fucking dream. A dark chuckle rumbled my bloodied throat. "I *would* love hell, wouldn't I? It's where I fucking belong." I twirled under a beat of '80's music from a speaker. If Blythe existed somewhere in this realm, and all I had to do was kill all the Onyxes on this level, then fine. That was just fine with me. This was just a big fucking video game, wasn't it? These zombie Onyx Harts had it coming, and I was player one.

They jumped over their stations, abandoning their rides and duties, meeting me where I was. And oh, I killed them with fury and reckless abandon. And with each kill I witnessed my father make, with each one of my bodies that fell at his hands, I hated him more.

Vladimir's voice called over a row of dead bodies. "I always wanted you, too, Dracul."

"Bullshit." I rolled my eyes.

"I am sorry that I hurt the ones you loved in my pursuit of your mother. Though do you not see the poetry in you doing the same now? Like father like son."

A huff of indignation left my throat as I stepped over a dead doppelgänger. "You're not my father," I repeated, wishing away the stupid, needy feelings in my chest.

"Well, you are my son," he replied, forlorn and sorrowful. I felt his emotions hit my face like a cold rag, and I hated every moment of absorbing his feelings. Before I could speak, laughter pulled my attention, and we were surrounded again. Only this time, there were more than I could have ever anticipated. I lit my fire and surrounded Vlad and me with a circle of flame.

"Over one hundred," he murmured, still standing proudly. But then I noticed the Ferris wheel as it turned slowly in the distance. Someone was sitting on it… someone with sunlight hair and curls I'd never forget. And my singed black heart jumped into my throat. "Minnie?"

And then I fucking lost it. Any restriction on my rage unleashed. My unbridled fire scorched with agony, searing skin and befalling every Onyx in its path as I ran over them, charging toward the wheel. They jumped at me, and I cracked their heads. Another two grabbed my arms, and I ripped out their throats with my teeth, still looking toward her. "Minnie?" I called out, reaching the base of the Ferris wheel.

She was in a plain light-blue dress with her hands folded in her lap. "Hi, Onyx. I've been waiting for you." She smiled, her chair coming to a stop, and the bar lifted. Minnie, *Minnie* gestured to the seat next to her, and in all my blood and gore and sweat, I took it without hesitation. It had to have been a mirage, but I didn't fucking care. When the bar in front of us clicked close, I startled to see my father looming in front of me.

"Your weakness, son," he said, his pain still radiating into me.

I huffed in disbelief. "Women? Yeah, I guess you were right."

"No," he replied, stepping back and letting the wheel kick back as four doppelgängers approached him from behind. "Shame."

I pushed at the locked bar. "Dad, look out!" I pointed behind him, but the doppelgängers grabbed him, and the bar fastened tight to my lap. "Fight!" I yelled as the machine tilted me back and up, up, and away from him.

But he didn't move. I watched in horror as I, or the bodies of me, ripped into his throat, and he fell to his knees. Minnie took my hand. I'd forgotten she was there until her soft hand wiped my tears. "You are enough, Onyx Hart. You have everything you need."

"Minnie," I sobbed, holding her hands. "I'm so sorry. I'm so sorry I couldn't save you."

"You did save me, Onyx. You did. The love you gave me was more than enough for that life."

I pulled away from her gaze to see a pile of wrath upon my father's body. "He brought you and me here. We're at the top now. You have to go," she urged, unlatching the bar.

"What?" I dried my face.

Doppelgängers snarled and hissed as they now climbed the wheel, shaking its bars. "You must go now. She needs you. Mortala needs you."

A gust of wind hit my face, and the pink sky was blocked in shadow. Then an enormous pale green dragon hovered above us. Its rider called down. "Take my hand." It was Elysium.

"I can't leave them," I shouted, back, grabbing Minnie's arm and looking back toward my father.

"You have to," my lost love replied, urging me forward. "Goodbye, Onyx."

"Goodbye, Minnie."

Words we never got to say. The dragon hooked its claws around my trunk, and with one beat of its wings, propelled us upward. Elysium reached down and pulled me onto the dragon's back, and I strained to look over the side as the doppelgangers overtook the Ferris wheel. "No!" I screamed as Elysium pulled me to his chest and I sobbed into his white beard.

My father had guided me through hell, only to die and to get me to her one last time. His final apology. And my last words to him would haunt me for the rest of my days. *You aren't my father.* While Minnie's words and hands were a balm to my shame, proclaiming I was enough, allowing me my goodbye. But clearly, I was a fool. A fool who'd just been played by my father one last time, only this time for my benefit and not his. He'd forfeited what he'd loved most, my mother, in favor of me.

My father.

And now I'd never see him again.

"Do you want my jacket?" I offered as we descended the wooden path down the mountain. It was flanked with streetlights that illuminated the flurries of snow as they flitted past. It was cold. It wasn't something I normally would have noticed, but it seemed I was still stuck in my old human form, and judging by Ezmerelda's scowl, so was she.

Rubbing her elbows, she kicked forward in her corseted dress. "My father was a railroad millionaire, and my mother a fortune-hunting debutant. When she secured a marriage to my father, I became her next asset."

We trudged forward, and I scanned the area, seeing nothing but trees and a clear path as we made our way down. I wasn't sure why Ezmerelda was sharing about herself. Perhaps her human form, or the train, was bringing up memories for her. I figured with how she helped me back there, the least I could do was listen and try not to be a prick to her for once. In fact, I was partially curious about her, not knowing much about her aside from her legendary and rabid status as the Red Vampiress, circus star, and lethal vixen. Talking would pass the time until I was closer to Blythe. "Sounds fun. The 1800s?"

"I was born in 1877. My mother was determined to marry me into European aristocracy and raised me like a prized pig for breeding." She examined her hands, seeing something in them that I didn't notice, before sighing. "I was fluent in German and French by age seven. With three governesses and hours of Latin, math, and piano daily." She straightened, wiggling her shoulders. "My mother forced me to wear a steel rod down my spine to straighten my posture. If I slouched, I'd be whipped with a riding crop. If I chewed too loudly, I'd be whipped. If I folded my napkin wrong, you guessed it—whipped."

"I'm sorry," I murmured.

She shrugged, smirking slightly. "When I was sixteen, my mother took me to Europe and paraded me around every duke and wealthy gentleman imaginable. And hell, I was one of America's richest heiresses, just as my mother always wanted. My pedigree traded for a lifetime layer of extra security for her." Ezmerelda spun in place, fanning her skirts and moving ahead of me. "The Duke of Something-or-other was to be my husband. Some old, bald, comb-over asshole. But I fell in love with a playwright. A very poor playwright, I might add. Winthrop Devenaire."

"I'm going to take a wild guess and say it didn't work out with him."

"*Her*," she corrected. "Winthrop was the man's name she published under. No, Winifred and I never got together. Though I did refuse to marry the duke, even after my mother locked me in my room without food or water for weeks. But... during those weeks, I explored more creative measures for finding my own way in life."

I raised an eyebrow at her as we rounded a bend. "Well, go on. Don't leave me hanging in hell."

She chuckled. "I agreed to marry the duke, but only long enough to run away. For weeks, there were strange flyers arriving at my door. Advertising some cirque, or circus, of sorts. Anyway, knowing what I know now, I never should have taken the bait. But I did and walked right into a phantom circus den."

"But you're a vampire, not a phantom, correct?"

Her tongue flicked over her teeth as if she missed her fangs. "Vampires have meddled in phantom circuses for years. They saw my potential and made me one of them. And well, I promptly murdered my mother when they did. She was my first kill."

I snorted a laugh. "Sounds about right."

"You going to tell me why you didn't follow through with becoming a priest? That sermon back there was awe-inspiring, I mean, I may pray again someday now. Probably not, actually, but almost."

"Funny. And why not? You mean besides becoming and archdemon? I don't know, I don't like getting up early on Sundays."

"Wow, Ghost. Was that an actual joke? Hell suits you."

"Same for you," I quipped as the ground leveled. "I almost hope you make it out of here alive."

"I almost hope I don't steal Blythe for myself and leave you here to suffer alone."

We both laughed then, the wooden walkway turning to ashy black ground. The smell of sulfur was heavy in the air. This was the version of hell I remembered.

"That smell is one you never forget, huh?" Ezmerelda asked. "And the screams. Do you hear them?"

Something deep in my bones buzzed, and I felt Ghost, my demon, slowly coming back online as we left the cold of the snowy mountain behind us and neared this black and scorched place. After a moment, I did slowly begin to hear them. The hollow screams of voices were older than time now—the plagued, the punished ones.

"Yeah," I growled, knowing he was near. We were getting closer. The atmosphere evolved again, and we were standing on a high blackened peak on what seemed like hardened molten lava. Though the stone path was narrow and the edges fell into what looked like eternity. In the distance, something was swirling round and round like a storm, a giant tornado waiting to funnel into destruction.

"The hurricane of souls," Ezmerelda whispered.

"How do you know so much about hell?" I asked, somewhat familiar with the cyclone of spirits we approached. Though how she knew of it was perplexing, the red vampiress had more secrets than she let on. Perhaps that was why she and Captain Vex were drawn to each other. Both so opposite, yet so the same. Did they see it as clearly as I did? I was sure the pirate captain did. Though Ezmerelda? I wasn't so sure. Maybe the vampiress and I were more alike than I'd considered. Perhaps that was why we had been sorted into the same level together. Though knowing her father was a railroad billionaire added another layer to the train, and I surmised she was likely more tormented by the situation than she'd let on.

"I know a lot of things," she said idly, looking around and past the hurricane of souls as if she were looking for something else. "He'll be here soon."

"Who?"

It wasn't the time for the red vampiress's coy games, but somehow, they didn't evade her, even as she stood on the very precipice of damned souls.

"That is the question, isn't it? Who will get here first?"

Sinking into the curve of the ship's side, I buried my head in my hands. I didn't want to stand and look over and see the swamp fading way, knowing I was leaving my pack of lunas behind like the coward I was. Like the coward Nephele said I was. She was right. Grandfather Jack would be so disappointed. Hot tears of failure stung at the corners of my eyes when a presence slumped next to me and nudged something cold at my elbow.

"Take a drink, boy. It'll ease your sorrows, or at least help you forget them. Not easy making it through The Swamp of No Need." Captain Vex gazed at me earnestly, thrusting the cool metal into my palm.

I accepted his offering and let the rum scour my throat with four big gulps. When I looked at him again, I was sure there was something strong in the alcohol because my first irrational thought was that Captain Vex was a handsome guy. He was weathered in the way any man of the sea might be, but with long, dark hair and an ornately decorated beard. He spoke like he was an old man, but he looked to be my age. Then again, I was hundreds of years old but still felt like a teenager sometimes.

"My pack is gone. They're dead because of me," I choked out, taking another drink to force the shake in my voice down.

Vex stroked his beard, and it jingled with keys and bells. His hand dipped to his neck, and he tugged on a familiar necklace. When he noticed my gaze, he smiled. "Got this from yer mouthy friend. Though his promise about a fire that never died was a load of horseshit, this wasn't."

A rough chuckle left my chest despite myself. "Onyx has a way of getting everything he wants."

"My kind of men, you Halloween Boys." The sea captain smiled and regarded his crew. They were hard at work hoisting sails as we sailed through… through what? Grabbing the board above to steady myself, I pulled up and looked out over nothing but black. As if we were sailing through space.

"Where are we? How did you even find me?"

"The necklace helped. Being a sorry sack of good-for-nothin helped, too. And oh, the jukebox scared off yer croc critters. Nasty things, but terrified of rock music, like most water folk are." He stood and wrapped an arm around my back. "Yer wolf pack isn't gone, son. And don't believe any of their last words. The marsh bewitches all of its inhabitants. I can see you stewing on thoughts you shouldn't be thinkin'. Your lunas knew what they signed up for. And I wouldn't put it past any wolven of Fenrir not to come clawing their way back, even from the pits of hell."

"I hope you're right."

Someone whistled from a beam, and Vex furrowed his brow, pulling out a set of binoculars from his vest and squinting. He swore, seemingly breathless.

"What is it?" I asked, straining to see much of anything except pitch black darkness beyond the illuminated ship.

"She's even more beautiful than I imagined." The sea captain sighed and murmured to himself. Shaking his head, he remembered me. "Choose your next moves wisely, son."

Finally, something came into view. A swirling gray cloud and air permeated with the rotten smell of sulfur. And beneath the spinning cloud stood two people. Ghost, I smelled immediately, though, oddly, he smelled more like… James Cove. Damn, if that wasn't an aroma I hadn't experienced in ages. And the other, a spicy, aromatic, floral fragrance that belonged to the woman who left the pirate breathless. As the ship approached, she ducked behind Ames, and he stood, shielding her.

The boat docked in midair, and I climbed a rope ladder down to my friend's waiting embrace. We held each other for a long moment, and I asked, "You all right?"

He cut a short nod. "You?"

"No, fuck no. Is Onyx with you?"

A small female voice whispered behind Ames. "Am I normal yet?"

He looked over his shoulder. "Back to being fearsome."

And then I recognized her as she smiled back with long fangs and blood-red eyes and hair. "Perfect." Ezmerelda stepped around us and took hold of the rope ladder, giving us a salute. Vex watched her, in awe, as she joined him on the boat, and I swore his shade of ruddy wasn't sunburn when she kissed him on the cheek.

"We've only got a small window of return here, boys, and I'm guessin' you haven't gotten what you came for," he called down.

"We'll see you again soon, Captain. Thank you for your help," Ghost called up.

"Anytime, son." He smiled as the sails dropped and caught a gust of wind from the spinning cloud overhead. And then they were gone, nothing but an extension of the darkness surrounding us.

Ghost and I stood alone while screams echoed around us.

"Do I even want to know what that is?" I pointed to the oily storm mass that looked like elongated faces swirling through a spin cycle in the black sky. But my palms were almost fully healed now, at least, thanks to werewolf genetics.

Before he could answer, a gust of wind hit our backs, and my blood pressure spiked, ready for battle. But though the sight was formidable, it was not one to be feared.

An enormous dragon hovered and landed with a thump, and its two riders exited its back. I recognized the slayer as his chair materialized and greeted him on the ground. And my gaze quickly scanned Onyx, seeing he was bloodied but in one piece. Sauntering over as if he were anywhere but hell, the vampire hybrid put an arm around both Ghost and me.

"You look like hell," I said.

He chuckled. "I always dress for the occasion." Turning, he addressed Elysium and the dragon. "What now? Wait for the big guy, or do we summon him?"

The slayer's chair sputtered something like a laugh. "No one calls forth the devil, and no one walks right into his circle, either. You wait for the shadow realm to deem your quest worthy and get you near him or…"

"Or?" Ghost crossed his arms and tapped his foot impatiently.

My mother's dragon voice floated through our minds. "Or you wait for him to find you."

Onyx walked to his mother and patted her long pale-green wing. "You guys should go. I'll see you soon."

A clipped order that had me wondering what version of the underworld my friend had been through. Had Ghost's and Dragon's trials been as wretched as my own? And what sort of sick fuck was the devil, Judas, who we'd trusted for so many years, to put us through this? To steal Blythe and be putting her through fuck knows what. The thought made my blood boil and my alpha rage inside me, ready to sniff him out and tear him apart.

I watched as my friend hugged Elysium goodbye and tried not to eavesdrop on their parting words as the slayer took his place upon the dragon queen again, and they took flight. Onyx stared after them long after they became one with the black.

"Do you guys want to talk about what just happened?" I asked, reminded of how the lunas and I would always debrief after a hunt or battle. My heart felt as if it were in shreds knowing they were gone, sinking to some torturous demise with giant crocodiles and marsh waters.

The guys both grunted their nos. I'd get them to talk about it eventually, though I wished they'd tell me now. I continued, rubbing Onyx's back. "Dragons, I've heard, can traverse hell. Your mom will make it out, and we might, too." I put a gentle hand on his back. "Don't worry."

He turned, his eyes glowing bright green as he assessed the screams swirling above us. The dried blood I smelled on his neck and knuckles was his, though I didn't see signs of harm. He had no cuts or wounds.

"I'm not worried," he said lowly. "I'm fucking pissed."

"Me too," Ghost agreed.

"Yeah," I growled, low in my throat.

"And I'm not fucking waiting anymore." Onyx took our hands, and we passed each other glances. "Our circles of hell spat us out here. Now we bring hell to him and we get our girl back."

And then we ran headfirst for the hurricane of souls.

CHAPTER 28

The Devil's in the Details

SO CAME THE END

Wolfgang pounded his fists into the demon, black blood spraying the already blood-drenched grass below.

James Cove screamed into the night, having slain another demon of his own. "More," he demanded, the archdemon hunger rising in his chest, though he didn't know it.

Onyx tossed a strangled demon aside. "Should we dump these in town square like they've done to the girls?"

"I want to meet who's sending them," Wolfgang growled. "There's a coward hiding behind these dark creatures."

"Yet none of you will consider that it's the new group of women in town. The Marcelene woman and her Samhain. Their Halloween celebration is the most suspicious of anything," James said, drying his hands with a rag.

Onyx marched past them. "I'm not about killing women. If we do, we're no better than this scum we just murdered. No, we stick to a code if this is something we do to protect the town."

"Speaking of which, tonight is All Hallows' Eve." Wolf wrapped his burly arms around the two men. "Let's see what's going on downtown. I heard people are dressing up and lighting pumpkins. A sign of hope in the night amidst all this tragedy."

"It would seem all of your precious Bible stories are true, James."

Onyx cast a half-blood drunken glance to the side. "Demons are here, plaguing our very town, dead at our feet. What other magic and mischief awaits us, I wonder?"

James tensed his jaw, not wanting to reveal anything about the stranger he had met in church or the deal he made with what he rightly supposed was me, the devil. And I'd upheld my end of the bargain. I'd helped them. The demons hadn't heard them coming, hadn't tasted human emotions. They were obtuse to their impending deaths. Deaths not possible by mortal hands, so I'd infused a little extra within them. Or rather, I'd only woken up what was already there.

You see, the Halloween Boys were extraordinary even before my intervention. Their potential was that of interest to me even before the mad vampire king Vladimir Drakon sent demons looking for his bride.

They sensed Onyx, of course. And Onyx may never know that his future bride's death was partially on his hands. Or maybe he did know, somewhere deep down, because he acted as if it were truly his fault. That shame would build and fester in him for hundreds of years. See, that was another interesting thing about taking men to immortal rank. While most flaws and virtues peaked and died within a lifetime of around eighty mankind years, these boys would have hundreds, thousands of years to develop both their gifts and curses.

What would shame do to Onyx Hart?

What would pride do to James Cove?

What would ignorance do to Wolfgang Jack?

I couldn't wait to see. I was sure we would enjoy watching them. We would follow them through time, aiding, cursing, doing whatever we liked.

Onyx took Wolfgang's hand and brought it to his mouth, running his tongue along his blackened bloody knuckles. "Demon blood doesn't taste so bad." He sighed, having no idea what was churning inside of him, only knowing that whatever it was turned him on.

"You're sick," Wolf replied lowly.

With a small growl, James grabbed Onyx's chin and pulled him to his chest. "Trying to make me jealous?"

"Is it working?" Onyx baited, looking at both of his friends like a meal. "Oh, it is, isn't it? I can almost feel your possessiveness."

"And I swear I can taste how fucking much you fucking want him," he snarled toward Wolfgang, who only crossed his thick arms and eyed them both.

Onyx stuck out his tongue, swiping James's lips lightly. "Perhaps I want each of you at once."

James looked to Wolf in silent and skeptical question, and the alpha shrugged his consent. Already they spoke in a language only the three of them understood. Fascinating.

James grabbed the back of Onyx's hair roughly and slammed his lips against his in a violent embrace. The carnage around them, the blood and gore, it aroused them each. I was staying firmly planted behind the tree line to watch. Oh, I did enjoy watching them in every event they took part in. Killing, fucking, all of it.

Then, with a rowdy push, James grabbed his friend and forced him to his knees. "Take my cock in front of your new suitor. Show him how good you swallow my cum down your throat."

"With pleasure." Onyx looked over his shoulder. "You just going to stand there, big guy?"

"How about you do what Mr. James Cove tells you to do," Wolfgang murmured, unzipping his pants. "And I'll do what I want with you."

Their exchange was brutal with need as James rammed his cock down Onyx's throat. Wolfgang moved behind the gagging man and forced them all to their knees after yanking down Onyx's pants.

Wolfgang stroked his generous cock before pushing it against his lover, meeting James's cold stare. "We could share. We could all have fun and keep doing this together," he said roughly. Already and always the broker of peace in their now forming crew.

And James couldn't help himself. Wolf was impossible not to like. The large man had an animalistic charm that was part his nature and part his golden soul shining through. The aspiring priest jerked a small nod before dropping his gaze to the werewolf's large cock as it eased into Onyx's backside.

The hybrid gargled on James and pushed against Wolf, wanting more, begging for more. The scene was horrifically erotic as they thrust and groaned together, knees muddied with demon blood. Dead bodies of monsters lying flayed around them, too poisonous and decrepit for even the flies to circle. No, they were alone, or so they thought. They didn't know I watched them like this, shadowed them like this. I could have been content to lurk in firelight forever and meddle in their affairs once in a while.

Even I couldn't have predicted the strange and fatal turn of events that would intertwine our paths for the rest of eternity. They were supposed to be a game, a show to watch, pets at the most. But what they'd become... If I had only known then...

Wolfgang's thrusts were long and hard, ending in an explosion of cum dripping down the backs of Onyx's legs as he reached around and pumped the vampire's release into his palm. All the while, James came down his friend's throat, looking to the twilight October sky with a grunt. As they dressed, collecting themselves, Onyx furrowed his brow as he assessed the man he'd just gone down on.

"What?" James asked in an irritated tone. "We're going to your little Halloween party."

"It's not that," Onyx said, sucking his finger before inspecting it. "You taste different."

A flash of worry, almost imperceptible to the human eye, steered James's expression. But he recovered as he zipped his trousers and re-shouldered his suspenders. "I don't know what you're talking about. Let's go. Leave the bodies here. I don't feel like hauling them to town tonight."

Ash Grove was a town in mourning but also one of a false sense of triumph. The disappearance of the girls was a tragic hit to the small and odd town, though the brutal killings of the monsters responsible carried out by unknown saviors gave them a sense of hope and justice. And with the newly resident witch coven's insistence, the town square was adorned in autumn decor and celebration.

Children bobbed for apples and women and men dressed in their finest attires. The shops were lit with flickering pumpkins and straw and all the lanterns burned auburn while men picked banjos in the street.

"*Well, this is different. I kind of like it,*" *Wolfgang surmised, sniffing out a vendor selling meats on a stick.*

Onyx's face dropped as he spotted a few of Minnie's old friends. "It's all right," he said, concealing his guilt.

"I don't like it," James growled.

A photographer with a thick handlebar mustache urged them together, holding his equipment with a flash of light, taking their picture. I quite liked that idea. In fact, perhaps I would start taking photographs of my own someday.

And like the uncanny shadow of a woman she was, Marcelene coiled out from her shop doors. "Hello, boys. I'm Marcelene, and this is my new shop. I believe I'll name it Magia Eclectics."

James raised an eyebrow. "So you're the newcomer and the reason for this Halloween occasion?"

"Don't look so thrilled." She giggled, her dark curls bouncing. "Besides, this town could use a little magic, don't you think?"

"I think we're doing just fine on our own," he countered.

"Dead and stolen girls and demons and ghouls in the woods would say otherwise, James," she answered ominously, and I smirked at the simmering rage I felt from James as I watched on. I was just another man in a suit, leaning against a shop door. The devil always wears a disguise, but you know that, don't you?

"You speak abnormally for a simple woman," James snarled, stepping forward. Wolfgang and Onyx intervened, putting hands on his shoulders.

Marcelene crossed her arms and narrowed her brown eyes. "And you speak with a tongue of the devil. I'll have no business with any of you." She flicked judgmental stares over the men. "But please stop by the caldron outside my shop for some pumpkin-spiced brew."

Now, I rarely intervened in the affairs of mortals. But these folks were different, and this place was different. There was a very dear reason why Ash Grove meant so much to me. And I found myself in that moment choosing sides. And the side I found myself favoring was not, in fact, the witch. Witches were no bother to me, typically. Their magic less grand than they boasted. Moonwaters and bundles of plants were no business of mine. But this woman had a little something superfluous, didn't she? A little touch of darkness she denied and a bit of ill-intent so heavily guarded. Interesting. This place was so fascinating, and fuck if next to nothing intrigued me anymore.

The festivities continued, and I enjoyed watching the town lit up in such a way. Though I knew it would be short-lived as something rumbled in the distance, something strange and abysmal. My curiosity turned to the young men, wondering which would notice first, taking silent bets in my mind. Hell, I even grabbed a popcorn from a vendor's stand. Rarely did remarkable things happen in my world, believe it or not. After eons, everything becomes dull, even worlds of magic. But the unpredictability of these men, this town, and the magic converging upon it was downright thrilling. And I'd meddled just enough to bring about a grand dénouement, did I not?

They stood at the outskirts, and it was James who noted them first, though Wolf's smell and Onyx's senses tuned in a moment later. Standing solid as stone and as eerie as their namesake, the ghouls formed a perimeter around the town. They'd been let in, lured by demon blood and screams. Ghouls were hunting dogs, rabid beasts either searching for their next kill or doing some master's bidding. And I had not yet enlisted any to my doing in eternities of time. But these were curious and wanted a taste of the town that drew in so many fiends.

The first one struck, stabbing a man playing a banjo with his long yellow claws, right through the gut. A woman screamed and ran, tripping over her skirts as another ghoul pounced on her. It was an attack of epic proportions, especially when the legion of demons joined in, seeing an easy way to seek retaliation on their fallen shadow friends. Onyx, Wolf, and James fought. Oh, they fought valiantly, but it wasn't quite enough, as the whole town fell into slaughter.

You're angry that I didn't intervene? Did you forget I am the devil? Massacres happened the same as wildfires destroying forests. It was the way of things, and it was a part of my duty to ensure that balance. Someone must. And as the screams persisted, the woman in purple ran into the center of town, holding the hands of her fellow witches, and they began to chant. "I knew she would be a problem," I murmured to myself, watching as James Cove beat a demon to death with his bare hands. Oh, I yearned to see what he could do as more than a man.

And then, suddenly, the sky flashed purple. Marcelene screamed and fell to the ground, and when I looked back to see fire igniting from Onyx's hands, the purple light encompassed him and his friends, and they fell to the ground, flame dispersing around them as it caught on the dried grass and snaked up a tree.

I walked closer, snarls from ghouls and shrieks from demons still chasing townspeople to every side of me. And when I looked down to survey the lifeless forms of James, Onyx, and Wolfgang, I sighed.

They were dead.

CHAPTER 29

Blythe

QUEEN OF HELL—ALMOST

> The gates of hell are open night and day.
> Smooth the descent, and easy is the way.
> But to return, and view the cheerful skies,
> In this the task and mighty labor lies.
> *Virgil*

Slimy, stringy orange gourd strings dangled in front of my nose. "Ew, stop." I shoved Zyre, and he bounced away, snickering as he gutted an enormously round pumpkin.

The devil smirked, digging into his gourd as I twirled my pumpkin around, looking for the smoothest surface to carve. "Not taking off your gloves even for pumpkin carving?" I asked. "This was your idea."

"I thought it would cheer you up," he grumbled, dropping seeds to the table.

"Watching you get messy is kind of cheering me up," I conceded, though my heart was still broken. I'd saved the guys, but at the expense of me being without them. Would they move on and forget all about me? Would they find a new girl…? The thought had me wanting to throw my pumpkin at the maniac clown twirling around downtown Hell Grove. The devil had set up a pumpkin carving station right in the middle of town. The orange, red, and yellow leaves were falling gently around us. God, it was beautiful here in this hell version of Ash Grove. But its beauty didn't take away from my deep ache for my boys. Ash Grove, even in all its autumn beauty, wasn't the same without them. Even if I made my home here in hell, how would I ever be the same without them?

"You're adrift in your thoughts, my dear," the devil said lowly, sliding his pumpkin next to mine and passing me a red-handled knife.

"Lost in hell," I muttered, narrowing a look at Zyre as he put a candle in his jack-o'-lantern. "You're an asshole for this bargain."

He slid the knife swiftly through the orange flesh of the pumpkin, making a triangle. "Some call me the devil, Judas, Hades, the evil one. But yes, I prefer asshole. Or sir. You ate the blackberries in my home. You eat, you stay. Never heard the stories before now?"

"Those tales usually involve a pomegranate."

"Even authors get it wrong sometimes. Perhaps that's intentional, perhaps a coincidence."

Rolling my eyes, I took the knife from his leather-gloved hand and started on my design, resisting the urge to jam it into his ribs.

Then he surprised me with his next question. "Do you recall much of your childhood?"

"No, I don't. But that's common of people with trauma. They block out memories."

"Did the good ole Dr. Cove tell you that?"

"You're really something else today," I muttered, piercing the pumpkin and imagining it was Judas.

He hummed to himself, rubbing his jaw as I avoided his intense stare. "Did you feel a pull to Ash Grove? Did the town let you in, an invisible town shielded from the world, full of monsters and the dead. Did you love it and feel like it was home the moment you arrived? Did its monsters flock to you, become enamored with you?"

Irritation and something else, that emotion I'd been pushing down, threatened to erupt as I gritted out, "You're going to say that the only reason they love me is because I'm death—"

"No," he interrupted earnestly, making my lower belly warm. "Because you're you. Because you are them, and they are you, and hell is your kingdom, and Ash Grove is hell shimmering on the earth side of the veil."

I met his garnet gaze then, and the magnetic pull between us became near undeniable. What was it about him, his words, this world? And what the heck did he mean by what he'd just said? Before I could respond and just as his eyes dropped to my lips, a cold presence appeared behind me, and the devil's attention went frosty along with it.

"My Lord, forgive me, but it is urgent." I turned to see the shadow demon. The one who'd been bringing my breakfasts and drawing my baths. It was difficult to make out his features, but from what I could surmise, he looked worried. What could have a demon from hell, servant of the devil, so concerned, afraid even?

"Watch her," Devil commanded Zyre, who nodded from his circle of pumpkins. "I'll be right back." The devil stood, but he stopped next to me, and after a moment of hesitation, he leaned down and kissed the top of my head before disappearing into a soft gray mist. My stupid heart shouldn't have leapt into my throat, but it did. Something was sparking, something was coming together in all his riddles, in the entire riddle that was Ash Grove, Belladonia, and Fenrir... It was so close, just on the tip of my tongue but somehow alluding me all the same. Why couldn't I figure this out? It was as if some heavy film lay over my perception and I couldn't shake it off.

Suddenly, my horns felt heavy and the orange-tinted autumn light dusted dark purple around me. Something shimmered in front of my vision, and the shape of a woman materialized. I looked to Zyre, who sat still carving another pumpkin and not paying me any attention, when a voice I recognized called out.

"Blythe?" Marcelene whispered.

"Yes," I whispered. "How are you here?"

"I'm not. I'm only somehow peering through the veil, and it so happens you're in the town square. Blythe, you must come home. You cannot stay with the devil—"

"What do you mean?" I asked, looking back to the spot where Zyre had previously sat. *Where did he go?* "Are the boys okay?" I couldn't help but ask.

Her brown eyes widened. "You have no idea, do you? Dear girl, I've only just sorted it out myself."

"No idea about what?"

But it was too late. Thunder crashed, and Marcelene screamed. The mauve light collided with red as if a rope reached through the veil and pulled her through until she was lying on the grass. She stood, brushing her dress, and hissed. "We meet again, devil."

"You have gone and angered me for the last time, Marcelene," Judas boomed behind me. I tried to run forward, to protect her, to hold her, but my feet steeled into place at his side while his wings fanned over my shoulders.

"What a wretched sight you two are to behold." Marcelene trembled, glancing from my horns to the devil's wings. "Both of you a wicked curse."

Ropes like red snakes sprang from the ground, wrapping around her neck and arms. I tried to scream, but nothing left my throat. The devil rendered me immobile, and I could only watch in horror as the hell fire and ropes drained the life from the crone. Red light slowly muffled out any trace of purple hue, and she fell to the ground, chanting, until no sound or sight of her existed anymore. And when she disappeared, my binds were loosened.

Turning on my heel, I reared back and punched the devil across the jaw as hard as I could. Ignoring the sting of my hand, I yelled, "Why would you kill her? Marcelene is my best friend's grand-mother; she was the first person who was kind to me when I came to Ash Grove."

"It was the witch's time… again. She has many debts to pay me." He took my arm roughly and pulled me to his front. "And you, my dear, are going to stay right here until I come for you."

Before I could argue or scream, the ground beneath me shifted from soft earth to cold concrete. I made to move, but my wrists were bound. Chained. The scream that left me was full of anger, terror, and hate as I realized where I was. Chained to the ground by the devil's power, in the middle of Ash Grove beyond the veil, at the brew pump.

CHAPTER 30

The Halloween Boys

THE MEAT LOCKER

Maybe when I took my friends' hands and plunged us into the screaming, haunting, fucking weird cyclone of souls, I'd had a few expectations.

One: that we might join the shriek fest for all of eternity.

Two: that we'd get spit out into the fiery flames of Mordor, where I assumed the devil sat like the evil eye of Sauron in some tower. I guessed that would make me and the guys hobbits in this scenario, and that was fucking wrong. Of course we would be elves or something equally cool in the Tolkien universe.

Anyway, what I didn't expect was walking down a dark corridor that slowly became slippery and cold until finally pushing open a heavy door into a huge room rife with fog and frost.

"What the fuck?" Wolfgang held his nose. "Where did you take us?"

"Not Mordor, I'm guessing." I strode forward, my step slipping on the frozen ground as swaying objects caught my attention.

Ames was already inspecting one as it hung by a large hook from the ceiling. He and Wolf spoke in unison. "Meat."

It took me a moment to gather what the fuck this was. "A meat locker?" I looked down the aisle, and it became clearer. Hundreds, maybe thousands, of raw, frozen carcasses hung from chains and hooks in the cold ice box. "Why are we here?" I asked, annoyed, thinking this was a nowhere and nothing place.

Until the answer came, and not from one of the companions I had traveled with. No, the voice that rumbled down the aisle of meat held the same cadence as a volcano erupting or a tsunami crashing ashore. "You are fools. Each of you."

It chilled my bones worse than the freezer could, and we all looked to each other before looking to him. This was for my wife, who'd been stolen, for my fiancée, who'd been slaughtered. This was for my boys, who'd lived through enough pain to be deceived by the devil himself. This was for Ash Grove. And this was for... my father. Who, at the end, gave up everything—his power, the love of my mother, who he'd done every wicked and vile thing in a thousand lifetimes to bring back. My father, who knew why he was accompanying me to hell and led me through a carnival of terrors to accept his fate of death by the hand of a hundred Onyx Harts he'd forsaken. To give me a moment with the girl he'd taken, to give me a chance at a life with the girl I loved and sought. He knew his greatest gift and show of love would be that of his life ending and his soul forever tormented in the chambers of hell. He chose that. In the end, Vladimir Drakon had chosen me.

And now the devil had taken my father, my fiancée, and my wife. The icy walls of this meat cooler were no barrier to the dragon fire pulsing through my veins. Fire gifted by my mother, and a cunning and ruthless mind given by my father. The lord of darkness and deception would pay, and justice would be served at the hands of the Halloween Boys.

This was it. The reason we had come.

The devil was here.

And hell rose to meet him.

BLYTHE'S FACE on my porch steps when she saw the dead foxes played through my mind. She was trying to be brave, but my wish for Blythe was that she'd never have to be brave again. That there would be no more horrors in her life to stand up against or find her voice in. I wished for no more gloomy forests to traverse like she had when she selflessly rescued Fenrir. Blythe was my luna.

Next, I thought of the face of another luna. Nephele didn't deserve a death by swamp monster in the dredges of torturous eternity. She was right in everything she said to me, whether she was bewitched by the waters or not. I was a disappointment. I had botched this entire mission, and my grandfather would be ashamed that I'd left her and the other lunas there like a coward. I chose selfishness for Blythe, and I would choose it again. There wasn't a number of crocodiles in this realm that I wouldn't slay for her, my hands bloody and my lungs screaming for her. My mate.

And now I'd fight the biggest foe of all. Worse still was that I had thought he was our friend this entire time. Had that been a hoax, too? Perhaps my foolishness had gotten us into this mess and now these were the consequences of a stupid, desperate plea I had made so very long ago. He'd come to collect his due.

The devil stood with his thick arms crossed and his red leather cape behind him. He was huge, bigger than me, and the most formidable of opponents. The guys and I had slain many foes, but nothing like him. As the chill air cleared, I noticed the glint of a red mask with horns. And for some reason, the fact that he wore a mask pissed me off even more.

I broke the silence, knowing that Ghost would wage war, Onyx would hurl insults, and the devil would, as usual, remain quiet. "You know why we're here." Still, he only stood. "You know what we want," I continued. The lunas, elders, and my grandfather had always taught me to first seek peace. Perhaps there was a chance, even now. And looking at my friends, I couldn't bear the thought of losing either of them to this battle. I also couldn't comprehend a reality where a fight like this worked in our favor. Had we simply fought through death to meet our end in a meat locker?

The blaze of warmth from Onyx's knuckles brushed against my forearm, a stark contrast to the freeze we were submersed in. Ghost's breathing was unsteady, revving up as if he were only moments from charging toward the ancient evil regarding us next to two hanging racks of carcasses. Regret weighed on my shoulders for so many things, and I couldn't help but feel this was all my fault. And it was up to me to make it right somehow.

"I would trade my life for hers," I spoke out, feeling the whip of Ghost and Onyx's gazes. But I only stared forward at the glinting dark red mask of an old evil. "My servitude, my alpha, whatever you want. Just let her go."

The devil's voice spoke lowly. "What use is a dog at my feet?"

And in a flash, a ball of fire launched at his head. It slammed against an invisible barrier and writhed and sizzled as it seemed to destroy the fortress meant to stop it. I passed Onyx a sideways glance. He only stepped out ahead of me with palms lit with dragon flame. "Put down your walls, coward. You've put us through hell. Now it's your turn. Or are you too old, too high and mighty, to fight?"

"He's afraid," Ghost rumbled from above me, already shifted into his archdemon form. The heat mixed with the cold of the locker and the blue hell smoke surrounding us. "Why go through all this trouble to keep us out? To lie to us for centuries?"

The devil took a step forward, the meat carcasses swaying on their hooks. "Allowing you this far was a courtesy in more ways than one. This will be your one offer, your one grace. Turn back now, leave Blythe to me, and we will never cross paths again."

The guys and I growled in unison, and I didn't have to pull my eyes away from the evil before me to know our answer to that.

Fuck no.

Our answer would always be her.

Death or nothing.

THE ARCHDEMON UNLEASHED every bit of rage I'd constantly been holding in. Like a rabid beast confined by an ill-fitting cage, I broke through the bars in a bellow of fury. My vision was deep blues of hell smoke as I sent my tendrils uncoiling toward my enemy. Explosions of dragon fire pierced his craven walls and sent them furling in ash like curls of blackened paper.

The alpha wolf transformed, not needing a moon. Perhaps Blythe was his moon. His love for her shining its lunar light upon his beast and calling him forth in her time of need. A werewolf, a slave to her light as much as the vampire hybrid and I were.

Wolfgang could rip through veils as an alpha, the elders had said, and that he did. Tearing through the devil's enchantments meant to keep us out and away from our claimed. They worked with precision, as if we'd discussed and practiced this very scenario. We hadn't. But after two hundred years, we often didn't need words. They knew acutely all of our strengths and weaknesses. We'd silently and collectively weighed the risks, and they knew as well as I that providing me first access was our strongest bet in this wicked game of cards. And the devil's poker face was sealed to his face in what I now saw was a leathered red mask. Taking his stance, he waved me forward like the arrogant prick he was. Like this was a scrimmage in Onyx's barn, as if this were another monster fight club under an October sky. I was about to show him how wrong he was.

"Wait!" Onyx called, and I only slightly paused as I stepped through the opening they held for me. He reached into his pocket, his other hand still blazing with spitting embers, and clicked something. "The acoustics in here are superb."

My eye roll should have joined the hurricane of souls because it could have gone on endlessly as AC/DC's "Thunderstruck" began playing through my musical idiot of a friend's rattly cassette player. Of course he had brought it to hell with him. That thing was like a cockroach and would survive the apocalypse.

But all right, I would never admit it, but it did give me a little push of nerve as I stalked up to the devil as he leveled me with a glower. "Show me what you've got, James," he spat.

And at the sound of my name, the old name carved onto my gravestone in Ash Grove, I went fucking berserk. The name and clothing he made me wear in an old train to nowhere. Blue hell smoke collided with him at the same moment I swung. My fist made contact with something firm and cold, but my celebration was short-lived as I pulled back with nothing but frozen meat juice on my protruding demon bones. "Running now, motherfucker?" I searched the meat locker, noticing how the red of his wardrobe and mask blended in with the hanging cow ribs. "Big bad devil so scared—"

Something grabbed my neck and flung me backward before darkness hovered above me.

"He has fucking wings?" Wolfgang shouted somewhere in the distance as the devil's strike cut across my chest. It burned and stung, leaching energy from my body. Hell ropes, the fucker wasn't going to play fair, was he?

The red mask regarded me impassively as he made for another blow. I rolled away just as something as solid as rock pounced him from the side and sent the two of them rolling into carcasses as they swung violently on their chains. It was Wolfgang, and he howled a feral and deranged sound as his claws dug into the devil's shoulders. The maw of the alpha snarled, seeking his opponent's throat. Goddamn, Wolfgang was a fucking beast.

The devil grabbed Wolf's snout with two leather-gloved hands, snapping it closed and pinning him down and punching him in the stomach. Wolf yelped, and I knew that punch carried more than strength as it glowed red on both the fist that carried it and the mark it burned into the alpha's middle. As I charged for the devil, Onyx beat me to it. He pulled him off Wolf by his cape with fiery hands. The cape burned, singeing through any power the devil had. Whatever it was, it was no match for Dragon flames. Damn, Onyx somehow was the perfect opponent against hell's dark magic.

"Oh, if it's not the king of nothing," the devil straightened, crossing his arms as he baited my friend, enormous in stature and power. "How are Mom and Dad?"

My companion's eyes blazed green as he flashed his fangs. Fire then surrounded him from head to toe in a manner I'd never witnessed before. He looked like hell itself, jagged and deadly. Every bit the cold vampire and the surging dragon. "About to be really fucking proud," he said lowly before making his attack.

Onyx moved with every ounce of his vampiric speed, evading the devil's reach and instead prowling behind him and sinking his teeth into his thick neck. Fire danced on Onyx's fangs and as I helped Wolf up, we both passed each other a raised eyebrow look of *oh, shit*. The pride I felt fighting alongside my boys like this... I couldn't describe it. And it seemed we were fucking winning, too.

While the devil was between Onyx's teeth, Wolf and I joined. While I wrapped him in blue smoke, Wolfgang pounded him with fists and claws, neither of us giving a fuck that the mix of Onyx's fire and the devil's red light hurt like shit.

And just as we were moments from victory, the room went pitch black, and the only sound we heard was the rattling of chains. When light appeared again, all the meat carcasses hanging on hooks transformed. Grotesque and hateful, they took the mirror image shape of our opponent, cape and red leather mask and all.

We were surrounded by hundreds of the devil then.

"Weak," Onyx said into the locker. "But we got this, right, boys?"

I met the gaze of not just my boys, then, but two lords. The Wolf King and the Vampire King, and I smiled. "Yeah, we got this."

And so we fought.

Through bloodied punches, red screams of pain, lashes of hell's ropes scarring my skin and blood dripping down our bodies, we fought. It could have been for hours, or for ages, but we'd do this forever. We'd make our own fucking cyclone of souls, and we'd fight the devil in all his incarnations forever.

"We can do this for all of eternity!" I cried out as I held a devil by the throat. "And you fucking know that. Give us back our claimed, or we will tear hell apart for her." With him in my grasp, I tore off his mask and dropped it to the cold ground.

I snarled at what greeted me. It wasn't the face of Judas, but only swirling shadow. "We're fighting fucking puppets. Shadow demons," I yelled to the guys in various stages of battles.

"What do we do?" Wolf called, ripping his maw into a shadow demon's side.

Onyx answered. "Kill them all to unlock the final boss, I assume." Eighties rock still trilled from his pocket.

"This isn't a fucking video game, dumbass," Wolf said with mirth in his alpha tone. "But that does sound like the only reasonable plan."

I gritted through shoving off three devils as they relentlessly attacked. "Except we're still outnumbered, and Onyx's fire is running on fumes."

We gathered in the middle of the aisle, surrounded by chains and hooks and dead shadow demons lifeless beneath their fallen red capes. The air chilled as we stood back-to-back, ready for another onslaught, perhaps the final one, as our greatest defense, dragon fire, waned. "Whatever happens," I said to my friends, my family, "I love you guys. And it's been a pleasure fighting with you all these years."

"Don't go sappy on me, Cove," Wolfgang hissed. "We aren't done for yet."

Always the optimist, even at the end. I had no doubts the devil would keep us here while he sent more and more shadow demons cosplaying in his form and imbued with his powers until we were dead and trapped. Pieces of hanging bones in his ice locker.

They began to launch themselves, slipping on the ground below, and we braced for the hit of a hundred or more—when the room echoed in screams.

One by one, the devils were covered in black shadow before dropping to the ground. Onyx, out of breath, dimmed the fire on his palms as we all leaned against each other, bloodied, tired, and wounded, watching the sight around us. The screaming continued as darkness swirled around each devil, dropping them, rendering them immobile. Until finally, one appeared in front of me, and I recognized the slender-framed damned as he cocked his head.

"For the train sermon," he wheezed.

I swallowed, cutting him a nod. "You're all released. Go, move on."

The damned stood a moment longer, and hundreds more joined him before he nodded slowly and vanished like vapor on a soft wind. They were free from my graveyard of agony and torment. All those men we'd slaughtered. All those souls I'd made it my mission to torture. Letting them die… I wouldn't call it forgiveness like my sermon said, but maybe it was something more like mercy. Maybe it was more like dying to myself and my desires. Neither were virtues I expected to gain from hell, of all places, but they affected me all the same. Maybe hell was the only school from where I could learn. The only place more wicked than me.

Then, like cogs in a clock, the room began to shift again. Our backs pressed closer together and we held on to each other tight, waiting for what would be revealed next. Suddenly, we found ourselves seated on the front row. I knew the dip of the uncomfortable hard wooden bench, the musty smell, and the mix of colored lights filtering in against stone walls.

We sat in the front row of Lamb's Blood Church.

And on the priest's throne sat the devil.

With Blythe on his lap.

CHAPTER 31

Blythe

BETWEEN THE DEVIL AND THE DEEP BLUE SEA

> The shepherds opened the door and told them to look in. They looked in and it was very dark and smoky. From within the darkness they also thought they heard the rumbling sound of fire accompanied by tormented cries. And the smell of brimstone wafted from the door. Christian turned to the shepherds and asked, 'What does this mean?' The shepherds told them, 'This is a byway to hell, where hypocrites enter in.'
>
> *John Bunyan, Pilgrim's Progress*

One moment, we were carving pumpkins on the steps of Lamb's Blood Church with the whole town—or was it just us in the town square? Or were we eating dinner and watching the sunset? I remembered him so clearly, looking over and giving me a rare, broad, sparkling white smile. *Isn't it beautiful?* I asked.

Yes, you are, he answered.

Wait, no, that wasn't right. Did that happen, even? And now his hand wrapped around my ribs. God, he felt so good. I ran my palms over his thick forearms and down to where his leather gloves clutched my middle as I sat on his lap. "Do you like my touch, Mortala?" he whispered seductively in my ear.

I nodded, urging his hand down. He smiled against my cheek. "Say it. Say it loud for me."

"Please touch me," I begged, my voice desperate with need. He didn't feel like a new lover, but a longtime partner as he spread my legs, locking my knees overtop his.

He eased my black silk nightgown up over my curves, and I felt the cool air of… where were we? It didn't matter. My grip found his arm again, and I forced him between my thighs. "Oh, look how eager she is for me. You all have not been taking care of her. Look how insatiable she is," the devil purred.

I giggled. He was talking nonsense. Who was even speaking to? My head was fuzzy, and I didn't know the day or time or where exactly we were, but I didn't care. Then his gloved touch swiped against my center, making my wetness echo throughout the space. "How's that feel, Mortala?" he urged.

"So good," I answered. "Please don't stop."

Something rumbled in the distance, and I tried to clear my head and sit up. "Shh. Just a little… church mouse," the devil said darkly. "Keep focusing on my fingers. Do you like when I thrust them inside you like this?"

And with a quick movement, three of his long and thick fingers pushed into me, coaxing a moan from my throat. Chairs, or something, were falling over. Mice could knock over furniture? It didn't matter. The only thing I could feel was his touch.

My climax built and built as he hooked within me, bringing forth a swift orgasm. I groaned my release, pressing my head into his shoulder and grabbing on to him for balance. His lap felt so good as I was grinding backward against him, feeling the length of his hard cock pressing into my back. And suddenly, the black lace over my mind lifted slightly. And so many things hit me all at once.

Being held in Judas's arms as we glided over hell's Ash Grove, laughing as we picked blackberries barefoot in the summer, rolling dice and playing cards... and the guys. My boys. My head was pounding as his garnet gaze found mine. "My love, would you like to leave, or do you want to stay?"

"What?" I asked, confused. Of course I wanted my Judas.

And then the black lace lifted a little more, and I remembered. Hell, Marcelene, our bargain, my Halloween Boys... I jerked back, falling out of his lap. "Let me go!" I screamed.

The flash of sorrow across his gaze, marring his impossibly handsome features, sank into my heart, and I wanted to take it back immediately. The absence of him hitting me like a boulder in the gut. But it was too late. "As you wish," he said lowly. "You will never see me again. Goodbye, Mortala. My reaper, my death."

I reached for him, but three other sets of hands found me, and I was wrapped up in them.

We've got you, little ghost.

Hold on to me, belladonna.

We're almost home, my luna.

And somehow agony, joy, regret, and elation coexisted and fought within my chest. Warring with each other, mixing into tears streaking down my cheeks, as the next thing I remembered was the fragrant smell of fall leaves, cinnamon, and crisp earthly autumn air.

Ash Grove.

I was home.

And I'd somehow left behind home, all at the same time.

HAVING them back in my arms, in the floor bed of Wolf's tiny cabin loft, and being back in my beloved real-life Ash Grove felt like a dream, a miracle, a gift... all wrapped up in some sort of Halloween curse I still hadn't unraveled. I'd spent much of my time sleeping, while each of my boys filtered in and out to lie with me and check on me, or to force Ames to let go of my hand and give me space.

There was so much to sort through in my mind, having been to hell and back and somehow still not feeling whole. How could that be? Their perfect faces hovered above me as I stretched my sore muscles.

"How did my body die but I still get sore?" I complained, trying to bring some levity to their worried expressions.

Onyx nudged his knuckles against my chin. "Yes, still have to treat your temporal form nice, even as an immortal, belladonna."

Wolfgang gathered my empty water cups and oatmeal bowls from breakfast that had gathered around my perch. "I know three guys who'd be happy to treat your body nice when you're feeling ready."

I giggled and took Ames's hand. "I've missed you all so much. When I went to hell and made that stupid bargain, I never thought—"

"Shh," Ames intercepted. "We have a lifetime to process the events of hell. Right now, what you need is rest."

My chest tightened as the late afternoon light filtered in alongside a chilly breeze through the open windows. Feeling them close was a luxury I'd never take for granted ever again. "You broke into hell and fought the devil for me, didn't you?" I'd gathered as much but hadn't asked outright. None of them seemed too keen to even speak of what happened, but I could only imagine the horrors they'd had to endure to retrieve me.

But their eyes were tender as they regarded me with more love than any woman, human or not, dead or alive, had ever received. God, how had I gotten so lucky?

"We'd do it again in a heartbeat," Ames whispered.

Wolfgang kissed my temple. "No more blackberry patches for you, though."

I swung a pillow weakly at the werewolf. "I was trying to save you idiots."

"We conquered the underworld. What do we need saving from?" Ghost raised a cocky eyebrow.

They were doing that thing they did again. Deflecting, making light of our plight, not allowing me to devolve too deeply into their true thoughts. Maybe they were trying to protect me and allow me to recover, or maybe their experiences without me were really so dark that they weren't ready to discuss them. Either way, the guys chuckled, and I bit my lip through my smile. Wolfgang and Ames left to speak with the lunas and elders of Fenrir, and Onyx lay on his elbow next to me, twirling a lock of my hair. He smiled, showing his fangs, and I couldn't help but fall in love with him all over again. "What are you smiling about?"

"Remembering you with horns."

He didn't mean it, but it felt as if a cold rag had smacked me across the face, bringing me back to earth as heavy emotions poured into me, pulling me outside of Wolf's little sanctuary and back into my own darkness. And the easy truth that I didn't even need to search for was that I missed my adornments. I missed my horns. "You saw those?"

"We did."

"When?"

His smile faded then, and he focused on my hair as he felt it between his thumb and forefinger. "Guess what?"

When I didn't answer, he tugged at my hair. Then he took my arm and gently put it between his lips. That definitely got my attention, and he smirked, giving me a soft lick instead of the bite I craved. "What?" I answered, giving him a playful shove.

He looked around, making sure no one else was in earshot. "I'm busting you out of here tonight."

I raised a skeptical eyebrow. "Oh? Where are you taking me?"

He snapped his teeth playfully in my direction, pushing me over a stack of pillows and tickling me lovingly. "It's October. Where else?"

WOLF CHASED after Onyx after their usual taunting, and I shook my head, grinning, as I followed the path of jack-o'-lanterns after them. Blue smoke swirled around my feet and then my wrist like a bracelet and my ring finger like a ring. "Beautiful." I smiled as Ames appeared beside me. His face was that of the man I hadn't seen in a year. An entire year had passed, and my skeleton man was back in all his sexy darkness.

Though something about the scene had me feeling major deja vu. Had I done this before, or had I dreamt it? My head was still fuzzy. I crinkled my forehead, and despite the white sheet over my head, Ghost tasted my confusion and laced his hand with mine. "Your mind will recover, I promise."

"The things I felt and did in hell… it all felt so real…"

"Magic of the likes of the devil is the most powerful and potent in all the realms. It's driven mad every being who's been touched by it throughout time. Don't be so hard on yourself. The fact that you're still standing, the fact that you have your mind intact, is remarkable. You are amazing, Blythe."

I squeezed his hand tight and looked over and up at his crystal blue eyes surrounded by black paint. "My skeleton man."

He tugged at my sheet. "My little ghost."

"Though she didn't have to take the pet name so literally, did she?" Onyx nagged as we caught up with him.

Wolfgang punched him in the arm. "Don't poke fun at her. She's delicate right now."

"I'm lazy right now, and this was the only costume I could come up with on such short notice." I glared at Onyx. "By the way, great job sneaking me out."

He shrugged. "You'd think Ghost put another tracker on you."

"Another?" I raised an eyebrow at my broody skeleton companion as Wolfgang laughed heartily. Something else they weren't telling me, obviously.

Ames punched Onyx in the side and he yowled through a laugh as my skeleton man put his arm around my shoulder. "You'll always be my little blue dot."

"Whatever that means," I smiled and flicked Onyx a playful stare.

Onyx kicked up flurries of dried leaves in the wind and turned. "They caught us sneaking out this time, but we've still got a week until Halloween. There's lots of spooky shit the two of us could get into between now and then."

Only a week until Halloween. I'd spent so much of October in hell… and yet somehow it still felt like home. Maybe the Ash Grove of hell was meant to make me feel this way. Maybe this was all a part of the trick. But I couldn't help but remember the Halloween festival of hell, the one that looked an awful lot like Hallows Fest, when we stepped out of the trees and into the celebration. Looking around, I realized who I was looking for and was afraid to even ask about the witch coven leader, so instead, I asked about others who weighed on my thoughts.

"Raven and Cat? Are they okay?"

Wolfgang wrapped his burly arm around me. "They're great, and I'm sure they'll find you soon."

My relief was palpable as we strolled the stands of shifters, inhaling the smell of clove and nutmeg, and passed by a coven of vampires who, for some reason, bowed to Onyx as they passed. "What's that about?" I asked.

"I paid them twenty dollars to do that in front of you. You know, so I'd look cool," he said, buying a caramel apple and passing it to me.

"How's she going to eat that with a sheet over her head?" Ames asked, amused, as I took it under my sheet with me to nibble.

"I'll always find a way for treats." I brushed against him, taking a chewy, bittersweet bite as we walked. And then another question I didn't want to ask came to me as we neared the willow tree. My heart constricted at the memory of how I'd left it burnt in hell… but here, it still stood, as eerie and looming as ever. "The witches… are they all okay?" I was such a wimp. I couldn't even make myself say their names. Marcelene and Yesenia. Maybe Marcelene had been a trick. Maybe the devil hadn't taken her.

And right on cue, when they didn't want to answer something,

Onyx popped in front of me, green dragon mask elegantly shimmering in the torchlight. "Wow, I've got a great idea." He took my hand and quickly led me through the crowd. I couldn't help but laugh at his bravado as a crowd of deer shifters grumbled as he shoved them aside, pulling me through Hallows Fest like a blanket on a clothesline in my stupid last-minute costume.

And even though I'd left hell, I still felt like I was there, and not in a bad way. I half expected Zyre to jump out, juggling something obnoxiously. Or… maybe part of my very perplexed heart hoped that someone else would pop out. Someone caped and quiet… What was wrong with me? Was Ames right and this was just the aftereffects of the devil's obscure and twisted magic, or was it something else?

I mean, it couldn't be anything else, right? People cheered for the Halloween Boys and parted as we all passed. The chaos, the orange and blacks, and all the immortals, from vampires to tall goat-beings walking on what looked like stilts to even a few rogue phantoms who hid from the guys' gaze, it was all so Hallows Fest, and it did fill my soul with a sense of belonging, just as it did last year when I first came.

Only last year, I had come alone. Hunted by one, stalked by another, or rather, stalked by a few others… and now one of those stalkers pulled me past the tents and stations and music, magic, and mayhem, to just up the hill and beyond the tree line, where only a couple of solitary pumpkins flickered their candles from their hollow crevices.

"What are you doing?" I asked. But I got my answer quickly, as Onyx pushed me against a thick oak tree, then tore off my sheet and tossed it aside. His lips met mine for a tender but frantic kiss under the moonlight. The feel of his body pressed against mine and every inch of exposed skin of my mini dress felt divine. And the leaves and sticks crunching around us let me know, despite the flurry of bats beating their wings behind my ribs, that we weren't alone.

Someone took my wrist and pushed Onyx's chest, taking his

place and pinning me against the tree. "My skeleton man. Still possessively stalking me, I see," I teased.

"Always," Ghost said darkly against my lips, his hands snaking up my front and cupping my breasts.

Wolfgang's rough hands pulled my shoulders, and he inched in behind me so I was leaning against him and not the tree. His touch skimmed down my sides and folded over my hips as I felt his hard length press against my back.

My skeleton man didn't miss a beat, kissing me as deeply as ever, kissing me like he had missed me, like I was his. I held on to his neck, and Wolf helped hold me up as my panties were swiftly removed and Ames's cock was lined up with my center. Wolf's rough hands and burly forearms lifted me as my legs wrapped around my mysterious skull-painted man. "That's it, little ghost. Enjoying the show, Onyx?" he asked over his shoulder.

"Very much," he purred, leaning against a tree and watching with a hungry expression as his finger trailed his lower lip.

"You want the skeleton man's cock?" Ames whispered in my ear. "Do you want to be fucked at Hallows Fest?"

I nodded, out of breath at the sensations around me. The air smelled like clove and coffee. The night was cold, and leaves crunched under us with every movement as music and laughter played just beyond the trees. Anyone could wander into the woods and find us. But I didn't care. "Yes," I breathed. "Please."

"Maybe we should take her on stage and fuck her there, too." Wolfgang growled, his coarse beard scratching against my earlobe. Before I could even respond to his dark desire, he reached around and ran three fingers down my slit. "Oh, she's nice and wet for you, Ames. Feel it?" Wolf's massive hand then stroked my wetness down Ames's waiting length, and my skeleton man growled.

I could have died a happy death then and there at the sight of that. "How about Wolf takes you from behind, and I take you from the front?" Ames asked between heated kisses.

My nod was enthusiastic as I met Onyx's smirk. I knew from that pleased-with-himself look that he'd accomplished what he'd set out to. Distracting me, cheering me up, getting my mind off hell and its… inhabitants. His plan was working for now.

And as both of my men nudged the heads of their dicks toward both sides of me, Ames pushed in, filling me and making me scream and melt into his chest. And as he thrust out abruptly, Wolfgang eased in an inch behind me, but instead of entering my ass like I'd expected, his long cock pushed into my wanting slit, too.

And then Ames joined him.

My mind went gloriously empty. The only thing filling my being was the combined lengths of my men. The exquisite aware-ness of Ghost and Wolf rubbing their cocks together inside me was nothing short of soul-blinding indulgence. There was nothing else but the stretch of taking them both, feeling them both push inside me at the same time, my body struggling to take the girth of each of them. The sounds that came from me were anything but digni-fied, but I didn't care, I became one with Wolfgang's strength as he lifted me up and down, taking over my movements for me, using me to grind atop both of them melded into each other.

Ames took advantage of the werewolf holding me and moved inside me, thrusting in time with every down motion. Our joint wetness dripped down their cocks and slicked me deliciously as we groaned together. Ames bit my lower lip while Wolf grunted his nibbles along the crook of my neck.

It was dark and sinful ecstasy, and every so often, when my eyes could focus past the erotic scene before me, I caught a glimpse of my vampire's hooded green eyes and parted lips as he watched on with rapt attention.

But more than just the experience of taking them both inside me at the same time was the feeling of having them back, the emotions of knowing they were mine and we'd all fought for each other so hard. But that came with the twinge of guilt I wished would vanish. The wonderings of where Judas was and why I couldn't get him out of my brain.

At my jaw, Wolf rasped, "Come on both of our cocks, little one.

Come on our cocks as we come inside you and fill you up with us."

"Oh my god." My head fell back onto his strong shoulder as he continued to propel me up and down, slamming me harder and harder onto their stiff lengths.

"That's right, little ghost," my skeleton man ground out. "You belong to us, don't you?"

"Yes," I whimpered before catching his lips again, feeling his fingers toy with my nipples in the cold air. My orgasm broke against them, as if they'd speared me from the inside, bringing about my perfect and beautiful October death. As I writhed and moaned atop them, I felt their releases shoot up into me, filling me fuller than I'd ever been. And then, oh god, the stretch of Wolf's knotting took effect.

I screamed, and Ames grunted, pushing farther into me as we were both subjected to the glorious torture that was our werewolf knotting. Only this time I wasn't alone in taking it. Ames had to endure it along with me. And the press and stretch of both of them had tears streaking my face, and suddenly, I was glad I had a sheet to put over me when this was done, because my mascara was wrecked and running down my cheeks, staining Ames shirt with tears and my bites against the fabric.

"It hurts so bad," I whined, wiggling, my sore pussy fighting for relief. And then my vampire was by my side, running his touch down my arm lightly. Suddenly, a wave of pleasure, no more discomfort, rippled down my body like a warm rain.

"No pain for you. Not today, my belladonna. Not even the fun kind," he coaxed, holding me, holding us through our aftershocks of pleasure. When my two guys softly released me, Onyx asked Wolf to hold me up, and he obeyed, hooking his hands under my knees, and spreading me wide.

My vampire dropped to kneel in the crunchy leaves and put my ankles over his shoulders. "Allow me to clean you up." He smiled that charming grin that roped me more in under his spell each time. My pussy clenched at the potential of his mouth and those fangs.

"Only if you bite me, too," I whispered, hearing Ames's and Wolf's small chuckles.

My vampire hybrid's emerald eyes sparkled with interest. "If you're going to demand it, I suppose I can't say no."

The first swipe of his tongue had me sinking into Wolf's arms as he continued his symphony of kisses on my neck. "Onyx," I breathed, just wanting to say his name. "Wolf, Ames," I groaned after.

"That's right, belladonna, we're all here worshipping you. And they taste delectable mixed with your vessence. All of you pair so nicely," he murmured against my aching center. "Still want to give me a taste?"

I knew what he was asking, and the answer was simple, easy, and tantalizing. "Yes."

And with a swift movement of striking electricity, his fangs sank into my swollen cunt, and he began to drink. He drank my second, third, and fourth orgasms, and I shuddered against him, my thighs clenching against his face. He drank me, my blood, and the guys' combined releases like we were the finest of wines. Groaning along with every mouthful of blood and passion.

I bled for him from my most delicate of places. Allowing him my blood, allowing my Halloween Boys anything and everything. My love for them was more than anything I could ever form into words. So instead, I'd offer them my body, my mind, anything they wanted. These boys had gone to hell to find me. There was no escape from these monsters I'd gathered, and for that, I was immeasurably thankful.

THEY WERE DOTING ON ME. The guys, the lunas, everyone. At first, it was sweet, but after a few days of nonstop rest and being waited on, having lunas awkwardly smile as I took walks… I started to feel like some kept lady in a historical romance. And my walks through Fenrir were sandwiched between my guys, talking away about stories of Hallows Fest past, inside jokes, and upcoming concerts and video games they were into. So normal. So… suspiciously normal. And through their chatter, I realized the pack at Fenrir's numbers were thinner than before. Where was Nephele? Where were the lunas I'd gotten to know in the spring? My questions were brushed off or met with Onyx's charm, and I was becoming increasingly annoyed.

They weren't telling me things. They were reverting back to treating me like the helpless damsel again. They had rescued me from hell, but I wasn't there chained to a wall… well, at least not most of the time. And the devil wasn't that terrible… okay, he was kind of terrible, but in an alluring kind of way. My time spent there, beyond the veil, was for a purpose, and I'd saved the guys, so I'd served my purpose. Life could go back to normal, right? So then why couldn't I stop thinking about him? And his stupid smile, his garnet eyes, and those hidden wings. The way he looked at me so earnestly. Not like some captor whisking me away just to piss off the guys. No, there was something else.

There was more beneath his riddles. There was a story woven through all of our interactions over this past year, a story I only had torn and random chapters of. Why was he always appearing, visiting me randomly, helping me, only to walk me through a fucking gorgeous side of the underworld—and then let me go.

He let me leave.

My memories of hell were coming in flashes of nonsense. I recalled the fires we viewed from atop his big tourmaline mountain. *You will stop the fires*, he'd said. Nothing he told me made sense or aligned with this fierce and terrible ruler that the guys and everyone else painted him as. Was it all a lie? And if it was, to what end? I couldn't point to one thing the devil had gained from his interactions with me. When I'd asked, in the vampire city of Belladonia, what he wanted with me, he'd replied so simply. *To get to know you.*

Then there were our sexual encounters… which I hadn't had the nerve to share with the guys yet. Not because I was hiding them, but because I couldn't even make sense of them enough to decipher what had happened. Ghost would say he bewitched me into enjoying it and wanting it. And I'd assumed the same. But then… what if he hadn't? What if my flashes, my visions, my dreams, were all from somewhere inside me and not planted by the devil and his tricks?

What if all this is real and not a lie? What if I'm not tricking you? Could you try to believe that? If only for a moment.

His silky-smooth baritone rolled through my mind, bobbing up and down like apples in a bucket of water. I was grabbing for memories with my mouth like a kid bobbing for apples. Coming up short and with a face drenched in cold water.

On this October day leading up to Halloween, I'd ventured into town with the guys. Though the way they kept glancing when I tried to wander away had me even more curious as to what they were hiding, and I suspected it was a lot. And more concerning, as I searched the sky and lampposts, I hadn't seen Raven once since being back.

Something was amiss, and I had to figure it out. I had to piece this entire puzzle together. And I couldn't rely on my Halloween Boys to do it for me. There was too much to explain. And I held all the cards here, didn't I? It was just a matter of playing the right hand. Cards reminded me of Zyre.

Don't you see what this is? Mercy, the riddle, the game is so clearly laid out it's almost too easy for me to keep quiet, he'd said in hell.

As was typical, the guys went about checking on every shopkeeper, helping change lightbulbs and hang orange foliage atop doorframes. They were the keepers of Ash Grove. I smiled at the small and innocent realization as I watched them among a decked-out town. All the plastic decor was back and tacky as ever, and I freaking loved it.

Though I did need a better costume than a white sheet with holes cut out for eyes for Hallows Fest.

An animal chimed behind me.

Meow.

When I turned, I saw Cat swishing her long tail and licking her paw in the cracked door of Magia Eclectics. Magia… I wondered if Yesenia was there… or if Marcelene… my chest tightened in memory of how she had come to speak to me in hell. The devil had killed her, hadn't he? But then the door to Magia was ajar and Cat was sitting there, as casual as ever.

I made a thumb towards the magic shop when I caught Ames's nosy glance. He looked to me and then to Cat before she hissed at him. He rolled his eyes in response, nails between his teeth as he climbed a ladder and began hammering a black and orange banner above the candy shoppe. Onyx and Wolf shook the ladder, laughing at Ames's annoyance, and I grinned. They were dorks. My dorks.

When I approached Cat, she disappeared into the dark and heavily scented shop. The grim reaper bellowed its *wah, ha, ha* on my way in, the same way it always had. Maybe part of the magic of Ash Grove was how it never changed. The decorations were the same each year. The diner floors would always stick to your shoes, the Halloween finery would smell like stale candy corn each year, and the townspeople and their shops would always hold secrets behind their kind smiles and felines in doorways.

And I was walking into a secret then and there, wasn't I? Just like I had a year ago. Just like I hoped to do every year until the end of time. Doors, oh, the doors. Would they always hold such possibility?

The space swirled with dark purple wavering upon the visible swirls of lavender incense. A record played in the background with "Season of the Witch" crooning through the old horn speaker.

And as I found myself distracted over the orbs of crystal balls lighting black as I walked by them, following Cat as she pranced away. An old woman's voice called over the front desk. "Well, if it isn't death on my very doorstep… again."

Startled, I met her brown eyes. "Marcelene? You're…"

"Alive? Oh, yes, dear child. The devil and I dance." She spun in a circle, flailing out her long purple skirt and wiggled her hips. "Though not the same kind of dancing as the two of you. A tango, is it?" she winked.

I cleared my throat as my face flushed, ready to change the subject. "I guess if you're still alive, I'm looking for a costume."

Marcelene's form was an old woman again, but I didn't want to mention the shift. She was still just as beautiful and feisty as ever, and I was thankful to see her here, so alive and well. The witches were a universe all their own, and though we often disagreed, I liked them.

The crone leaned on her elbow and raised an eyebrow. "One other than the one you're wearing now? Neither of us is alive, and we're more alive than ever, all at once."

"I'm not wearing a costume," I replied, exasperated. I looked down to check my fitted ensemble.

Marcelene snickered as Cat jumped up onto the counter.

"Well, I have some gossip for you, Blythe." Cat arched her back in a stretch. "But I've figured out who you are. Well, Marcelene and I have. And I'm going to throw a live mouse at Raven for not telling me when I see him."

"Wait, what?" I asked, approaching the front table.

Marcelene took my hands in hers. "I should have seen it the moment you entered my shop… But I suppose that is your gift, isn't it? No one sees you coming." Her glimmering brown eyes met mine. "Not even you."

"Should we tell her?" Cat asked.

Marcelene scratched the feline's ear. "I think Death already knows."

My chest was tight as my breath came in short bursts. Lace-covered walls rose in my mind, telling me to stop, not to explore these dark areas of me, these memories…

Wait. Memories?

Marcelene tilted her head and surveyed me before a smile grew across her wrinkled face. "I like your horns."

I swallowed, my throat dry, and felt the heaviness on my head like a crown that suited me, like the horns had always been there. I reached up, feeling the curve of them as flashes of black strobed in my mind and heart. Then suddenly the incense wasn't lavender but blackberry. Blackberry so sweet and tart…

And then I remembered.

CHAPTER 32

Judas

LAST CHRISTMAS

> If I loved you less, I might be able to talk about it
> more.
>
> *Emma, Jane Austen*

I should have left. Or simply gazed at her through the raven's eyes, as I was accustomed to doing. But she was right there as the snow fell, sitting on the floor in a tiny farmhouse, so close to me. What would she do if I just… said hello? My Mortala was in there. That I knew. And it took every ounce of my strength not to tear down the walls and whisk her away, damn the consequences. Would the memories all come rushing back? I was more than prepared to take her then and there, if so. If she only spoke the words. Fuck the Halloween Boys. They didn't deserve her. They didn't comprehend who or what she was or that she was mine before time even began.

The idiots went to the kitchen, and I took my time startling her, sipping whiskey to calm my nerves. To calm my nerves? I hadn't been nervous since… since never. She noticed me and rose onto her knees, raising the skeptical brow I'd elicited hundreds of thousands of times. It wasn't the alcohol warming me then. *Hi,* she said, I think. I could only offer her a nod and curated stone face.

Do you see me? Remember me, Mortala. Say you remember.

"So, you're a devil, more powerful than anything, but you're helping them. Why?"

That was what she wanted to know? That's it? I swallowed the bitter burn of hurt. How long would I have to watch her like this? *You're right, Mortala. This doesn't make any fucking sense, does it? Wake the fuck up.*

"You don't think me to be altruistic?" I rumbled, pushing the emotion down.

She defended them and threatened me, and the hurt spit like fire and ash, churning within me, wanting to grab her and drag her to hell and fuck her on the trip down, reminding her of who she belonged to. Calling herself Death… she at least knew that much. At least that resonated. Perhaps Mortala wasn't too far from this amnesia of the spirit. This was a game, a game I had to play. A farce I'd promised my bride I'd play with her. What is one game among millennia of devotion? She couldn't see herself, and I couldn't either, until she was revealed on Halloween night with the veil at its thinnest. Death, the master of the hidden. A long and drawn-out game of hide and seek. Of course she'd found her way to Ash Grove. Hell through the veil. She'd always loved it here. How long had I searched for her? And here she was, kneeling on the floor before me, as stunning as ever, even without her glorious horns. Death couldn't see itself coming, just as I couldn't sense her. Revealing it all and not allowing it to unfurl in the manner the fates designed could have catastrophic consequences for us all. It could separate her from me again. Her attraction to the Halloween Boys was the same as mine, the pieces of her they held… I couldn't trifle with this delicate turn of events. No, my meddling was what had gotten us into this mess, and I'd had hundreds of years to regret my arrogance that first Halloween night. The night I lost her. I wouldn't dare repeat my sins. She would remember. Perhaps I couldn't outright tell her, but I could lead her to me. A breadcrumb trail of her and me is what I'd leave her.

So I taunted her, walking over, adoring her on her knees. She spoke to me like a queen. *Don't you see?* "I'll claim what's mine when the time comes. Be sure of that, Reaper."

Raven cawed as I tossed my glass into the blaze and gritted my teeth as I left her there. My heart shattered with the glass, the fire licking my wounds, and the memory of her big eyes haunting me thoroughly on my apparition back to a hell without her. Without hell's queen.

My counterpart.

My death.

And on my way down, a memory plagued me.

It was 1942, and she sat at a bar, smoking a long cigarette and slipping her heel on and off her foot as she waited. Tipping my hat at the bartender, I took the barstool next to her, and she didn't deign to even look at me.

"Curls suit you as well as horns, my death."

A slight curve in her blood-red lips formed as she puffed the cigarette. "Sir, I'm afraid you're speaking nonsense. Horns? Why, I'm quite fearful right now."

The bartender cleaned his hands with a rag and looked me over with a skeptical stare. "Miss, everything all right here?"

She raised her eyebrow in challenge. My Mortala loved her cat and mouse games. My bride loved making me chase her all around the world, throughout time. And I'd find her. I always found her. Today, a bar in the 1940s. Tomorrow, a colosseum in Rome. Time in the human realm was our playground. Our powers combined were unstoppable. We could destroy worlds if we wanted. But instead, we played games like this. If I had known this would be one of our last games for a few hundred years, or that the next time she left, I'd be searching for so long, I would have held her close and never let go. But instead, I spoke low in the smoke-filled bar. "It's fortunate that you enjoy the sweet sensation of fear, then, isn't it?"

With a smirk, she waved off the bartender. "Two whiskeys.

Neat, please." He eyed her a moment longer before nodding and sliding us our drinks. "You found me quickly this time."

"It helps that I never lose you."

"Don't you?"

"And I never will." I took her lace-gloved hand into my leathered one and kissed her knuckles. Years later, as I searched for her, I'd whisper the words into a songwriter's ear, hoping that wherever my bride was, she would hear it and she would remember. Perhaps I'd find an under-qualified and unassuming author to attempt to string together this story as well. The tale of Death and her monsters, Death and her Devil.

"Leather and lace," Mortala breathed. "Always."

"Always."

The carved pumpkins' lights were dim flickers now, not even standing at attention when I walked by. Even they were disenchanted with me. I'd had her back, had her here, and I still could not keep her. Perhaps in our time apart, she'd grown tired of me. Perhaps the flickering flames within our own little hell's jack-o'-lantern had dimmed. It would be a befitting hell for me, I thought. A life without her. Or worse, a life where she didn't want me. Where I'd have to watch her hate me, despise me, and wish to never see or know me.

I tried to give her as many clues as I could. Tried to spur some remembrance. But nothing. I had failed.

"Don't look at me like that," I murmured to the blackbird as I ascended the mountain. Yes, I could have flown or just fucking snapped my fingers and been there. But I wanted my muscles to hurt. Wanted to feel the pain and agony of the climb, because it didn't touch the torment inside my dark and twisted soul.

I had failed her.

I had failed the Halloween Boys, who I'd promised to look after, and who I'd reluctantly come to feel a sort of fondness for. How could they not have pieced it together? Had my centuries of aid and friendship meant nothing to them? I'd searched for a reaper, knowing it was Mortala, knowing she could not only break the curse but rejoin me at the throne. Unquestionably, my motives in the hunt were not all noble. They were more for me than them, but hell, I was the devil, after all. I didn't lock them in their circles of hell, though I was tempted. Nor did I punish them for retrieving her.

Her nod as she sat on my lap would trouble me for eternity.

Do you want to go?

Yes.

Raven squawked, circling me like the dead animal I was, or felt like. "You should have stayed with her," I called out. "I told you to watch after her."

At the top, the jagged tourmaline stones were glassy and bright even under the storm clouds and smoke from the fires. Raven responded, perching on one of the rock peaks. "You need me more right now. And my promise to not tell her feels impossible right now, because if she knew, it would set everything right."

"She must come to the answer on her own, or it is not the right time," I replied lowly. "And I do not need you." I sighed, looking up at the remarkable familiar. *Our* familiar. "But I so appreciate you, Raven Crow. And so does Mortala."

"What will you do?" he asked, sounding dejected. Such a sensitive and kind creature of darkness we shared between us.

I leaned backward onto the crystal stones. Magical mountain this was, hell's finest, and my heart tore and burned along with the fires in the distance coming closer, closer. The underworld was unbalanced without her, the same as I was. And the answer to imbalance was always destruction. There was no other way. And instead of sitting among its rumble, I would sleep. When would I awaken? A hundred years? Five hundred? Would Mortala want me then? The only thing I knew to be true was that if and when I woke, I would be immersed in the flames of the eternal fire. Our side of Ash Grove would be gone, and perhaps the magic would be gone from the one earth side as well.

Yes, dear friends, I had failed.

I had failed everyone.

CHAPTER 34
The Devil's in the Details

THIS IS HALLOWEEN

A flash of black darkness echoed through Ash Grove, illuminating every being in only an outline of white before it faded. I looked to the witch in horror and rage. "You dare summon my bride here?"

Marcelene shuddered, her magic failing as the purple sputtered out and she fell to her knees, gasping for breath. "I summon death. Yes, someone with some sense should come to these peoples' aid or their downfall."

Oh, this witch was going to be a problem.

My bride's presence was cold at my side. A hood over her horns, her robe blackened and flowing out behind her. Every bit the reaper of nightmares and the most beautiful and haunting creature I'd ever beheld. Disregarding the witch, she instead looked to the four fallen men on the ground, something lighting in her eyes. And then Mortala spoke, and even the ghouls hushed. "There is too much death. So much drawn to hell. Hell has tampered with this mortal place heavily. It is far too connected through the veil. Something must be done."

"It is only a few dozen mortals," I bargained.

"Every life matters. Otherwise death wouldn't matter, would it?" she wagered back, challenging me as she knelt next to James Cove and stroked his black hair tenderly. "I taste their emotions on my tongue, feel their *emotions in my bones, smell their fear and anger so strongly in my nose… I will save them. They will have parts of me, too, and I will find them again, find these pieces of me. Though the people here…" She looked around at the screams and fright. "The most I can offer is a swift death and lingering spirit."*

Holding her arm and helping her stand, I wanted to shake her. Did she even know what she was saying? "You'd be giving up this form and renewing o'er, Mortala. You cannot. You would have to find these Halloween… boys… and claim them as you choose in order to return to hell, to have your full being restored. Bestowing them with your essence would alter everything for lifetimes."

She smiled. "I wouldn't mind claiming them. Though I will miss you, my dear sweet devil. I love this place. It is hell. It is Ash Grove, and it is a piece of me. So these boys are a piece of me. This game will be fun, won't it? And they will join me. Join us at the end, I hope. Look after them, and say you'll look for me?"

Tears filled my eyes. Tears of sorrow and rage that she was doing this. Splitting us in two to make amends for hell's proximity to this town, for my lack of oversight and disinterest in preserving the mortals here. She was right. It was our fault, our responsibility in a sense—and death had come to set things right. Though a hellish outcome came with a wicked price. Nothing was free, even in distant realms such as these.

I swallowed my pain and held her hands, resting my forehead against hers. "I will search for you every moment of my existence, Mortala."

Mortala took a deep breath and looked around the town, taking it in one last time. "I like what they've done with it. Halloween." She tried the name on her lips. "Yes, I believe I'm a fan of Halloween."

With a deep ripple of black, like entering a tunnel and blazing through, she was gone. And her absence hit me like the grief of a hundred lifetimes. I pointed to the witch and back to her shop. "You are bonded to hell, and your magic stays there."

Before she could answer, a man grabbed my ankle, pulling himself up before rubbing his long hair from his eyes. "Please," Wolfgang begged. "Help my friends. I'll do anything."

A growl rumbled through my throat. He picked the wrong time to make a bargain with the devil. I would be helping them. I'd been helping them. But now I was bound to them in ways they'd never know or understand. They carried pieces of her now, gifts she gave to make them the guardians we both sensed they already were. The werewolf inhaled, and I knew his alpha senses were coming into play stronger than ever now.

I extended my hand. "You have a deal, Wolfgang Jack." We shook, and the ground rumbled. James stood before grabbing his head and bellowing as his body began to change.

He shifted into his ghost, his archdemon. Tall, muscular, and terrifying. Women screamed and ran as his blue hell smoke snaked out, grabbing ghouls and burning them in pain.

I took a step back, and Onyx rose, then, fire erupting from his palms and his fangs gleaming in the firelight. His shriek was of a different sort. One of pain, of remembering who he was and all he'd lost. Though death, my bride, was a tricky sort of temptress. They wouldn't remember her directly, only her lingering aftermath.

My bride was so evident inside each of them. The gift's she'd bestowed would stay with them forever. I longed for her inside them, watching their movements, entranced by the way they mobilized and immediately began their killing. They were so bloodthirsty. She would have been so proud to see it. The Halloween Boys were ruthless, villainous, and dripping with evil. Ripping through ghouls and demons as the remaining townspeople cried and hid. The ones who were still alive, at least. Though it didn't matter. They were trapped now. Some in body and those dead, in spirit.

And then the scene shifted with one last gift from Mortala. The spirits of the deceased rose from their bodies, roaming, searching. The witch stood next to me. "The town is cursed now. No one can leave, and these people left alive are worse off than the ones who are dead. And now… now we have them to contend with." She motioned toward James Cove's archdemon as he tore through a ghoul's throat as Onyx set a group of them on fire, all while Wolfgang howled a killing blow onto another.

"No one has lost more here today than me. And now, Marcelene, you are in my debt." I leveled her with a rageful stare that she met head-on.

"So be it," she answered, and we turned to watch the carnage together. Moments later, Ghost would kill her, and she would forget.

The first Halloween.

The Halloween Boys.

THE THREE GODDESSES *surrounded me as I leaned next to Mortala's empty black throne in the stark white room.*

"You just let her give her energy to those mortal men—"

"Sort of mortal," Brigid interrupted, her long hair glowing like the sun.

Danu, the third goddess, never spoke. She only looked on with a long face. I envied her perpetual silence and wished I never had to utter words myself.

"It's what she wanted" was all I could answer, feeling the emptiness of her throne. "I will find her. I always do."

"And what of hell while you search? It will deteriorate." Ceridwen crossed her long arms. "This is no good. You are the guardians of this realm. What of these new monsters?"

"They call themselves the Halloween Boys, or that's what the town now calls them. Catchy, isn't it?" I avoided her gaze. "I'll look after them. I vowed I would."

Then Danu spoke, and we all turned, shocked. Were these the first words she'd spoken in a millennium? Longer? "Death," she said, looking down and swaying in all her gray hooded robes, "has chosen her four horsemen. It is as it should be."

The gazes of the goddesses looked on hauntingly before leaving me alone. Alone with her empty throne.

CHAPTER 35

Mortala

THE DEVIL'S RESTING PLACE

> We loved with a love that was more than love.
> *Edgar Alan Poe*

"What's your favorite food lately?" I asked, running my touch over his skeleton-bone hand. He only ever took his gloves off for me. I was the only one who knew his hands. I was the only one who could hold the long bones next to my flesh. We lay on the red quilt under a beautifully dreary sky above our town.

He chuckled lowly. "The witches say that I appear wherever blackberries are. Books full of stories and lore about it." He turned onto his elbow, running a bone finger through my hair, his crimson eyes impossibly gorgeous. "But much to what I assume would be their dismay, I have no malicious intent. I just like the fruit."

A giggle tore through my chest. "I'll have to bake you a blackberry pie, then."

"I'd rather eat your berried cunt," he purred, pinning me down and climbing on top of me. "I enjoy baking. I'll make you one."

"Judas." I cupped his strong jaw. "You are so evil... and I love it so much."

He kissed my cheek. "So are you, my death. Incredibly so. Deliciously dark and sinisterly divine."

A THOUSAND TINY memories flooded back, and I couldn't catch my breath to even sort through them all. I wasn't being bewitched at all. The entire time, each vision was in remembrance. Memories. They were all memories. I paused with my hand on the knob of Magia Eclectics. "How do I get back to hell?"

"You're already here, child," Marcelene said with her soft kindness.

"The doors, the gates, they're all yours. Always have been. Try clicking your ruby heels together, Dorothy." Cat tucked her paws under her chest, looking amused with her *Wizard of Oz* reference. "Oh, he's mad. Better hurry."

I knew who she meant, but I couldn't stop to explain, and a sense of intense urgency blocked out all other thoughts at the moment. "Thank you both," I whispered as the grim reaper laughed its mechanical drawl behind me, and I stepped into hell's —and Ash Grove's—town square. They were the same on different sides of the veil.

How had it not all clicked into place before now?

A cough tore through my lungs, and my eyes burned as soot filled my nose and crackles sounded around me. Spinning, I saw my town drenched in plumes of smoke as orange and red fires licked above rooftops in the distance.

The fires had ascended. Where was the devil?

A familiar caw sounded above me, and when I turned, his long beak and humanoid body, complete with his little leather vest, stood, with open arms in greeting. Despite fires and time and space and memories flooding my pounding head, I squeezed Raven tight.

"You're here," I marveled. "Where's Judas?"

"He is the mountain again," Raven said, sad and plain. "I couldn't stop him from his slumber."

"Then I'll have to wake him up," I said. "Take me to him?"

"The closest I can get you is the bottom of the tourmaline. To fly up, I have to accompany you as the crow. You and I are the only ones he allows up there."

I swallowed, my eyes filling with tears and now from the smoke, as I remembered. "You're ours, aren't you? *Our* familiar."

His facial expressions were imperceptible through his plague mask, but I could have sworn his eyes grew fond and he smiled as he tilted his head in a small bow. "Forever at my lord and my queen's service... Mortala."

I took his long, feathered wing in my hand and held it tight. Raven had, this entire time, been an extension of Judas's love. A hint, a clue, of the love we shared for so long. Finally, it had become clear. But was I too late? It felt I might be, as I remembered the mountain and how the devil would go there to disappear with long sleeps. Essentially abandoning the world, letting hell fend for itself. And giving up on me. And it was my fault. I couldn't even blame him.

He'd been reaching out this entire time, showing me the way, offering himself to me, and I'd been so blind. Or maybe, on the contrary, I needed to accept the love I'd found in the Halloween Boys before my eyes were truly opened to who and what I was... and there was such magic in that, wasn't there? They were all pieces of me, and I was pieces of them, and we were all one. Ghost,

Dragon, Wolf, and Devil. They were mine; they were me, and we were all made for each other.

And what a cruel fate if Judas was truly locked away now. If I'd missed my opportunity, and now he was gone... and our roles would change, then. I'd have to manage hell while waiting for him. No, I couldn't let that be. As the fires thrashed into the town, raining ash around us, Raven held me close, and we tumbled into the black, until appearing at the base of the jagged black and stormy mountain of my sleeping devil.

The devil's resting place.

RAVEN CAWED OVERHEAD, circling higher and higher. This climb was mine; this mountain was mine. And maybe I was destined to be the luna that slept in his caverns forever in waiting... just like the tales of Fenrir said.

The stories are all about you, he'd told me.

And as I began my climb, as the sky above me seethed and reverberated and smoke stung my lungs, screeches sounded behind me. No one was here to protect me, I realized. And an even more disturbing and terrifying realization hit. That everything the devil had told me had been true. Instead of fighting against and weighing his words, they settled into a place of dreadful acceptance. He'd told me that every ghastly creature I'd encountered on the other side of the veil existed here in hell, and looking out among them, a stark terror fell over me.

They didn't know, or they didn't care, who or what I was. Just a girl climbing their lord's mountain as fires encroached on us all, pushing them in and toward me, gathered like sheep in a herd. I stared out at a hundred or more ghouls, the legions of demons, the shadowed creatures, and the red slitted eyes of beings I'd not seen before.

The stories weren't true. I wasn't going to sleep in my devil's caves for eternity. I was going to die at the base of them. Raven squawked, alerting me, but I already knew, and I kept climbing as monsters hissed behind me.

Chasing me.

They'd always been chasing me. For dark lords, for evil intent, for whatever reason. I came to Ash Grove a girl who was running. Running from my past, running from demons, from horrors of earth and hell combined. Alone, scared, ready to give up.

Until I met the Halloween Boys.

And they showed me, each in their own unique ways, that I was more and that I was worthy of love. I was worthy of staying in one spot. Of standing still and letting the evils have their go. And my boys were there for me, always reminding me that I had the power inside me the entire time. And they were right. They were right in the deepest and truest of ways. Because I was more powerful than anyone could have imagined. Despite my fear, despite my past, I was strong.

And not because I was mated to them or mated to the devil, but because I was me. Blythe Pearl and Mortala. Death, a reaper, and just a normal girl with darkness surrounding her. Both women, both versions of me, were valid. Both were beautiful and deserving of adoration.

A small voice called from below, and when I met their eyes through the limbs of the cold gray ghouls frozen in watch with dripping teeth, the willow tree spirit waved. I waved back as the demons disregarded my little friend and barreled after me.

"I shared with you my light. Now it's your turn. Tag, you're it!" The willow spirit giggled like a child, so at odds with the gnashes of teeth and rips of claws into rock that sang around me. When I found my footing, I let go of the rock I clutched and turned to face them as they climbed after me, spitting and snarling. The rest of them fanned out below the base of the mountain like ants as they scattered from the fires crashing forward.

"No more running," I said to myself, feeling my horns heavy on my head. A ghoul and two legioned demons scaled onto the overlook and launched themselves at me. I didn't know what to do.

But at the same time, I had all the answers. The answers weren't in a neat and explainable box. Nothing in any realm was. So many things just *were*, weren't they?

Blythe hoped for a savior or for a swift death. She shuddered inside me, afraid, remembering her stepdad, remembering the terror of his strikes, recalling the chase and the ghouls in the night. Blythe Pearl was haunted by nightmares of trauma and floods of fretfulness from their evil.

I honored that. I didn't tell those feelings to shut up. I didn't ignore them. No, instead, I held her hand, deep inside my soul. "I know you've been so afraid," I told myself. A ghoul struck, and I reached out a hand. He froze in midair, shaking and screaming. My horns felt lighter, then, and a small smile curved my lip. I squeezed Blythe's hand in my soul. "But I'm here now, and I've got us. I'm strong enough to save us, to be our own hero."

She squeezed my hand back in reverence of all we were together, each version of us—past, present, and future. They all existed within me at once, and they were each important and powerful in their own way. But it was time to grow. It was time to be the evil woman with horns.

The keeper of doors.

The legend of Belladonia.

The stories of Fenrir.

The savior of Ash Grove.

The queen of hell.

"I am Mortala," I said in a profound, echoing voice, stepping forward and addressing every snarl and hiss of darkness. "I am your reaper. I am death. I am the ruler of hell."

They stopped their thrashing and snarls and went silent before me as I remembered their claws and teeth and every haunt I'd endured at their mercy.

And it was time for my justice.

"You will all stay exactly where you stand and feel each flame of the fires until you are a grove of ash." My chest lightened, and I breathed a small laugh. Ash Grove.

And as they obeyed, frozen by my command, I turned, knowing a door would be waiting for me, and it was. Ornately decorated and deep blood red. I walked through it and onto the mountain top.

There wasn't a moment to marvel at what I'd just done, become, or accepted. Because the weather raged like a hurricane atop the slick tourmaline crystals. They shined like mirrors, and I saw my reflection. I couldn't help but notice the frightful creature I'd become. Long black horns twisted above my head, and my chestnut hair fell in waves down my shoulders. I was the woman from my vision on Halloween last year. The one on her throne, with Raven and her four men.

Yes, each of them.

"Is this the place?" I called above the storm to Raven, placing my palm on the slick black crystal mirror side of the mountain wall.

He called out a yes, landing in an enclave to shield his wings from the rain. "Judas," I whispered. "I'm here. Wake up."

Despite the frigid chill of the rain as it pricked against my skin, I felt the heat from the fire climbing the mountain. Hell was burning. Our home was on fire. When nothing happened, I sighed. The embers flicked around me, and water poured above me as thunder angrily crashed against flame. Resting my head against the cold side of the mountain, I conceded defeat. "Where is my leather?" I breathed, remembering our song, our wicked prayer. Oh, the lifetimes of music we had made together, the folklores they'd written of us. All wrong, of course, but stories through time all the same.

Suddenly, I was dry, and the fire paused at my back. The mountain shifted, and arms wrapped around me. Looking up in shock, I met his garnet gaze. "My lace," he whispered. "My death."

"Yes," I whimpered as the lips of my devil collided with mine. He tasted like tart blackberries on the saddest final day of summer.

He picked me up, spinning me around and pressing me to the

smooth mountain face. He ran his leather-gloved knuckles down my cheek, and I leaned into his touch with a sigh. "How do you know I'm not bewitching your mind?" he rumbled, seeming half-ardent and half-wary.

I took his wrist in my hands, realizing even both of my hands couldn't reach around it and touch. He was so big, in every way. Larger than life, than time and every realm. The devil and death. He was mine, and I was his. It always had been and always would be. He was fire, and I was thunder. Gently, as he watched with those downcast brows, I tugged off his glove, knowing what I'd see, knowing what my memories had shown me. The thing he showed no one else. The secret no one knew but me.

Even still, seeing the skeleton hand, so large, easily the length of my waist, was a horrific and delightful shock. I ran my fingers down the bones, feeling their smooth coldness. "These," I whispered. "I've missed these."

"They've missed you," he replied gruffly, removing his other glove and cupping my jaw with the bones of his grip. "Shall I show you just how much, my queen?"

"You may," I whispered, already shivering at the trail of touch as his skeletal caress skimmed down my sides, making my clothing melt away like ice in a warm drink. And suddenly, his wings darkened the sky, shielding us under a red tent.

"You are my burning willow. You are my hell; my place of eternal torment and sorrow. I am your devil, your guardian. I should love nothing, but I love only you," he rumbled, his declaration more powerful than any storm. We were naked, thrust into crimson-tinted darkness, in old and new ways. We kissed like we'd always and never kissed before. The devil's skeleton hands stroked my breasts and dipped inside my sex, coaxing a moan from my lips as his teeth pulled at the flesh of my neck.

It felt as if the world was spinning, as if hell was silencing and reigniting all at once. Everything he'd been holding back unleashed against me, and we were the night sky, the crashing thunderstorm of deadliest proportions. A holy and evil celebration of the worst and deadliest of loves. A love that died and came back to life. A love that found more pieces of herself in the Halloween Boys and danced with the devil in hell again. A love that stopped running and turned to the vices pursuing her and burned them alive. This moment alone with him, horn and bone, flame and mountain, was everything.

When his cock finally thrust into me, the stars behind my eyes lit into a flurry of red embers of fire raining from the sky. Hell was back. Hell was us. His long and strong boned hands held my horns in reverence as his garnet gaze found mine tenderly and tears streaked my cheeks. "My Mortala," he breathed, moving in and out, coaxing another and another detonation of bliss while his own release pooled down my thighs in holy offering to the mountain that couldn't hold my devil.

"My devil," I answered. "Judas."

His eyes drifted closed as he pulled me nearer, my legs entwining with his while his wings cut us off from the realms of bliss and torment. Making love to him was both agony and ecstasy. We'd found each other after all this time, and I knew we would again and again.

As we floated down from our passion, he set my feet on cobblestone. How long had we been merged in sex reunited? It could have been hours or days. "Are you ready?" he asked, running his lips along my horns. Even with the height of them, he towered over me, cocooning me in his wings.

Ready for what, I wasn't sure, but I knew the answer now was yes. I was ready. He ran a leather-gloved thumb along my lower lip and offered me one more tender glance and a soft kiss before unfolding his wings. My clothes felt heavy against my sensitive skin, my skin that still remembered every prick of his bone touch and delicious embraces.

And maybe I wasn't ready, because when I turned, letting the sunlight hit my face, I was back in Ash Grove, and I first met the shocked eyes of Yesenia. She stood, arms spread over the door of Magia, Cat in front of her, as three big men demanded to be let inside. At her expression, they turned, and my heart warmed at the sight of my beloved Halloween Boys.

First, they took in my horns, and I saw the look of love and relief wash over their beautiful, distinct faces. A demon, a wolf, a vampire-dragon. And then they looked over and above me at my companion, their gentle expressions hardening into death's wrathful stare.

The last moments happened in slow motion as the shadow of the devil stretched out in front of me. His wide and enormous shape, his wings up and outstretched, casting sinister art of a damned angel against the gray and dry leaf-speckled cobblestone. The guys, without hesitation made their attack, despite my too-slow pleas that they stop and listen.

The devil moved in front of me.

And then sunlight flooded us again as I locked eyes with Yesenia and a bored-looking Cat in front of Magia.

The Devil and the Halloween Boys were gone.

CHAPTER 36

Ghost

REVEREND PRIEST

> I do not mean to be sentimental about suffering – enough is certainly as good as a feast – but people who cannot suffer can never grow up, can never discover who they are. That man who is forced each day to snatch his manhood, his identity, out of the fire of human cruelty that rages to destroy it knows, if he survives his effort, and even if he does not survive it, something about himself and human life that no school on earth – and indeed, no church – can teach. He achieves his own authority, and that is unshakable
>
> *James Baldwin*

He didn't drag us back to hell or damn us to our respective levels of misery. I supposed he could have obliterated us with a word. Those words so skilled at entrancing and seducing our mate. The sight of Blythe holding his arm made me want to saw that arm off, no matter how powerful he was, no matter the repercussions.

But no, we weren't back in the meat locker or on some damned train to nothingness.

We were back where it all started.

In a familiar barn, rebuilt from its prior incineration, on a well-worn plot of farmland.

The devil had brought us back to Onyx's barn.

For monster fight club.

Wolfgang was growling, hardly containing his fury as he and Onyx zeroed in on the devil as he crossed his arms and leaned silently against the barn frame. It was night now, and the same bonfire we always built for these nights was blazing in the distance.

"We can talk, or I can beat your asses first. Your choice," the devil rumbled in his deep and otherworldly timbre.

"Oh, now he gives choices," Onyx spat, flames trilling up his forearms. "Where was Blythe's choice when you took her?"

"I did not take her. She came to me—" The devil dodged a hit from Wolfgang, whose fist instead splintered an old wooden beam behind him. "But indeed, I did not let her leave."

"You bewitched her mind and took advantage of her body," Wolf seethed. "We witnessed it ourselves in that fucking grotesque display."

My feet were firmly planted as I stared him down. If looks could kill, he'd be a dead man. "Say it, Ghost. Go on," the devil goaded, rearing back and punching Wolf across the jaw before leveling his abdomen with blows. Wolf stumbled back before charging forward again. This time, Onyx landed a flaming slash of fire across the devil's bare chest.

He let himself burn and bleed before us and growled, "I forced nothing on her."

"Liar," I replied lowly, stalking forward. My demon was close to the surface of my skin, ready to erupt. I felt him in my shaking voice and palms. But right now, I wanted to address the devil as a man. Perhaps kill him as a man, too. "Just like our entire friendship, our brotherhood. All of it has been a lie, hasn't it?" And then verses from the Bible, the book of Psalms, spilled from my constricted throat. *"For it was not an enemy that reproached me; then I could have borne it... But it was thou, a man mine equal, my guide, and mine acquaintance."*

Devil straightened, blood dripping down his muscular chest as I ambled forward. His jaw steeled, and he looked down at me with a dark and threatening gaze.

"Silence. Yeah, that's the Judas we know. Or do we know you at all?" Onyx mocked from the corner, arms still lit and green eyes glowing. Wolfgang paced in the doorway, ignoring the blood trickling from his lip and eyebrow.

And when I approached the devil, I didn't hesitate to land my blows. I punched him across the jaw. He still stood with his arms crossed, as if I'd done nothing but toss a feather in his direction. "Hit me back. Come on, fight, you coward."

"Okay," he rumbled, and I braced for the hit I so desperately craved. The fight to end him. Maybe to end me, too. I didn't fucking care. "Silence, as I searched for her."

I looked to the guys and back to him skeptically. "What?"

"Silence, as I ached for her." He pressed a leather-gloved hand to his blood-stained chest. "Silence as I mourned death and sought death."

"He's lost his mind." Onyx said. "He's speaking nonsense."

Wolfgang stilled his pacing and cocked his head in interest.

"Utter nonsense." The devil chuckled, giving us a rare glimpse of his teeth and something of a harsh smile. "I said the same. When she came to you on Halloween. When death paid a visit to Ash Grove. The sister city to hell. Hell through the veil. She fell in love with it, and somehow, she fell in love with you as well."

The guys and I exchanged glances again, but there was no mockery in them. Something in the way he spoke sounded... true.

"She is Mortala. She is my bride. The queen of hell. And... she is our mate. All of us. For you exist within her and she within you."

Cool air rushed in from behind, where a black archway

appeared. And there she was, walking out of it. The same as ever. She'd always been a stunning vision dressed in black, all curves and everything delectable a woman could possibly be. Only she had her horns back now. Only she was the woman on the throne we'd seen last Halloween night. She was Mortala. She was a reaper. She was death itself.

She came to me and tucked herself under my arm. I carefully avoided her horns to kiss her hair that smelled of nutmeg. "It was you all along, little ghost, wasn't it?"

She swallowed and took in the sight of the bloodied room, her battered men whose confusion had finally lifted. "I guess I've never been able to resist any of you."

Not caring who was watching, I took her face in my hands and kissed her deeply, flicking my tongue against her and lapping up the sweet taste of her happiness and arousal. "I don't care if you're the queen of hell. You'll always be my little ghost."

She smiled that heart-melting smile with those sweet as fuck dimples. "Now we know why I taste your emotions, too. Sweet honey." She licked her lips before holding my hand and turning to the guys. "You're all mine, you know. I claimed you all a very long time ago, and when I came to you on Halloween and set all of this in motion, I didn't know it would take so long to get back to you. But we're here now."

"Your four horsemen of death," Judas rumbled softly, though the way he looked at her was nothing short of holy adoration. And then I definitely knew this was all real. This was all right.

"My Halloween Boys." She smiled, leaning into Onyx's and Wolf's touches as they surrounded us.

"Our Halloween Queen," Onyx added.

Something shifted, then, in the crackling ash of the fire in the October breeze of night. That Blythe had always been ours, and we hers. That Blythe had offered herself to save us, and she had found us again. Righting our homes, aligning our dark souls, and igniting inside us who we were meant to be and what we were all meant to be together. Because of love, and because of Halloween, it had always been her. And it would always be her, and us, and October in Ash Grove, for all of time, in every realm.

Forever.

CHAPTER 37

Blythe

TRICK-OR-TREAT & HAUNTED HOUSES

> She'd always loved Halloween. A magic night. A night when anything could happen. Monsters could be real. Magic could whisper in the air.
> *Cynthia Eden*

"She should really be naked for this," Onyx said, fangs glinting under the dim church lighting.

Wolfgang took a sip from his flask. "I agree with that."

"Why?" I giggled. "Besides the fact that you boys are insatiable."

"Stop making her talk. The face is the most important part of the process." Ames grinned from behind his black and white painted face. "We have some surprises for you tonight, little ghost."

"Why are we all skull-paint and KISS cover band but Judas gets to look cool and mysterious in his red cape and leather gloves?" Onyx whined as Ames touched up my makeup with a flick of his brush. I kicked my legs up on the pew of Lamb's Blood Church, looking up at Judas, who sat on the priest's chair like he always belonged on a throne. I supposed he did. I supposed all of us did in our own dark ways.

"Because I'm the devil. Halloween is for me. Did you boys learn nothing in church?" he added on with cocky self-assurance. The guys moaned their laughs.

Wolfgang passed Onyx his flask. "Finally someone with a bigger ego than the King of Belladonia over here."

Onyx elbowed his friend, and, surprised, I asked, "You're king now? How could you not tell me that?"

The vampire shrugged, running a hand through his jet-black hair, looking every bit the dark angel in face paint that I fell in love with. "Must have slipped my mind in all the *fun*."

"I bet Vladimir is livid, huh?" I asked, noticing his and Wolfgang's faces drop as Ames cleared his throat, swiping black paint along the underside of my jaw. "What did I say?"

"He's, uh, my dad isn't around anymore. But it's okay. We made up in the end." I reached out for his hand, and with a soft smile, he wrapped his fingers around mine. "Plus, Queen of Hell sounds a whole lot cooler than King of Belladonia."

"You're sure you're okay?" I whispered, ignoring his mask of charm. His green eyes softened, and he gave my palm a squeeze.

"I'm more than okay, belladonna. Are you?"

I met the glance of each of them, from the garnet eyes beaming down at me to the amber ones of my wolf, the crystal blues of my demon, and the emerald stare of the newest king of vampires. They were all mine. And somehow, we'd all become these new versions of ourselves together. Like it was always meant to be this way. Like our love and our little family had brought out the best in each of us.

"Yes," I answered, my throat constricting with emotion that was hard to tame.

Onyx smiled, and Ames kissed my temple. I knew they felt it and tasted it, the feelings of the words I couldn't manage to say.

When we descended the church steps and the grounds littered with pumpkins, Ash Grove was alight in Halloween flair. From every lantern blazing with fire to an excess of pumpkins and crunchy leaves to step on. Children ran past, digging through their pillowcases of loot, and I breathed inthe October air. It was finally here, the most magical day of the year in every realm.

Halloween.

The Halloween Boys, complete with their devil and their Halloween Queen, prowled down the street of ancient and hell-touched Ash Grove as Raven fluttered above us and storekeepers stood outside their shops, dropping handfuls of candy into kids' baskets.

Wolfgang thrust a hollow plastic pumpkin bucket into my hand. "Trick-or-treating with us is a tradition you're never getting out of. Even if you're, you know, death and master of the under-world or whatever."

"Or whatever?" I giggled, feeling the weight on my shoulders ease for the first time in… well, ever.

Onyx pinched my ass, and I yelped as he walked backward in front of us. "Look at your arms, my queen."

When I looked down, they were glowing neon green in the places the paint had touched. I wore a tight-fitted black mini dress to let Ames paint me as a skeleton all over. The dress even had a hood with holes to accommodate my horns, and with the glowing paint covering me from head to toe and my hood raised, I felt very much like what I was. The grim reaper. Before reaching the first shop full of waiting candies, I noticed Judas and Ames talking as they lagged behind Onyx, Wolf, and me. My eyebrow raised in quiet question, and my skeleton man smiled, joining my side and slipping his hand down the small of my back.

Tingles lit my skin, but when I looked down the path we had come, Judas was gone.

"He's skipping ahead," Ames assured me with a rough voice in my ear.

"More surprises?" I asked, the corners of my black lips curving as I realized he was glowing under his skull paint, too. "Thank you for forgiving him," I whispered.

But there was nothing I could hide from the guys, as Onyx's keen vampire hearing caught it. "So quick to forgive the devil for doing the same damn thing I did."

"Yeah, we'll never forgive you for stealing our girl. The devil gets a pass." Wolfgang shoved his friend, and they exchanged playful blows as Ames shook his head and watched on.

Ames nudged me toward the first open shop. "Technically, we Halloween Boys owe you and the devil our lives, our gifts. Without the two of you, none of this would be," he said appreciatively, casting a gaze over the guys and to downtown Ash Grove and beyond. My chest swelled with love. How far my sweet archdemon had come since we'd known each other. From a caged and restless being full of rage to something a bit softer, something stronger in himself. "Quit looking at me like that, or I'll have to fuck you right here on the steps of Willis Hardware. I think the old man would find that inappropriate."

The skeleton man smacked my ass, and I laughed, walking up to say the words they all loved to hear. "Trick-or-treat!"

I thanked Mr. and Mrs. Willis as they waved after us and we hit the other downtown shops.

"Nothing feels better than Halloween night." Onyx spun, unwrapping a caramel bar. "The smells, the spooky, the feeling of fear and excitement in the air. Oh, and the sweet memories of being taken by death so long ago." He shot me a wicked grin. "What a ride. Huh, belladonna?"

I didn't know why, but even more emotion clutched at my soul. Remembering my vision of my boys lying on the ground, lifeless, and then realizing it wasn't a vision at all, but a memory. Recalling the vision of the burning forest, where I looked to Raven and asked *Who did this?* and he answered *you did*. Those were all real, all from me, all hints to who and what I was. And now, finally, I saw it all for its truth. Now, at long last, I saw myself for who I was and accepted every part of it without running.

"Let's hurry," I told them. "Because I want to make it to the last night of Hallows Fest."

The guys exchanged looks and agreed as we made our way into the adjoining neighborhood of downtown. The moon was a spotlight on the wet pavement plastered with red maple and yellow ginkgo leaves. We stopped at a familiar empty little house, and the guys proceeded to drape it with toilet paper. I stood at the end of the driveway rolling my eyes. "I'm pretty sure Marcelene is trapped in hell, yet you're still vandalizing her home?"

"It's tradition," Wolfgang purred, kissing my cheek as the guys laughed.

They were hopeless brutes, truly. Hopeless little lost boys who'd gone to hell and back for me. They were the villains of the story and had a trail of blood and evil deeds behind their names. And I loved them more and more with each passing breath. They'd been worth every moment of doubt, every moment of confusion at solving this riddle of me, of Ash Grove. And finally, we'd reached the end of the page together. At least the end of this chapter, this book. We had endless more stories to write together for all of time.

And surely in each new installment of our tale, my boys would be getting into mischief, and I would be somewhere nearby, laughing and shaking my head. We trick-or-treated for a few more houses, then walked up a dark hill to a looming, multi-point black house.

The guys grew silent on our walk up, and I stopped at the gate. "I don't think anyone's home… plus it looks creepy here."

"Thought you loved creepy?" Ames asked, his skull paint still neon under the moonlight.

"Obviously," I replied, wrapping my arms around Wolfgang, who eagerly took in the affection and nuzzled into the top of my head. "But they don't look like they have candy for trick-or-treaters."

Onyx opened the squeaking sharp-pronged iron gate and grinned. "Really? I think they look like the sort of house to hand out full-size candy bars."

"And fill the entire yard with pumpkins," Ames added, following after him.

Wolfgang led me down the path and up the porch stairs. "Plenty of room in the backyard for a fire pit, too."

"What are you guys playing at?" I asked, crossing my arms as they all stood in a line at the black front door, looking guilty as hell even under their skull makeup.

Ames rubbed the back of his neck. "I know you said you're not a white picket fence girl. But what about a spiked wrought-iron gate girl?"

Onyx reached into his pocket and dangled keys in front of my nose. "I hear it's haunted."

Ames snickered. "It's certainly about to be."

"Don't tease me," I chided. "Are you guys saying…"

Wolfgang squeezed my ribs from behind and gruffed into my ear. "It's ours, little one."

Ames opened the door to a dark candlelit corridor and smiled a rare and beautiful smile. "Welcome home, little ghost."

Before I could fight the warm tears on my face or burst through the entrance to explore, Onyx blocked the way and held up a finger. "Not so fast, my eager darling. We've devised a game of how you're to explore and experience your first and last home."

"A dark ritual of sorts." Ames smirked and backed into the house. "The holy father says all new dwellings must be christened."

Wolfgang eased me inside, then closed the door and turned me around. He put his hands over my eyes. "Keep your eyes closed and count to one hundred, then come looking for us to receive your tricks and treats."

"Like we said, it's haunted, so you may stumble upon a ghost…" Ames's voice said from somewhere in the distance.

"Even a vampire who wants to suck your blood," Onyx added in his best Dracula impression, and I bit my lip to stop from giggling.

"Perhaps a werewolf hungry to eat you whole," Wolf added roughly from up the stairs. The floor beneath them creaked with each step, and I heard doors squeaking overhead. Multiple stories of haunted, creepy goodness, and I couldn't wait to explore our new home.

Our home.

When footfalls and floor squeaks fell silent, I moved my hands from my eyes and took in the space. Gothic black and purple wallpaper adorned the walls, up to the high pointed ceilings and iron chandeliers dripping with clear jewels. Ornate rugs covered dark hardwoods, and everything looked so antique. Some of it I felt I recognized.

Furnishings from the floating castle in Belladonia. The end tables and artwork from Lamb's Blood Church, and a bear skinned rug in the homey living area by the raging hearth. Every room I passed kindled revelations in my mind, visions I now knew weren't only daydreams or disassociation or some fantasy world I was building in my head. The visions were true, and they were of things to come. By the fireplace, I flashed to a scene of wool stockings and a big black holiday tree decorated in bones and pumpkins.

When I passed by the copper-accented kitchen, I saw a hazy image of Wolf stirring a pot and Judas pulling breads from the oven. Wolfgang chattered away, sharing a story and Devil smiling softly on, removing the rolls from their pan.

The doors to a study filled with books were open, and another vision sprang to life. Of Ames sitting in the armchair, ankle on his knee as he read a hardback. Across from him, Onyx played at the piano, another relic from the music room in Belladonia. Our song gently echoed through the house, caressing the walls, and warming my heart. And as I ascended the spiral staircase, the first door at the top opened slightly and all on its own. Maybe doors spoke to me now, or maybe the house was truly haunted and the spirits were ushering me inside. When I took in the candlelit bedroom with the plush lavender bedding, fireplace, and flowers, I laughed through my tears and picked up my stuffed bat from between the pillows.

The gruff voice of my werewolf pulled at me from the doorway.

"Not fair of me to hide in your room instead of mine, but I just couldn't wait to see what you thought of it."

With the ceiling's peak and the long window that was as tall as him, Wolfgang didn't seem too big for this place, for once. I swallowed down my emotion and clutched my stuff as he excitedly gestured to a familiar black vanity. "Donated by Judas, with all your makeup. He organized it the way you like." I could have died, and cried, and died again at the thought of the devil arranging my makeup in the way I liked.

Wolfgang moved to a tall wooden cabinet. "And this..." He opened it with a flourish, and something clambered inside. A box of tissues.

I reached it and pulled one out to dry my tears. "Wait, is this the magic cabinet from Magia Eclectics? How the hell did you get this?"

Wolf chuckled. "It wasn't easy, but we stole it, basically," he shrugged. "We didn't want to insult you by giving you your own room. Of course, you'll be sleeping with us, or we'll be sleeping together, whenever you want. But we just thought that after everything you've been through, you'd want a space to call your own. And to get away from Onyx occasionally."

My throat tightened with tears and laughter as I found my way into his warm arms. "I've never had my own home before. No place has ever felt safe. Until now. Until you guys."

He kissed the top of my head. "You're always safe with us, my sweet luna."

Taking his wide calloused hand in mine, I tugged him into the hall. "Let's go find our moody thieving vampire."

Wolfgang chuckled. "You sure you want me to come? I think the master plan was that we all got you to ourselves in this hide-and-seek haunted house game."

"You're mine." I smiled. "And I'm not letting any of you boys out of my sight ever again."

Down the hall, we passed by more stolen artifacts from Ash Grove, hell, Belladonia, and Fenrir. We found Onyx's room draped in dark green silks and filled with guitars reflecting the fireplace blaze.

He stood and took a sip from a martini glass, looking at us with that stare that would make any mortal turn and run. I loved that feeling of fear he could bring about so easily. "It seems I've lured two sweet victims into my lair," he purred, pulling me close and running his knuckles along my cheek.

Wolf closed in behind me, running his touch over my hips and Onyx's arms. "Not sure how sweet this one is," the werewolf replied lowly. "Might have to taste her and see."

And taste me they did.

Onyx sank his fangs into my neck as Wolf hiked up my dress over my ass, sliding his girth between the backs of my thighs. My orgasms wrecked through me at my vampire's sucking, electricity shocking through me at every swallow. And when they both entered me, it only added to the already insurmountable ecstasy.

Blood trickled down my neck onto silk sheets, because somehow, we ended up on the bed, and my pussy burned from the stretch as they both moved in and out of me. Their grunts and whimpers as they spilled deep within me brought me to another peak that felt like a dream. Onyx bit and drank from my breast as Wolfgang kneaded my ass and lapped up the wound on my neck. The mixture of Onyx's sultry and sharp seduction and Wolf's brute strength and passionate lovemaking had me tumbling into a thousand waves of elation.

When they'd finally had their fill, at least for the moment, Onyx kissed my lips, and a surge of energy flowed through my body where I'd previously been limp and sex drunk. "As much as I'd like to keep you here this way, belladonna, I know there's a cantankerous demon awaiting his claimed."

Grinning against his bloodstained fangs, I turned and kissed Wolf, tangling my fingers in his wavy hair. "Come with me?"

"We'll find you," Wolfgang replied softly.

Onyx helped me to stand. "This Halloween night is far from over, my love."

Excitement trilled through me as I left them in Onyx's room and padded barefoot up another flight of stairs. Ames would want to be in the highest part of the house, like in Lamb's Blood Church. My attic-haunting demon's door was ajar, and I smiled as I entered his room, seeing it lit in purple and blues from smoky stained-glass windows stricken with moonlight. The old-timey vintage four-post bed, the old antenna television, and the rickety coffee table were all straight from his church. My simple and steadfast man.

His hands snaked along my ribs from behind, and he buried his nose in my hair. "You dare come into my attic smelling like blood and sex and fear?"

Ghost's archdemon voice echoed and took my breath, mixing it with anticipation and desire. Dipping his hand down my stomach and flicking his fingers over my tender sex, he murmured, "I love where your thighs touch, and I love when they're wet with you and with them... Wolf and Dragon have sent their demon a gift, haven't they?"

Leaning back into his hold, I spun around and found his soft lips and tongue. "I'm glad we finally know now why you taste like honey," I whispered, hoarse with want.

"A gift from you this whole time," he answered, dropping to his knees and peeling up my mini dress. I flushed at his assessment, taking me in, bare and dripping from Wolf's and Onyx's passion.

"Am I having Ghost or Ames tonight?" I asked, running my fingers through his hair.

His crystal blue stare met mine, and he smirked beneath his skeleton face paint that glowed purple in the cool light of his attic. "How about a little of both—the man and the monster?"

His response surprised me. My archdemon had always been at war with his human form. Just last Halloween, he was confused when I asked for the man over the demon... yet tonight, he'd made peace with them both. This Halloween, he offered me every part of who he was.

"That sounds perfect," I whispered. And with that, he opened his mouth an unfurled his long forked demon tongue. My thighs clenched together in need as he inched it between where they touched, lapping up the remnants of my sex with his friends.

"Their flavor mixed with yours…" He pushed inside me, and I moaned, holding on to his shoulders for support. But he withdrew and stood, towering over me. He dipped down and licked my lips with his demon tongue. I took it in readily, tasting me and Wolf Onyx and Ghost.

He laid me back on his bed and devoured me slowly and hungrily. Inching his tongue in and out of my pussy, bringing me to the edge and sending me spiraling over his cliff of pleasure again and again. Then finally, when I begged for his cock, he obliged, crawling over me and sinking inside, moving in and out as our moans married, blurring everything that existed but us. Me and my archdemon, my ghost, my monster who haunted me and had brought me out of hiding. My man who had lured me to Ash Grove so long ago and then did it again without even knowing.

All I could do was murmur my I love yous and accept his in response as we collided in bliss and I readily accepted every drop of his black cum inside me.

After we'd cuddled, tangled in each other as we always did, he pulled me to stand and tugged my dress back over my head. "We're not finished with you," Ghost whispered in my ear, sending chills down my spine.

"This house, Halloween, my boys, what more could there be?"

He took my hands and pressed his forehead to mine. "So much more, little ghost," he said with a tone of mirth I rarely got from him. He was happy. We all were. When he pulled back, he gestured over my shoulder, and when I turned, I realized we weren't in his attic anymore. Instead, we were in Lamb's Blood Church.

On the priest's throne, where Ghost had taken me last Halloween, sat *him*. My devil. My Judas. The final horseman to complete my sweet little collection of boys. The corner of his mouth lifted in a sinister smile, and Onyx and Wolf joined my side.

"Fancy meeting you here," I said into the echoey cathedral. "You know, last year, we did some pretty despicable things in this church."

"Did you? Sounds like a new tradition has begun," Judas rumbled. "Show me. You know I love to watch. I've been watching you all for so long."

Onyx ran his fangs along the crook of my neck. "Let's put on a show for the devil in God's house, shall we?"

Locking eyes with Judas, regal and reclined, I lifted my arms in silent invitation, and the boys obeyed, removing my dress.

The devil rumbled. "Our death, she is breathtaking, isn't she?"

"The most beautiful little ghost," Ames replied, catching my lips with his. Before I could respond, Wolfgang had scooped me up, and I was carried to the base of the altar. A wicked sacrifice before Hades himself.

The devil looked down on us as the guys positioned me how they wanted. I was their doll. I was whatever they wanted me to be, as I straddled Ghost, my massive archdemon. Taking in his cock, forcing myself to push lower and lower through the burn, as Onyx mounted me from behind, taking my backside. It was too much, and I couldn't do it, couldn't handle the pain and bliss. And when I screamed out, a ragged hymn as I caught the devil's eyes, my mouth filled with Wolfgang's thick cock. He shoved it down my throat, threatening to knot me breathless. As the devil hummed his encouragement of that plan, my other two boys pounded my pussy and ass.

This was wretched and corrupt and wrong. Being fucked senseless at the base of a holy altar with the devil in the priest's throne, watching on so leisurely. It was depraved. I felt so evil, and I loved every sinister moment of being claimed by all of my monsters.

They were mine and I was theirs. And we'd continue this dark ritual in this very church for every Halloween that was to come. It was our family tradition now. The visions of the hundreds of years of this flashed across my mind as my orgasm rattled me to my core and my moans echoed through the rafters. A trick, a treat, a dark and unholy celebration by firelight—that was our love.

When the guys had spent me, wilted and useless, they carried me up the altar steps. And like a caught maiden for a monster, they laid me on the devil's lap in some sick and twisted offering that was so befitting for us. Though he didn't take his own pleasure from me—I had a feeling it would come later, when we were alone—he cupped my face and kissed me tenderly. "You are wretchedly marvelous, my bride."

"Let's go to bed," I said hoarsely to the room, eliciting chuckles.

"Halloween has only just begun, little death," the devil responded. "And tonight, we spend it together. All of us."

I wasn't sure what he meant as I got dressed and followed them down the pumpkin-laden steps of Lamb's Blood Church. And then I heard it.

The music, the celebration, the flurry of people and monsters alike. "Hallows Fest and hell have come to downtown Ash Grove," the devil rumbled in my ear. "Do you like it?"

"I can't believe how perfect this is." I covered my mouth. Shifters, vampires, and pirates all mingled and laughed in the lantern-lit streets. The air was thick with cinnamon and fall's crisp invitation to winter. Outside Magia Eclectics, Yesenia and Marcelene waved with their covens as they stirred their caldron of pumpkin spice. "You let Marcelene go?" I asked, raising an eyebrow at my tall and silent devil, who only gave a half shrug.

"It's Halloween" was his simple reply.

Even Ames was smiling as he shook hands with pirates. Onyx nodded at the vampires who bowed to him, and Wolfgang embraced the wolves from Fenrir, who joined us around an enormous bonfire in the heart of town.

A red clown wearing a gaudy sparkling sequin blazer popped out from behind a tree, startling me, and the guys jumped to my defense. "Haven't I killed Zyre once already?" Wolf asked, grabbing him by the collar.

"Doesn't hurt to do it again," Onyx answered as the clown laughed manically.

"It's okay," I called them off. "He's... fine," I said reluctantly.

Zyre tipped his hat at us and smoothed his shirt. "You figured out the riddle, played the final hand of cards. Way to go, Ace."

And for some stupid reason, that brought a smile to my face. But I could hardly revel in my joy as more surprises lurked around every corner. Spirits in their 1800s attire passed us by, waving and greeting us. The curse was broken, but the ghosts still stopped by to say hello on Halloween night. It was Ash Grove, after all, and the tradition of ghost stories lived on.

My throat tightened with emotion when a girl and her mother and father stopped to give me a hug. Ellie Mae and Mr. And Mrs. Moore all regarded me with such pride in their eyes. "I'm so happy to see you," I told them.

"Us too," Ellie smiled, looking beautiful in a sky-blue dress. "Have you been looking after my dolls?"

Wolf, Onyx, and Ames bit their lips to hold back laughter as I mustered up my response, holding her hands lovingly. "Ellie, I have been to hell, I've fought ghouls and demons, I've even contended with the devil himself... and nothing scares me more than your house of dolls. I'm sorry."

The small crowd busted out with laughter. Wolven dried their eyes, and even a couple of vampires cracked a smile while my boys were beside themselves with hilarity.

Onyx found surprise guests of his own. Queen Cassiopeia and Elysium shook hands with the devil, as if he were just any man on the street. Though Elysium did turn a few shades paler than usual, and that made me giggle.

Queen Cassiopeia, in all her regal beauty, hugged me tenderly. "It is nice to see you again, and looking so much like yourself, Mortala. Please come see me soon. I'm sure there's much we can speak about."

I assured her that I would. I rubbed Onyx's back lovingly as we visited with his mother, knowing and sensing the absence he felt without his father present.

But before we could speak on it, a small shrill voice slithered behind us.

Lolth, with her hair hanging in her face, regarded the new vampire king. "I suppose I'm your familiar now," she lamented to Onyx.

Wolfgang and Ames snickered as Onyx fumbled for words. "He'd love that," Ames answered for him, squeezing his friend's shoulders.

"No. No, thank you, Lolth," he answered, elbowing the demon in the ribs. "I already have a familiar."

"Who?" I asked through tears of laughter as I wrapped myself up in my silent and solemn devil's arms. Even he was amused in his quiet way.

Onyx put an arm around the werewolf and ruffled his long hair. "Wolfgang, of course."

"I am *not* your fucking familiar," he growled, though he was laughing, too. We all were.

Raven cawed overhead, and the devil and I watched him lovingly. "Speaking of familiars," Judas said in my ear, "we have a very fine one."

"Yes, we do," I answered, noticing Ames's familiar, Cat, nearby and listening to every word. The nosy little thing.

She pranced over, and to Ames's horror and amusement, rubbed up against the devil's ankles. He chuckled and reached down to pet her ear. "You're a good familiar, too," he said, "though Ghost does not give you nearly enough credit for your cleverness."

Cat purred. "I agree. However, now that the graveyard is empty of the damned, I'm going on a vacation. I deserve a tropical cruise at Ghost's expense."

Rolling his eyes, my skeleton man replied, "I suppose we'll just have to fill the graveyard back up to full capacity to give you something to do."

Onyx's eyes gazed up with glee. "And now without the curse holding us in place, the possibilities for occupants are endless."

I giggled as the devil gave me a squeeze. "I do love when you all plot murder."

"We have one last surprise." Ames tugged at my hair, and Onyx and Wolf breezed past us, looking mischievous.

"I don't know how many more surprises I can take." I dried my eyes. It was more joy, more wondrous life and darkness, than I'd ever experienced. We were all finally together and finally home, with each other. The veil lifted and shimmered as hell took part in the festivities of Halloween, too. Ash Grove and hell were one and the same, just like my Halloween Boys and I were.

Suddenly, a female voice spoke into a microphone over the crowd from the brew pump's stage. Somehow, the old gas station had been magically transported to the center of town, and the crowd of beasts and ghosts, witches and monsters, all cheered at the sight of Ezmerelda, the Red Vampiress herself, announcing the band of the night.

The devil clutched me tight, and I leaned back into his embrace as she spoke. "We missed the show last year, but tonight, this Halloween, everything is different, isn't it?" She found me in the crowd and winked. "It is my immense pleasure to introduce tonight's band… the Halloween Boys!"

The crowd went insane as my guys took the stage. Wolfgang on the drums, Onyx and Ames on vocals and guitar. They played, and they fucking rocked. And it was everything Halloween should be. Their show, my devil's arms. The world under a thin lace veil was still and humming with October magic all around us.

All of our missing pieces had at last come together.

CHAPTER 38

Judas

LEATHER AND LACE

> The farther we've gotten from the magic and mystery of our past, the more we've come to need Halloween.
> *Paula Guran*

Ash grove hadn't changed over time. As a force ancient and steadfast as I, that was reason enough for the fascination. Everything changed. Every town and person, every landscape and mountain range would be different in the next year, the next decade. By a century later, it would be almost unrecognizable. But not Ash Grove. It stayed the same autumn snow globe, frozen in time, with the same elderly folk tipping their hats and the same rambunctious, troublemaking children. Granted they'd come to accept automobiles and modern technology, but the heart of the place, the other side of the door to hell, my home, always remained the same.

It was why I enjoyed photography and baking, I supposed. They were each art forms that held something as the same forever. An image would remain locked in time eternally the same way a recipe would ignite the same flavors of hundreds of past years over your tongue and through your mind in an instant. What a commonplace sort of magic.

Yes, I liked things that didn't change, because they reminded me of my love for my bride. Something no earthly or unearthly realm could shake. Oh, how I continued watching her even after our joining together that sacred Halloween night. The night that hell and its counterpart lifted the lace cloak and danced together as one. The night that all parts of my Mortala and everything the reaper of death touched fell into the fullness of its exquisite darkness.

She remembered. We all remembered.

And much as I told her, I was but a guardian, so were her horsemen. They, along with myself, were custodians of death. Ever at her service, kneeling at her feet, worshipping our queen. She chose to reside mainly in the house we'd found for her with all its transplanted magic from the fallen King Vladimir's castle and gifts from hell and Fenrir. It suited her, it suited us, and though I was not one for anything new, I did enjoy watching her there.

I'd gaze through the hundred candles she'd always have lit in her room and watch her stroke Raven's wings as she told me of her day as she undressed. Perhaps I would come to her and surprise her that night, perhaps I would make her wait another day and I would simply watch her sleep and await which of her boys would find her in the evening moonlight, insatiable for more of her almost as much as I was.

Mortala would find me in hell just the same, never forgetting her people there and treating them as an extension of the town, the home she adored so dearly. We would fly and we would visit our mountain. Her presence had calmed the fires and laid the foundations for a grove of ash. Ash Grove was hers. Whatever she wanted in this life or any life, was hers for long as power thrummed through my being.

And my fondness for Ghost, Dragon, and Wolf never faded. Sure, I'd toyed with the idea of keeping her to myself for a millennium or two. They could have waited as I had. Though the pain it would have caused her would not have been worth my momentary satisfaction of reclaiming my bride. She had chosen them, had found parts of herself within their souls and given to them pieces of hers. They were parts of her, and me, and interwoven in the fabrics of the realities of our beings.

Gods in their own right, rulers of their own kingdoms. More powerful and meaningful than even their most arrogant of thoughts could imagine. Even still, I watched them in wonder, awaiting their discoveries of what more they'd find within themselves. Now that their chains had been removed and hearts had married with death and all of us, where would they go but further and further in ability and guardianship? Beings of myth, they were. Beings of myth who still ordered midnight pizzas to their gothic castle and played games on the television far too loudly for my taste. But she loved them, and they loved her, and I loved them all.

Yes, I supposed the sermons were wrong about that. Surely the devil can and does love. And the evil ones are far more complicated than the stories depict, and perhaps hell was not so bad once you'd lived through it once or twice. Death came silently and with no warning. One could not see her nor predict her arrival. And what a breathtaking gift that was. The magic of starting new, of dying, of handing your bargains over to the devil to be thrust into a monstrous journey to the deepest, scariest parts of oneself. That wouldn't be too bad of an idea for me to pass along to Father Joseph for his next sermon, would it?

Many things changed. Change was the natural way of things, the order of life. Though beyond life… into death and beyond… those limitations didn't exist, and some truths stayed true, unshakable and unmoving as a mountain of glass. And one of those laws was Death and her four horsemen, evermore. And that I would always be her leather, chasing after her lace.

I would watch every season unfold just as I'd watched the Halloween boys behind lantern flickers and campfires.

CHAPTER 39

Blythe

HAPPY HALLOWEEN

> I'll tell you what freedom is to me: no fear
> *Nina Simone*

That day, it was a cell phone ringing, that reminded me of why I loved my life. By the time I'd fetched it from my purse, I'd missed the call, and instead had received a flirtatious text message in the group chat from a werewolf caught in breakfast duty in Fenrir.

Moments later, a rolled-up crossword puzzle would slap in front of me as my vampire king entwined his ankles with mine as he sat across from me. Onyx gazed up at me with those long lashes and emerald-green eyes lit with something other than sadness now.

And he was there, too. Watching. The devil was always watching me. I knew from the way my coffee, no matter how long it sat out, never got cold. I knew it from the red tint of every mirror I gazed into and from the letters left on my black silk pillowcase at night. Hell was not the same without me, he'd say, before appearing in my doorway during my nightly bath. Never predictable, always coming and going as he pleased. It was the way we were. Cat and mouse, push and pull. I'd run, and he would chase, catching me with leather-gloved hands and removing my lacey underthings.

Wolfgang would eventually take his usual groove in the booth next to Onyx, and they'd flirt and banter and torment the waitress until the bells on the door would jingle and suddenly, *he* would appear. My knight, my skeleton man, my archdemon, my ghost. Taking his spot next to me and smelling my hair, cupping my jaw to kiss me deeper than is proper to kiss in a diner. And we never cared enough to stop.

The smell of maple syrup, autumn leaves, sex, and possibilities radiated around us like a fall breeze in a graveyard. Our gothic home the creepiest and most haunted, our love the thing of legends and myth.

Death and her four horsemen, the witches whispered around their cauldrons of pumpkin spice.

Nothing but trouble. The old men of Ash Grove would shake their heads over their newspapers.

Both groups would be right. And though the trees would grow bare again, like they did every year, we'd look on to Belladonia and the Bleeding Heart Ball. We'd await Laverna and the celebration of spring in Fenrir with our beloved wolves. And then, after summer, when the blackberries were at their most sour... we'd know that hell was nearer. We'd feel it in our bones—the thinning of the veil—and we'd catch glimpses of it through its mirror image of Ash Grove. Finally, the two sides of the coin at harmony with the other.

And my boys and I. Ghost, Dragon, Wolf, and Devil. Well, we'd always have Halloween. Together we *were* Halloween. Stories of us were ghost tales and horror novels full of mystery. Of how death came and gave pieces of herself to the men she loved.

How remarkable and ordinary at the same time, that I had to go searching for it. That in finding my way to my guys, they, in turn, pointed me toward myself. Though maybe in everyone we love we are simply finding missing pieces of ourselves. Maybe they help us remember who we truly are. Maybe that's magic.

That was something so strange and wondrous. A blissful and dreadful eternity spent with my villains. The monsters I had fallen in love with. And the monster I became and grew to love, too. With us, our monsters would forever win. Their villains would always get their girl, and every day of forever and ever, would be Halloween.

And they haunted happily ever after.

The End.

Dearest Spooky Reader,

I have been thinking about this author's note since I wrote ghost in 2022. Strange thing to have on my mind, probably, but it's true. And it's also true that it may be odd to have an author note at the beginning and again at the end of the book, like Ghost did, but everything about this series as been peculiar and too much.

One reason this note has been on my mind so heavily is that it's something I don't know how to write. How do I convey what this series has meant to me? How do I accurately tell you in a page or two that The Halloween Boys and your love for them saved me and forever altered my life?

Maybe you don't know this, but in 2019 I was diagnosed with cancer. Death was something I had to heavily contend with for the first time. My escape was reading, and the stories I devoured gave me strength. I held onto the hope that when I got better, I'd put stories out that could be an anchor for people, too, like those books were for me.

From hospital rooms and tense phone calls, Blythe materialized somewhere in my psyche. The personification of death so beautiful and meaningful. Not as something to rage against but as a haunting reminder of what life truly means.

To making peace with the monsters that chase you, to learning that there's always another door to open to some other world. I hope these books have been a door for you, dear reader. Because sometimes hell is a wicked trail of sorrow tailored just to us…

The journey in writing this series was like cleaning out a haunted attic in my soul. It kicked up dust and introduced me to spirits I didn't know I needed to meet. There have been readers who have reached out saying that this series has changed their life. Some have said that seeing certain characters' representation healed parts of them that they didn't know they needed healing. I can't even begin to convey what that means to me that anyone would feel that way about my work.

Really, I still can't believe anyone even reads these.

I hope that The Halloween Boys have helped remind you in some small way that magic is real, that darkness is beautiful, and that everyone we love is a piece of us, a lit pumpkin patch pointing us back toward ourselves on the coldest autumn nights. I hope it reminds you to love the opposing parts of yourself, and to make friends with your monsters, and set free your ghosts.

Thank you for welcoming these stories with such open and lovingly dark hearts. That they've been a success is some sort of dark magic. None of them follow the blueprint of what they should have been and each release I bit my nails thinking *wow, that halloween boy really went off the rails, didn't he?* But for some bizarre reason you stuck around and read them all, didn't you? Thank you for doing that. Truly, I'm so happy that you did.

With so much love,

Kat

Acknowledgments

TO GHOST

Thank you for teaching me to love my severeness and lonesome nature. For showing me that it's okay to bend and soften for love. You taught me that even my hundreds of years long perceptions of myself and others can be blessedly wrong... and for that I am so glad. (But really, you didn't have to scare me with dead birds and demon dreams so often.) Nonetheless, you protected me when I truly needed it, and I'll never forget that. You'll always be my graveyard companion.

TO ONYX

We raged against each other a lot, didn't we? You are such a hurricane of emotion and self loathing just stumbling your way forward into love and acceptance. Sounds familiar... like maybe you were my mirror this whole time. Thank you for that. For burning it all down when I couldn't. For being a voice for the voiceless. For showing me that emotional hurricanes can also build while they destroy. You've accompanied me to morgues with your cassette player on full blast. I'll love you forever.

TO WOLF

Thank you for giving me magic and love when I didn't even know I needed it. You threw out half a dozen outlines for your book, continually and gently whispering, make it simple. Magic is easy. For in the kindest way forcing me into the light and making me embrace the gentle and tender within the darkness. I know you'd tear through veils for anyone who needed it and you taught me how to do the same. Through the swamp of self doubt, you carried me. With you there will always be a willow tree and talking spirits.

TO DEVIL

Your lesson for me within this bargain we made was as intricate as the levels of hell we explored. At the very least, I knew and still know, I was unprepared for all you had to offer. You didn't do anything the way I thought you would, everything was backwards, and when I thought I knew— you gleefully showed me that I had no fucking clue. The more I learned the less I knew. And that's the way you wanted it. And for that… thank you. Together, we showcased something different, didn't we? You appeared in my hell as a teacher, a guide, and I am so appreciative of that.

TO BLYTHE

You know I can't even talk about you without getting emotional. Your strength and beauty— death in lipstick— healed so many broken parts of me. For snuggling stuffed animals and commanding legions of demons, for being a scared little girl and a goddess of darkness, you taught me about duality and death while being unabashedly yourself. A door will always open to you, and now after spending all this time with you, I believe the same for me. To the doors, and how I know there's one ready and waiting for me, wide open to Ash Grove anytime I need it.

To E, for never doubting that I had it in me. Thank you for being the Wolf to my Onyx.

To the friends who became family and the family I chose and love dearly.

Dakota Wilde my best friend and the bestselling author of Hell House. How does anyone write without a fellow author friend to keep them writing on the hard days, send them doughnuts on the really really hard days, and be the first cheering them on after a win? Our demons brought us together last October and for that I am so thankful. They say demons bring misfortune, but mine brought me a soul sister.

Sav, my friend and PA for your meltdown management and virgo goddess organization. You told me after Ghost to push up all my deadlines and finish the series this year. I did it! And I made you help me!

To everyone who made this series possible. Beth at VB Edits and Proofreading— I still can't spell dyphlla and I never will be able to. Why did they have to be called that? Why am I like this?

Shannon at Shanoff Designs— responding calmly and promptly to every cover question, for lending your art and talent to these pretty covers. Thank you so much.

My covens on Patreon and Facebook. Seriously, some of the most amazing people have found me through this series. Your excitement and love for the story kept me going in ways you'll never know. It was the magic I needed to keep writing on many dark days.

To my ARC team, you guys rocked every release. Sharing, hyping, I can't thank you enough.

I don't want to say goodbye, and I'm not, not really. Because I know the boys and Blythe are always with me. They're with you too, if you want them to be.

BECAUSE FOR ALL OF US— EVERY DAY IS HALLOWEEN.

Trick or Treat With Me

- Sign up for my newsletter to be the first to know about new book releases
- Join my patreon for early e-books, extra scenes of The Halloween Boys, secret projects, and more.
- Join me on #spicybooktok TikTok:
- See fan edits on Instagram:
- Follow for updates and quotes on Twitter:
- Follow me on Amazon for upcoming books:
- Join my reader coven on FB
- Please consider leaving a review on your favorite platform

Business or press inquires please email katblackthorneauthor@gmail.com

Also by Kat Blackthorne

The Halloween Boys

Ghost

Dragon

Wolf

Devil

Wicked Ecstasy

The other villains of Ash Grove

Come For A Spell

Familiar Taste

Lady Venom Takes a Mistress

Gothic lesbian romance set in The Halloween Boys Universe

Hot Queens

Contemporary polyamory

Hotwife

Hot Life

Let it Snow Queen

Browse by Trope for more

at katblackthorne.com

www.ingramcontent.com/pod-product-compliance
Lightning Source LLC
Chambersburg PA
CBHW020134310726
48970CB00006B/1871